Other Angie Amalfi Mysteries by
Joanne Pence

To Catch a Cook
A Cook in Time
Cooks Overboard
Cook's Night Out
Cooking Most Deadly
Cooking Up Trouble
Too Many Cooks
Something's Cooking

BELL, COOK, AND CANDLE

AN ANGIE AMALFI MYSTERY

JOANNE PENCE

AVON BOOKS

An Imprint of HarperCollinsPublishers

This is a work of fiction. Names, characters, places, and incidents are products of the author's imagination or are used fictitiously and are not to be construed as real. Any resemblance to actual events, locales, organizations, or persons, living or dead, is entirely coincidental.

AVON BOOKS
An Imprint of HarperCollins*Publishers*
10 East 53rd Street
New York, New York 10022-5299

Copyright © 2002 by Joanne Pence
ISBN: 0-06-103084-8
www.avonbooks.com

First Avon Books paperback printing: January 2002

Avon Trademark Reg. U.S. Pat. Off. and in Other Countries, Marca Registrada, Hecho en U.S.A.
HarperCollins® is a registered trademark of HarperCollins Publishers Inc.

Printed in the U.S.A.

10 9 8 7 6 5 4 3 2

*This book is dedicated to the many wonderful people
who have so warmly welcomed
me and my family to the Treasure Valley.*

Chapter 1

Little did the people who walked the city streets know of the hidden life that teemed around them, a dark, deadly substratum that knew no compassion, generosity, or humanity. Humanity—hah! A weak, self-serving concept if he ever heard one.

Only an occasional noise in the darkness, a sudden shadow thrust across blood-filled cracks in a sidewalk lit by street lamps, gave unheeded warning that there was more to existence than what they knew, those day-walkers, more than what they saw every day, more than what they felt. How surprised the blind would be if they could see as he did all night, every night.

A dark-gray sewer rat slunk out from the shelter of a stone wall, raised its nose to sniff the night air, and froze, paralyzed with fright. The watcher smiled, his mouth wet with anticipation.

The rat's sharp claws dug hard against the sidewalk, and its black eyes bulged. Abruptly, as if roused from its stupor, it scurried toward the gutter that ran under the old church, its powerful hind legs pumping fast. But too late.

High, sharp squeals shredded the evening silence as talons ripped through the rat's neck and chest. Blood squirted from the wounds in the fat, twitching body and splattered on the creature that fed on it.

Angie Amalfi waved good-bye to her latest customer as she and her friend, Connie Rogers, walked across the street toward her new silver Mercedes-Benz coupe. Granted, the CL600 two-door was a step down from the Ferrari Testarossa she used to drive, but it was a much more practical car. A family car almost, and she had a good idea of the family she wanted it to be a part of.

Anyway, her Ferrari was toast. Literally. No sense crying over spilt . . . cinders.

Beyond the car loomed what had once been a beautiful Catholic church in San Francisco's elegant Pacific Heights neighborhood but was now begrimed and sinister. Built at the turn of the century out of stone, the Church of Saint Michael the Archangel was one of the few structures that had survived the city's big 1906 earthquake and fire. After the not-quite-as-huge quake in 1989, however, it was condemned. The archdiocese decided against spending the money necessary to shore it up to make it safe again, but preservationists in the city campaigned against the church being torn down, and building inspectors wouldn't allow it to be used. So there it stood, doomed.

Angie wasn't particularly concerned about old churches at the moment, however. Not when she was biting her tongue so hard she would look like she had a mouthful of raspberry Jell-O if she wasn't careful. And it was all because of Connie.

She looked back over her shoulder at her customer,

flashed a big smile, and gave a friendly wave. Barbara Knudsen, the wife of an assistant district attorney who had just been appointed to the bench, waved in return before stepping back inside her house and shutting the door. She was throwing a big party for the new judge, and the two of them had come up with an idea for a Comical Cake: an oversized smiley-faced gavel rapping down onto a replica of a Monopoly *Go Directly to Jail* card.

"She's a nice lady," Connie murmured.

Angie couldn't hold it in any longer. "I couldn't believe that you mentioned Lolly Firenghetti to her," she cried. "Have your brains turned to Noodle-Roni? What in the world were you thinking?"

Stunned by the attack, Connie stopped in the middle of the street. "What's that supposed to mean?" Blond, in her thirties, and divorced, she owned her own business, a gift shop called Everyone's Fancy. From the time they first met, she and Angie had been close friends. Until now. "I was trying to help."

"Help me?" Angie, brunette with auburn highlights, in her twenties and single, would have waved her arms, but she was too busy fishing her car keys out of her Coach bag. "By telling a customer about my competition? Benedict Arnold gave more help than that!"

"I was sure she knew there were other companies that did made-to-order cakes. I just wanted to convince her that yours is better."

"She acted as if she'd never heard of Lolly's business."

"Is that my problem?" Connie asked.

Angie wasn't sure. She also wasn't sure why people

wanted humorous cakes to celebrate serious occasions, but since they did, her business was growing geometrically with each party she attended, Lolly Firenghetti or no. "Let's forget it," she said, disgruntled.

"Well, it'll be interesting to see if she sticks with you or goes with Lolly's company," Connie observed as they continued again toward the Mercedes.

Angie could all but feel the smoke coming out of her ears. "Interesting? You aren't taking my new business at all seriously, and I don't appreciate that one little bit!" Angie pressed hard against the car's unlock button on her key ring, then grabbed hold of the key to the ignition. Her finger began to sting.

The key was new. She'd had duplicates made when she bought the car, and one of the duplicates was on the key ring. Apparently, the edges hadn't been ground smooth, and a sharp edge of metal punctured her finger. Blood began to well up.

"Damn!" Angie muttered. "Now look at what you've done."

"What I've done?" Connie headed toward the passenger's side, her nose in the air. "You're the one who asked me to come here tonight."

"You were supposed to give me support, be a kind of chorus for me and my business. Like, say, the Supremes for Diana Ross. Wait, they split up. Well, you know what I mean." Not wanting to get blood on her pearl-gray leather seats or royal-blue Versace suit, she took a moment to fish a Kleenex from her purse and press it against her finger. "I didn't expect you to find my cakes some kind of joke."

Connie's foot tapped impatiently. "Frankly, anyone whose business gets its start at a funeral shouldn't be surprised when people find it more than a little humorous."

Too irritated to reply, Angie got into the car and shoved the tissue into her jacket pocket. It slipped out, caught by a breeze. Part of her speechlessness, unfortunately, stemmed from the fact that what Connie said was true.

Her business had begun only three weeks earlier when a friend's elderly grandmother passed away and the friend asked Angie to create a special cake for a post-funeral reception. Since the grandmother had loved chocolate to excess, the granddaughter wanted a chocolate cake. To Angie's horror, her friend then asked that the cake be covered with purple icing and trimmed with a black border.

At first, Angie thought her friend was joking. Luckily, she didn't laugh, because the bereaved was dead serious, so to speak, about the macabre tribute, and was catapulting her grandmother into eternity in the poorest possible taste.

Angie not only complied, but also added a few calla lilies to one corner to offset the *Rest in Peace, Pearl* curlicued across the center.

It had to be the most hideous cake ever created. If she could have dropped it off at the reception and snuck home, she would have.

Much to her amazement, some members of the funeral party were deeply moved. Others commented favorably on her wry humor. She didn't know whether to be flattered or appalled or to deny all responsibility.

A mourner asked if she'd be willing to create a comical sheet cake for an office party. A coworker was retiring, and the staff wanted a cake that looked like a nursing home with the words *Not Long Now, Buddy* written in black.

Ha, ha.

Angie quoted an outrageous price. She hadn't studied cooking and baking at the Cordon Bleu in Paris to come up with Metamucil Manor retirement cakes. To her amazement, the woman accepted.

That led to a cake for a baby shower. The parents' last name was Baer, and they asked for a bear cub in a baby blanket. Two cakes later, Angie decided to regard her cakes not as mere confections, but as whimsical works of art, similar to ice sculptures at gala events. She drew up some business cards, and Comical Cakes was born.

Now, careful not to cut herself again, she slid the key into the ignition and turned it. The car's engine cranked but didn't start. She stopped and took a deep breath.

"This place is pretty creepy," Connie said, wriggling to make herself more comfortable. "I feel like someone is watching me."

"You're being silly. There's nothing creepy about this street. It's a beautiful neighborhood." Angie tried the key again. Nothing.

"Usually streets have lots of lights and houses, with children playing and dogs barking." Connie pulled her python-print coat closer and strapped on the seat belt. "This one has a decaying church taking up an entire city block."

"What is wrong with this car?" Angie glowered at the unlit dashboard in frustration. "I don't have time for this! I have a Comical Cake to design!"

"I didn't think new cars were so temperamental,"

Connie said, gazing out the window at St. Michael's Church. "My old car works perfectly. I should be home with it instead of here being unappreciated this way."

Angie gritted her teeth. "I appreciate you coming with me," she said after a while as she rummaged through the glove compartment for the car manual. New cars were so sophisticated they almost drove themselves, but that didn't help if you couldn't get them started. "I would appreciate a little more support next time, that's all."

"Maybe being stuck in this spooky place is payback for your business's funereal beginnings," Connie said, sounding both worried and scared.

The manual was the size of a small town's telephone book. Angie tossed it back, slammed the glove box shut, and tried again. "Will you stop that already! What's with you?" Miraculously, this time—thank you, Lord!—the engine caught.

"Nothing is 'with' me! Nothing at all." Connie faced forward, sitting stiffly in the car seat. "Just get moving. I don't like it here."

"You aren't the only one!" With the engine purring, Angie took a moment to check her finger again under the map lamp. As much as she wanted to get away, she didn't want any bloody spots turning this into an OJ car if she could help it.

The finger was fine. As she shut off the lamp, she noticed that no streetlights illuminated the area near the old church.

She reached over and hit the door lock on the driver's side, locking both doors at the same time, and pulled away from the curb.

* * *

The lacerated corpse of the rat dangled by its tail from his fingertips. Thirst and hunger satisfied for the moment, he tossed it into the gutter and wiped the back of his hand across his mouth as he slunk closer to the street. He had watched the women in the luxurious car with interest—with very much attention, judging by the effect one in particular had had on his body. It had been a long time since simply looking at a woman could make his blood flow this way. Usually, he had to be doing much more than looking, even more than touching. He sucked the blood slowly from each of his fingertips as the car disappeared in the distance.

A tissue fluttered to his feet; he bent over and picked it up. *A sign*, he thought.

I am Beast. I am Destroyer. I am where lust, terror, and death converge.

I am Nightmare.

Chapter 2

San Francisco Homicide Inspector Paavo Smith had wasted most of the morning in the Hall of Justice lost in thought, glancing from time to time at the picture he'd pulled from his desk drawer. Angie had given it to him some months before with the expectation that he'd keep it on the top of his desk, not tucked away inside.

Whenever he looked at her smiling face framed by shiny brown hair with red highlights, her soulful brown eyes, small nose, and generous mouth, something inside him twisted. It was a good twist, he had to admit, but not one conducive to work. In fact, nothing about his current relationship with Angie helped his concentration in any area, and he had to put an end to this situation.

He returned the picture to his desk and shut the drawer. "The hell with it, Yosh," he said glumly. "I've got to do it. There's no getting around it anymore."

"Are you sure about this, Paav?" His partner, Toshiro Yoshiwara, gave him a piercing stare from the desk parked across from Paavo's. A big man, broad and muscular, with close-cropped black hair and a thick neck, Yosh stood only a couple of inches shorter than Paavo's six-foot-two-inch height and just barely managed to squeeze into his office swivel chair.

"I know I can't keep on this way. She's driving me nuts." Paavo wasn't one to wear his feelings on his sleeve or even to admit to them. Talking about them to Yosh wasn't easy either, but even a tough cop had to open up to someone sometime. That's what partners were all about.

Yosh put down his pencil, turning away from the Form 10A9 he'd been typing, and swung his chair to face Paavo. "You two have been together quite a while." He paused, then added, "I guess a man's gotta do what a man's gotta do."

"So it seems." Paavo hated the trite phrase, one he'd heard too often used as an excuse for some of the most heinous acts imaginable.

"When will you do it?" Yosh asked, his face sympathetic.

"I'll have to wait until the time is exactly right. It isn't something to spring on her out of the blue."

"No, that's for sure."

Paavo lifted his head as Homicide Inspector Rebecca Mayfield strode into the large, open room that made up the homicide division of the Bureau of Inspections, her partner, Bill Sutter, dragging in about ten steps behind her. Thirty-five years old, Rebecca, Homicide's only woman detective, wore her sandy-blond hair pinned back in a twist. Her navy-blue sport jacket, starched white shirt, and khaki slacks showed off her tall, well-toned figure. She moved with an unconsciously athletic, no-nonsense gait, as sexy as it was businesslike.

Sutter was the forgotten man on the force—nonde-script, waiting for retirement, bland, and constantly wearing the expression of a person in need of a double dose of Pepto-Bismol.

"Don't say anything about this, okay?" Paavo said quietly to Yosh.

"My lips are sealed," Yosh answered. "But maybe you're feeling this way because we don't have a big case to work on. You might just be bored."

"I don't think I'm about to change my life out of boredom," Paavo said.

"You never know. I'm half tempted myself."

"What's with you guys?" Rebecca asked. "You're sitting there like you just lost your best friends."

"Maybe so," Yosh said, glancing in Paavo's direction.

Paavo didn't answer but walked to the window and stared out at the lights of the freeway snaking south and east, leading cars out of the bowels of a city where death occurred so quickly, so brutally, and so damned often it was becoming harder and harder to deal with. Maybe Yosh was right and his decision regarding Angie was part of the bigger picture, a much broader need for change.

No, that was too easy an explanation. This was about Angie and him, nothing more.

That same freeway also brought cars northward and westward, into the city, but Paavo didn't look at those lanes. He didn't want to think about them, only the ones leaving, the ones escaping.

As he studied the scene below, a chill struck him, one of those that Angie described as someone walking over your grave. That was not at all the feeling he'd ex-pected. For the first time, he wanted to live life to the

fullest. He felt as if he'd only been skimming the surface and was ready for much more.

He spun away from the window and the eerie sensa-
tion it gave him.

Yosh was staring at him, a strange look on his face.

Serefina Amalfi stormed into her youngest daughter's
apartment like a running back for the Forty-Niners.
"I'm so disappointed in you, Angelina!" Short, with a
round body, round face, and dyed black hair tightly
pulled into a stylish bun, she plopped her boxy black
purse on the coffee table and proceeded to remove her
black scarf, overcoat, and gloves. Even her dress was
black. Not a good sign.

Angie still carried the dishrag she'd used to dry her
hands after washing cake batter off them. "What did I
do, *Mamma?*"

"Not what you did, what you haven't done. How did
I raise such a *stupida?*"

Angie knew she was in for a long haul. "Would you
like a cup of coffee?"

"Do you have any of your pecan shortbread cookies?" Serefina stopped her diatribe to ask, and joined
Angie in the kitchen.

"No. I've been busy with my cakes. I haven't had
time to bake cookies." Angie put on the coffee.

"You and your cakes! Who wants silly cakes?" The
wooden chair squeaked as Serefina lowered herself
into it. "Cakes are to eat, to melt in the mouth, not to
look at and laugh!"

Biting her tongue so hard she feared permanent in-
dentations, Angie opened the refrigerator. "I can offer
you a sandwich, or I'll make a frittata."

Serefina clasped her hands together. "I'm too upset to eat."

Angie seated herself at the table. "Okay, what's this about?"

"You. And Paavo."

Angie was shocked. "Paavo?"

"You went through so much with him just last month. He learned about his *mamma*, his *papà*, and what did you do about it? *Niente!*"

"Nothing? I did as much as I could." What was her mother's problem? "I was there for him, I tried to help him."

"But"—Serefina leaned toward her, eyeball to eyeball—"did you get him to propose?"

Angie could have shrieked. "Marriage was the last thing on his mind when he was going through all that."

"It should have been the first thing on his mind once he got over it. *Testa dura!* Where have I failed as a mother? You should know that already." Serefina threw her head back, arms out, and announced to the ceiling, "*Madonna mia*, such a daughter I have, an embarrassment to Italian women *in tutto del mondo!*"

Angie placed a cup of coffee in front of her mother and plunked a bottle of brandy beside it. Serefina enjoyed her coffee royals, as she called them, and Angie was ready to join her. "Paavo will propose when he's good and ready."

Pouring generously, Serefina instructed, "You have to help him get ready."

"I am, *Mamma*. I'm doing everything I can."

Serefina gave her a long-suffering look. "Angelina, you have a lot to learn."

* * *

The dark, run-down Victorian looked like a place the Addams family might have called home. Three stories tall, it had a steeply pitched roof and turret on the top floor. Zoe Vane followed the directions she'd been given to the west side of the building. Sure enough, cement steps led down to a heavy wooden basement door.

How cool was it to knock? She didn't want to look like some dweeb. She turned the knob, and to her surprise, the latch slid open. She pushed the door wide and strode inside, a blasé, been-there-done-that expression on her face.

A big man with a shiny dome of a head, beer belly, and black Nehru jacket buttoned tight against a bloated neck caught the door and stared at her hard, then slowly lowered pitbull eyes to her short black leather skirt and over-the-knee black leather boots.

"Who do you think you are walking in here?" His voice was low and gravelly.

"Hey, there, my man." She tossed out the words at a fast, urban clip. "I didn't know this little rendezvous spot was so classy it had someone just to open up the door. You know what I'm saying?" She put a fist on her hip and let it sway.

"You got an invitation?" he asked.

She rolled her eyes as if contemplating leaving. "Look, I heard this is a happening place and I'm new in town. Where was I supposed to get this invitation?"

"You got some ID?"

She blinked in astonishment. "You carding me?"

Uncle Fester's double gave her a leering smirk. "No. I just want to know your name. Let's see it."

She handed him a ten-dollar bill. "Call me Alexandra Hamilton."

He grinned. "Now you're catching on."

Once inside The Crypt Macabre, as the club was called, she felt she'd stepped into a Hollywood movie—a room thick with smoke from tobacco and the distinctive scent of weed, Marilyn Manson shrieking over the sound system, and pulsating strobe lights creating herky-jerky surreal images.

Shoulders back, her white-powdered face slack as if world-weary, black-shadowed eyelids half closed, and plum-glossed lips arched in a slight sneer, she took leggy strides deep into the room. Halfway, she stopped, hips thrust forward, and ran her fingers through raven-black hair, pushing it to the side in a way that made it flop over in greater disarray.

Her black blouse was only half buttoned, showing a considerable amount of cleavage, and a black, silver-studded dog collar was fastened around her neck.

If all this didn't get her noticed, she had no idea what more to do.

"Who are you?"

She lifted heavy eyes to the young man at her side, slowly dropping her gaze over his black-leather-clad, rail-thin body, then up again. His black hair was spiked, his eyes lined with red pencil, and his lips colorless. Three silver studs paraded along one earlobe. He looked like something out of Madame Tussaud's. She pouted sullenly. "Who wants to know?"

"They call me Rysk—that's like *risky* but with a *y*."

An arrogant toss of her head caused her hair to fall onto her face. She raked it back as she spoke. "If you're trying to impress me, it's not happening. I know *risky* has a *y* in it."

He smirked and put his hands on narrow hips. "It's, like, two *y*'s."

"I didn't come here for a spelling bee." She turned away. This young punk was a waste of time.

"Who are you?" he repeated, stepping around to face her, blocking her path.

He stood too close. He was tall, but with her high heels, she nearly looked him straight in the eye. "Don't you get it? Or are you the census bureau?"

He folded his arms and moved even closer, letting his elbow bump against her. "I ask the questions around here."

Nobody but nobody touched her. "Who the hell do you think you are!" She stepped back, her hands fisted.

"Relax," he said.

"Go to hell." She twisted away from him, easing into the crowd. *Bastard,* she thought, trying to calm herself. She needed to focus, not to waste her time with nobodies. One particular man's notice was what she was after.

Blaring music, the constant on/off blinking of the lights, and the heavy, stale air made her head throb and her eyes smart. She tucked in her chin, her gaze moving slowly, carefully. These were not the beautiful people of the city, despite the music and strobe lights. They were the nerds, the troubled, society's rejects. Many of the males still had remnants of teenage acne and the gangly, loose-limbed look of a boy not yet grown into a man's body. The women were also mostly young, their faces made up garishly, funeral-parlor style, much like hers. Their often chubby bodies were clad in romantic floor-length black or wine-colored velvet dresses or in dark slacks and grungy T-shirts with demonic images or symbols of death. Not even heavy Goth makeup could hide soft, flabby skin and chunky, unappealing bone structure.

Their expressions were generally vacant or blandly happy, as if they were under the influence of Ecstasy or other drugs.

She wondered if any of this crowd had an idea of the danger they were exposed to by simply being here.

An almost overwhelming desire filled her to grip their shoulders and shake them, along with the firm knowledge that it wouldn't do one damn bit of good. *Stupid, stupid children.*

She clenched and unclenched her hands, breathing deeply as she willed her eyes not to tear up in anger and frustration.

Then she saw him, lounging on a sofa, surrounded by the only truly beautiful women in the entire club. His hair, like almost everyone else's there, was black and combed straight back from a widow's peak in the center of his forehead—probably plucked into a perfect shape. His face was white, but with the look of one who stays out of the sun while eating healthily—a much more alive look than the bloodless tone of his cohorts.

His shoulders were broad, and his arms and chest surprisingly muscular. His dark-brown eyes were deep set and soulful, and when he spoke to a woman, he would touch her face or hair like a father touching his child and then smile as knowingly as a lover reliving intimacies. She could almost see why so many of the women at his feet hung on his every word. It made her sick.

She turned away, her head light. Before coming here tonight, the mere thought of him had filled her with fury. Now to see him, to be so close she could almost touch him, smell him, breathe the same air, made her physically ill.

Someday she was going to kill him. Of that she had no doubt.

Paavo couldn't sleep. His chest was tight, and he gasped for breath. He checked through his small one-bedroom house for gas leaks, and finding no problem, opened the bedroom window wide even though the night temperature was in the forties and the air was heavy with ocean fog.

That day, he had called Angie a couple of times, but she was busy planning a cake for some new judge's party. It would be crowded with potential customers, the kind of people she needed to impress. She'd deliver the cake tomorrow night. Maybe after that . . .

The situation with Angie had to be what was troubling him, causing this strange heaviness in his chest. He pulled a rocking chair up to the window and sat in front of it, rubbing his arms against the chill as he looked out at the night.

Angie awoke with a start. The clock by the bed showed four A.M. She listened, wondering what had caused her to wake.

The usual apartment sounds softly murmured in the background—the hum of the refrigerator, the ticking of a Georgian-style wall clock in the dining room, the occasional rush of warm air pushing through the heating vents.

A vague awareness of a troubling dream rattled in her head, but she pushed it away. Nightmares were the bane of solitary sleepers, and she didn't want to chance remembering.

Concern about the judge's cake and the reaction of the city's politicos must have been the cause of her waking. She wouldn't be able to bake anything, let alone cleverly decorate it, if she didn't go back to sleep.

She turned over and tried to ignore the uneasiness that seeped into her bones. The clock radio's digital display showed five A.M. before sleep came to her again.

Night fell slowly in San Francisco, its ever-present fog carrying crystals of light long after the sun set beyond the rim of the ocean. Once the starless sky turned black, bright city lights illuminated the most populated areas, but the other streets were shrouded in darkness.

A few streetlamps and a handful of patrol cars weren't enough to keep the streets safe, to keep the monsters that lurked on them at bay. The creatures that preyed on the innocent were closer than anyone imagined.

Mason Markowitz knew that well. His body was gaunt with lack of food, but he could not eat; his hair had gone white with the things he'd seen, but he could not turn his eyes away.

He stood on a street corner, lured again to the old church for reasons he could not rationally explain or justify. He'd witnessed strange things here, dead rats, lurking beasts, and even two young women, arguing, wrapped up in their worldly concerns.

Coldness had descended on him as he'd watched them go, and he feared what lay ahead and all that he must do. He'd been drawn here by evil, attracted to this place as he had been to others, but nowhere had he felt the dark forces so strong or so dangerous.

Beyond all doubt, here the darklings of night roamed, the horrors of every nightmare walked. Although an army of exorcists laden with rituals and sacred chrisms should be used to expel the possessing demons, few believed in such ceremony any longer.

Instead, Markowitz alone must cast them out, or failing that, he would at least deprive the demons of their unnatural hosts.

Chapter 3

 He drew the crumpled Kleenex from his pocket and carefully smoothed it out. A speck of blood stained the white center. He shut his eyes as he rubbed it against his cheek, remembering the two women and in particular *her*. The tissue felt soft . . . soft as a woman's skin. It was a sign, he thought, a sign for the convergence of lust, terror, and death.

Folding the Kleenex, he tucked it safely away and placed his left hand on the Book. Fiery heat flowed from it, and he threw back his head in rapture.

How long had the ancient text awaited him, knowing that he alone would be chosen to fulfill its prophecy? Once he had felt isolated, a pariah. Soon he would be all-powerful, and those who scorned him would be sacrificed.

Now, in the darkness just before dawn, he opened the heavy, ancient volume of the *Ars Diabolus* and, as in past readings, was engulfed by a feeling of strength, power, and promise. Here, by candlelight in the basement of the once consecrated church, a church soon to be reconsecrated to the night, he began to read.

You, Mortal, have received the call of the Infernal Prince and must now prepare your way to your Destiny. To become Dark Lord, Master of the Night, you must follow the Dark Path.

Already, you have been in the Dark Presence of the Servants of the Infernal Prince: Lord Belial, Lord Asmodeus, Lord Beelzebub, Lord Megaros, and Others Whose Names are not to be revealed.

Already, you have assembled Great Mounds in the Deep Night to Summon Power, you have entered the consecrated places of the Enemy to perform the Infernal Prince's Rite, and you have trod the Dark Way of Blood Sacrifice.

Know you, Mortal, that to become Dark Lord you must assemble your Court of Five: the Four Dark Ladies and the One Queen. With them and through their Pentagram you shall be granted Power and shall Reign with the might of the Dark Plane upon this world forever.

Go, then, and gather your maidens.

Angie wasn't at all pleased with Connie. She'd promised to come by the apartment after work. Together they would take the happy gavel to the judge's party and set it up. The problem with comical cakes was that they were oversized and delicate. If this one started to slide and the frosting mooshed together, she'd end up with what looked like a happy mud ball. How would she explain that to the judge's wife?

She'd waited for Connie as long as she could, then headed for the judge's house alone, hoping Connie would be waiting outside it to help her. No such luck. Her irritation grew, and she stayed in the car a moment, taking deep breaths and trying to calm herself.

The closest street parking to Judge Knudsen's home was in front of the empty church she'd parked beside on her last visit. If she lived here, she'd do all she could to get the city to resolve the situation—either to tear the building down or to use it. It seemed wrong to leave it vacant and subject to vandals and other intruders. The Catholic Church had a rite to desanctify a church when one had to be abandoned, so that evil people could not misuse sacred ground. This was all in all a good idea, she thought—and something the Church had most likely already taken care of.

The building vanished from her mind as she carried the big cake into the house and set it up, thankfully unharmed. Not so discreetly placing some of her business cards nearby to drum up more business, she left the home before the party began and decided to call Paavo about dinner tonight. She had planned to go out with Connie, but since Connie had stood her up . . .

As she walked back to the car, the statue of St. Michael the Archangel at the top of the old church caught her eye. It was as if he was looking down at her and frowning. Connie had been terribly nervous here the other night. Maybe that was why she hadn't shown up tonight.

Angie would have laughed off Connie's fears except that her superstitious Italian mother had raised her on stories filled with strange night creatures in closets, in basements, and in old churchyards. As much as her

very American practical self didn't want to believe in
bogeymen, deep inside her, she couldn't quite shake
the thought that they just might get you if you didn'
watch out.

She forced her mind away from such scary ideas and
focused on more important things—like her outfit fo
dinner with Paavo. He'd been talking about going
someplace nice. Definitely the red and white silk strap
less dress . . .

Were those footsteps behind her? Running footsteps'

Her senses sprang alert, a chill racing down he
spine. As she turned, hands grabbed her shoulder.
from behind.

"Got you!"

She screamed.

"I haven't seen you here before," said a pale young
woman with hair so blond it was almost white. He
floor-length, white gauzy outfit seemed more like a
nightgown than a dress. Wine-red lips provided he
only color. She moved with a languid air, as if she'
taken too much of a narcotic.

Zoe Vane smiled. She'd seen the woman the othe
night with the Baron and had sought her out. "You
outfit is out of sight," she said. "It's hot."

"You like my dress?" the woman asked. "I'm glad
somebody thinks it's pretty. I think it's pretty."

"So, what do they call you?" Zoe asked. "M
name's Zoe Vane."

Heavy eyes, the pupils tiny pinpricks, gazed up a
her. "They call me Mina. Mina Harker."

"Mina Harker?" Zoe's blood turned to ice. Wha
was going on here? She smiled. "That's cold chill time

I like it! You must be one big *Dracula* fan, right? Me, too."

The woman looked puzzled. *"Dracula?* I don't know about that. I'm not one for movies."

Zoe swallowed her retort and forced her streetwise demeanor back again. "There I go, running off at the mouth when I don't have a clue what I'm talking about. My mistake."

Mina regarded her quizzically, then put her hand on Zoe's arm and leaned into her. "You like my name, don't you? Most people tell me it's a pretty name."

"Sure, girl. It's real pretty." This woman was weird. Zoe needed to get to the point fast. "Tell me, have you known the Baron long?"

"No, not very long. He's so cool. So sexy. So good-looking. Don't you think he's the coolest guy you've ever met?"

"Cool. Very cool."

"I think so, too." Mina sighed and batted her eyes at Zoe. "I don't like his friend, though."

"Which friend is that?"

"You know, Fieldren. You've got to know Wilbur. He's kind of squishy. I don't like him but the Baron does. Fieldren lets me know when the Baron wants to see me, so I guess for that reason alone I should like him." Her giggle made Zoe realize the woman was even younger than she'd thought—maybe only eighteen or so.

"Do you know what the Baron does?" Zoe asked, changing the subject. "I mean, how can the Baron afford this big house? And this constant partying?"

Mina grinned. "Well, duh! He's a Baron. He doesn't have to *do* anything. How can you not know that?"

Good question. "I'm from Chicago."

"Oh," Mina said, as if that explained everything.

"So, where is our dear Baron tonight?" Zoe asked, looking around the room once again.

"I'm not sure. I thought he was going to be here. I was so much looking forward to seeing him again. He's so cool."

"So I've heard. Tell me, do you live nearby?"

"Nearby?" Mina giggled again. "These days, I live here."

Connie laughed so hard tears came to her eyes. She doubled over, holding her stomach, unable to say a word.

Angie put her hand to her heart and collapsed against her car. "Are you trying to kill me?" She didn't find it funny in the least.

"What a reaction! Were you scared or what?" Connie wiped her eyes, trying to control herself.

"I wasn't scared. You just startled me a little."

"With that scream? Every dog in the state heard you. You must have thought I was Lolly Firenghetti attacking you for starting up a rival comical cakes business." Connie started to laugh all over again.

"I'm glad you find it so funny!"

"I'm sorry." Connie tried to stop, but she wasn't very successful. "It was the setting—that creepy old church. You were so lost in thought, you didn't hear me walk up to you. I couldn't help myself."

"You certainly could have helped yourself! And St. Michael's is a venerable church. It's not creepy."

"Oh, no? There's a sign on the gate down the block that says GRAVEYARD. Scary stuff."

Angie smoothed her hair. She was sure it was standing on end. "Old graveyards are interesting, that's all."

"I don't think so!" Connie said. "And neither do you."

Angie folded her arms, the idea for a little revenge forming. "Come to think of it, I'd like to go inside to check out some tombstones. They might make intriguing cake decorations."

"You're kidding, right?"

"Not at all. Of course, if you're too scared to come with me . . ."

Connie blinked a couple of times, then she slowly and somewhat resolutely raised her chin. "Lead the way."

Angie smiled to herself as she marched toward the iron gate. Connie stuck close behind.

"Maybe the gate will be locked," Connie said hopefully.

Angie easily lifted the gate latch. "I guess nobody worries about grave robbers anymore." The gate required a hard shove to open, and the rusted hinges creaked their protest. She held the gate wide to let Connie enter. "After you."

"No," Connie drew back. "You can have the honor."

Grinning to herself, Angie walked inside and found she had entered a garden. Since there were no streetlights on the sidewalk near the church, the area around the gate was dark, and the garden even darker. Trees cut off the moonlight, and overgrown bushes loomed all around them. It took Angie a while to find the path that she imagined must lead to the graveyard.

"I don't think this is such a good idea," Connie murmured.

"Sure it is." Angie crept deeper into the garden, then

stopped. "Did you hear that sound?" she whispered, her voice low, quivering.

Connie, quaking, grabbed her arm. "No."

Angie chuckled. "Me, neither."

"Darn you!" Connie cried, giving her a shove. "That does it. Onward to the graves, Elvira, Mistress of the Night."

Angie suppressed her laughter as she walked faster and faster. Suddenly, the shrubbery opened up, letting more of the moonlight shine onto a patch of ground marked by seven tombstones, all topped with crosses.

"I wonder if they were priests," Angie whispered as she bent close to a stone. Although she'd been joking about little tombstone cakes, she had to admit the idea wasn't bad. But what occasion could they possibly be used for?

"Don't step there!" Angie said as Connie approached.

Connie jumped back. "Why not?"

"You were standing right on a grave. I wouldn't do that if I were you."

The wind whipped up and made a low, crooning sound. Connie shrank further to the side. "Angie, let's get out of here."

"But this is so great! The atmosphere is wonderful. I should soak it in so I'll be ready if someone wants an early Halloween party." She moved to a larger tombstone and crouched down but couldn't make out any of the letters.

The crooning sound grew louder, then suddenly stopped. All turned absolutely still.

"I can't take this, Angie," Connie said, whipping her head from graves to markers to rocks and trees. "Let's go."

Silence.

Connie turned back to the tombstone Angie had been looking at. She was gone. "Angie?" Connie's voice scarcely worked.

She heard nothing.

"Angie?" Connie wailed, close to tears.

No answer.

"Angie!" she shrieked.

Suddenly, Angie jumped out of the bushes behind her. "Boo!"

Connie let out a terrified squawk. When she could breathe again, she glowered at her giggling friend. "All right. You got even. Let's go."

The iron gate clanged shut. The metallic echo danced down their spines. "What was that?" Connie whimpered, unable to move.

"I don't know."

"Did you do it?" Connie demanded. "Is this more of your idea of how to get even?"

"Believe me, I didn't do a thing."

Connie edged closer to Angie, not realizing that Angie was edging up to her.

"Probably just some pedestrian saw the gate open and decided to shut it," Angie said. "Being a good citizen and all."

"You're right." Connie didn't sound too convinced.

"Maybe we should leave now." Angie's mouth was dry.

"Good idea."

The two started walking slowly hand in hand toward the gate.

From inside the church came a loud creaking sound followed by a hollow boom as a door slammed shut.

"I . . . I thought the church was empty," Connie whispered, her hand tightening on Angie's.

"So did I. It must be the wind again," Angie whispered back.

"But . . . there is no wind now."

They looked at each other long and hard and then turned and began to run, hands still clutched, Connie in one direction and Angie in the other. Their grip unbroken, their arms stretched, and then a hard jolt caused them to spin back together and collide.

Not only had they stepped on graves, they now sprawled over them. Angie was chilled to the bone as she lifted her eyes. From this angle, she could read the gravestone's cheerful message. *All flesh is grass.*

Connie was the first to her feet. She grabbed Angie, tugging wildly at her. The two plunged headlong through the churchyard, practically doing high jumps over anything that might trip them, somehow finding the garden path in the darkness and hurtling through it to the gate.

The iron gate was shut. Connie pulled at it, but it didn't open. Angie reached for it as well, trying to help, slapping Connie's hands away from the latch until she could finally yank the latch back and push the gate open.

Bouncing and jostling against each other, they squeezed through, ran to their respective cars, and drove away in a mad dash.

His heart was full.

He visualized her once again with the moonlight streaming down on her face as she walked through the churchyard. She was perfect in every way.

His silver maiden. His virgin.

He was hungry for her, hungry for the taste of her flesh, her rich, warm blood, the throbbing of her living heart in his hands.

The quiet street enveloped him in darkness as he faced her apartment. His eyes glowed red, and his body pulsated with desire, yearning for a coupling stronger and more satisfying than any mere mortal could ever know. When the time was right, she would be his in every way.

The lights in her apartment switched off. Visions of her alone in her big, welcoming bed came to him. Perhaps he would be in her dreams tonight as she was, always, in his.

Chapter 4

Luis Calderon was in his late forties, divorced and bitter about it. The other homicide inspectors speculated that single-handedly he kept the Rose Pomade Company in business with his foot-tall pompadour. Calderon liked it when he was a teenager, and he wasn't about to change. Of course, the color wasn't Grecian Formula black when he was a boy, but no one dared point that out to him.

Different in every way from Calderon was Bo Benson—African-American, mid-thirties, streetwise, suave, and unabashedly single. He dressed like a Calvin Klein ad, went out with a new woman every week, and had a face and physique so appealing that women's heads swiveled like turnstiles whenever he walked by. The guys in the bureau liked to say Wilt Chamberlain's record had nothing on him, and they weren't talking basketball.

"Look at you two sitting around yakking like a couple of clueless college professors," Calderon said to Paavo and Yosh, who continued to catch up on paperwork in lieu of any interesting homicides coming their

32

way. He dropped into his chair with a thud. "Don't you guys have any work to do?"

"Work? Hell, no." Yosh leaned back and put his feet up on the desk, hands clasped behind his head. "We'd rather watch you two do it. Much more fun this way."

"Yeah, well, I'm glad somebody's having fun here," Calderon said, half snarling as he threw his notebook onto his desk. "You wouldn't be having any if you saw what we did."

"It sucked, big time," Benson agreed. He took a bottle of Evian from his desk and opened it. "I'll be looking real hard to get my hands on the son of a bitch."

"What've you got?" Paavo asked.

Calderon took off his jacket and rolled up his sleeves. "An Indian girl, Lucy Whitefeather. Only nineteen years old. She was real pretty, long, black hair. Shit!"

Paavo was surprised by Calderon's tone. It wasn't like him to sound so personal about a victim.

"She was last seen waiting for the bus to take her home from a City College night course," Benson remarked. "Everyone said she was a good kid. Going to school at night, working days. And some bastard killed her. She'd been missing all night, but her folks thought she was with a boyfriend. Her body was found this morning by garbage men in an alley just off Lobos, across from Ocean View Playground."

"Sexual assault?" Yosh asked, sitting upright, feet on the floor, as the seriousness and tragic nature of murder filled him.

"Looks like. Assaulted and strangled. But that wasn't the weird part. She was surrounded by burning candles, little votive candles like you see in church—"

"Weird," Yosh agreed.

"No," Calderon chimed in. "The weird part was that her heart was cut out."

"Cut out? You mean it's gone?" Paavo looked from him to Bo.

"You got it," Bo said. "It was like something you'd see in one of those horror movies, the ones with demons and witches and Christopher Walken."

"My favorites," Yosh said.

"Not mine," Bo admitted, head shaking. "Gave me goosebumps."

"Hell, now I gotta deal with a chicken partner," Calderon grumped, pouring himself a cup of strong, black coffee. "Or should I say *goose?* He's probably going to be seeing Freddie Kruger in every closet."

"It was spooky, man," Bo protested. "Her laying there, naked, that candle wax around her, a hole in her chest—"

"Bawk, bawk, bawk!" Calderon flapped his elbows.

Benson shook his head.

"Sounds like some kind of ritual," Paavo said. "Do you think that's what you're dealing with?"

"That's what I *don't* like about this," Bo replied. "A ritual in an alley doesn't make sense. Other people could wander by, notice something going on. It was too much of a chance to take."

"She was most likely killed someplace else," Paavo suggested, "and brought there."

"She had to have been. There wasn't enough blood for it to have been done there." Benson lifted his dark eyes. "Still, to carry around dead weight, then set up all those candles—it makes me wonder if the killer didn't have others helping him, others as sick as he is."

"Let me know if I can help," Paavo said.

"Not you, Paav," Yosh said. "You've got other things on your plate right now."

"Such as?" Calderon asked, interested.

"Angie." Yosh winked, then glanced at Paavo and began to hum the tune "Tonight" from *West Side Story*.

Paavo didn't say a word. Yosh cackled, then made a gesture as if he were zipping his mouth shut.

Real helpful, Yosh, Paavo thought, the urge to strangle suddenly strong.

Calderon lifted his eyebrows and faced Paavo. "What's the problem?"

"No problem." He turned to his desk and began pushing papers around as if he was looking for something important. He knew he wasn't fooling anyone.

Calderon and Benson continued to look at him expectantly. Suddenly, he couldn't handle the closeness of the homicide bureau and walked out without another word.

Stanfield Bonnette leaned casually against the kitchen counter and watched Angie switch on her KitchenAid. Her neighbor from across the hall stood about six feet tall, slim, with puppy-dog brown eyes and silky brown hair that often flopped onto his forehead. He dressed well, today in a pale-green Izod short-sleeved pullover tucked into belted natural linen slacks, with polished brown loafers. In his early thirties, he occasionally worked in a bank. It should have been consistent work, but reliability wasn't part of Stan's vocabulary.

"I don't think I'd want to eat a cake that reminds me of a dentist's office," he said.

"Good, because if you touch this, you die." She had gotten a request that morning from a dentist's wife for a Comical Cake for her husband's retirement. Angie had come up with a set of dentures and the words "Bite into a Happy Retirement." Unfortunately, she had no idea how to bake a denture cake and was in no mood to put up with Stan's suggestions.

At her fierce expression, he backed up. "What are those big, round cake pans for?"

"They're for Saturday's project—a wedding cake." Serefina's nagging visit came to mind. *Nothing like adding insult to injury,* Angie thought, as she scraped the batter from the sides of the bowl. She stood back, hands on hips of her peach-colored jumpsuit, as she watched the mixer do its job.

"Since when does a company called Comical Cakes do wedding cakes?" He sidled up to the cake batter and stretched a forefinger toward it. Angie slapped his hand away.

"Apparently, it's the third marriage for each, so they went for a cake that says on each layer, in iridescent colors:

'Remarriage—
the Triumph of
Optimism over Experience'."

"Not a bad line or three," Stan said.

"It's a gloss on a saying by Dr. Johnson or some-body like that," she added. "Traditional bakers wouldn't go along with the couple's wishes."

"They do have reputations to maintain," Stan said.

"As if I don't?"

He didn't answer but reached in the cookie jar for some sustenance. It was empty. "Have you given up baking for yourself because of your business?"

"It's taking up all my time, in case you haven't noticed." She turned off the mixer and poured the dentist's cake into two round pans. She would attempt to shape the cake after it was baked.

"I'm starving," Stan said as he opened the refrigerator door. "I didn't eat yet today." Halfway inside, his voice echoed as he said, "Doesn't seem to me that baking ugly cakes should take up all your time this way."

"That's just what I needed to hear!"

"It's true, though." Since no interesting leftovers beckoned, he shut the door, folded his arms, and stared glumly at the cookie jar.

Yes, she had to admit, it was true. Her fledgling business was taking up her time, but wasn't that the way with any start-up? You devoted your life, heart and soul, to the enterprise, whatever it was. Well, she was doing that now and loving every minute of it, whether Stan or Serefina or Connie or anyone else liked it or not. At least Paavo stood by her.

"You know what, Stan, I'd have time to bake for me—and you—if each cake didn't take so long. For example, when I bake the wedding cake, I'll need three ovens. And I only have two"—she pointed to her fire-engine-red, professional-size Viking range—"but if I could use your oven, the baking would go that much faster."

He snorted. "I hate to be petty about this, Angie, but I don't see how letting you use my oven would help at all. Look at the time you spend doing this. How much are you making from it? Sixty cents an hour? Not to mention the danger."

"What danger?"

"Didn't you hear about the strangler?" At Angie's

questioning look, he continued, "It was such a horrible murder. Really creepy. They found the body of a woman, a young woman, and—here's the really scary part—her heart had been cut out."

"How awful!" Angie was shocked and also surprised she hadn't heard about it. She'd slept poorly again last night, probably because of her adventure in the graveyard, and hadn't even put on the radio, let alone read the newspaper today. All her time seemed to be taken up either baking, delivering, or designing cakes.

"It was probably some kind of ritual killing. I've heard that with some of these satanic cults, they keep people alive while they do horrible things to them. What if she was alive when they started to cut out the heart?" He lowered his voice. "Tha-thump, tha-thump."

"Will you stop!" She threw a potholder at him.

"I can imagine all these ugly, evil people in robes standing around some poor young woman. It must have been so terrible for her—"

"Enough already! You're scaring me now!" Her escapade in the creepy churchyard must have jangled her nerves more than she'd realized.

"Why didn't your boyfriend tell you about it?" Stan plucked an apple from a ceramic bowl on the counter. "Shouldn't he warn you of such things?"

"I haven't talked to him yet today." Angie hoped the conversation was closed.

He took a big bite, chewed, and swallowed. "If I was your boyfriend, I wouldn't let you go out delivering cakes to strange people late at night unless I was with you. It's too scary out there right now. Stay home, Angie. Give this up." He glanced woefully at the apple, then back at the refrigerator. She could almost hear his unspoken plea: *Cook!*

"I can't stay home hiding under the bed every time someone is killed in a city this size." She said this as much to convince herself as Stan. "Things like that happen, unfortunately."

"You could stay in my bed anytime, Angie." He grinned.

She rolled her eyes and opened a box of confectioners' sugar for the icing.

Loud staccato raps sounded at the door. Paavo's knock.

Angie hurried to it. "Paavo! What a surprise."

He kissed her, then kept his hands on her shoulders as his pale-blue eyes studied her a long moment, his expression serious. He was a tall man, with broad shoulders and a slim but powerful build. His short hair was dark brown, his high-cheekboned face was hard and chiseled. It was the kind of face that crooks, thieves, and murderers might cower from, but Angie saw it as nothing less than handsome.

"Is something wrong?" she asked.

"I just wanted to see you." His hands tightened, ready to draw her closer, when Stan appeared in the doorway to the kitchen.

"My, my, look at what turned up," Stan said, slouching against the doorjamb, apple core in hand.

Angie's neighbor's mere existence was enough to put Paavo's teeth on edge. "If it isn't Bonnet," he said, trying to keep the irritation from his voice.

"You might want to call me Mr. Bonnette since I'm going to be Angie's partner."

"What?" Angie gawked at him.

Paavo was relieved by Angie's reaction. He hated to think she'd completely lost her senses over this new business.

Stan strolled further into the living room. "She'll be using my oven, and I'll be seeing that she's all right when she goes out at night." He paused. "She didn't even know about the strangler."

"It just happened last night," Paavo said to Angie, wondering what tales Bonnette had been telling her.

"There's some ritual-performing strangler loose in the city?" The thought horrified her. "Stan's right?"

He hated to admit it. He wanted to simply tell her to get that loser out of her house so they could be alone. "You need to be careful, just as always," he said.

"So, maybe Stan should go with me at night," she suggested. "At least until you catch this guy."

Having to agree to that was bamboo-sticks-under-the-fingernails time. "If there's no one else around, he's better than going out alone." *But not by much,* he wanted to add.

A bell chimed from inside the kitchen, and Stan scooted away from Paavo's glare.

"*Our* cake is ready, Angie," he chirped. "Come help me test it. I'll find a toothpick for us."

"Don't touch it, Stan!" she cried, ready to run after him, but hesitated, glancing at Paavo.

This visit wasn't going the way he'd planned, Paavo thought. "You're busy. I'll get going." He would have liked to touch her, to at least run the back of his hand against the softness of her cheek, but the thought of that nerdy little blowhard in the next room was so irritating, he just wanted out of there. "Don't forget our dinner date tonight."

"Oh, that's right!" She had almost forgotten. That wasn't like her at all. She never overlooked anything where Paavo was concerned—or at least never had before.

After hurrying him out the door, she returned to the kitchen. Stan had already removed the cakes from the pans and cut himself a big slice. He sat at the small kitchen table, plate in front of him, fork poised to dig in.

"What are you doing?" she shrieked.

"Just testing to see if it's done." He speared a mouthful. "Did I ever tell you I love warm cake?"

Connie Rogers sat at Angie's dining room table, discreetly yawned, and forced her eyes to focus on the papers in front of her.

Earlier, Angie had put in an emergency call to Connie. Even if Stan hadn't ruined the test cakes, her idea of a set of dentures just wasn't a good one. While waiting for Connie, she printed out a bunch of computer graphics and sketched her own pictures of teeth—lots and lots of smiling mouths filled with Dentyne-bright displays.

"When you think about it," Connie said, after going through the printouts and drawings several times, "teeth are really kind of ugly. Big, white, hard shell things protruding from shiny pink gums. Yech."

"If the dentist's wife wants teeth, she gets teeth," Angie said, nose deep in magazine ads for toothpaste and denture adhesives. "Judging from her house, they've been good to her."

"I can imagine. I think I've paid for at least three rooms of my dentist's home all by myself."

"What about fangs?" Angie mused.

"I don't see your Dr. Pain as Dracula," Connie replied. "Maybe you should settle for a set of choppers with *Eat Me* across the top."

Tossing the magazines aside, Angie put her head in her hands. "I give up!"

"You'll come up with something," Connie said. "You always do. It'll be fine."

"I always do? I'm the one with so many failed businesses I'm the family joke! Daffy Duck gets more respect."

"You just haven't hit the right business yet."

"I hope this is it," Angie said wearily. "I'm running out of ideas."

Connie nodded. "I can imagine."

The two studied the pictures a while longer. "You know what," Angie said, lifting a computer graphic from the stack. "I like this single tooth best of all. He's kind of cute, and he's got a nice smiling face."

"The boxy-looking molar?" Connie asked. She bent close to study the drawing. "How do you know it's a *he?*"

Angie pushed her out of the way. "Look, we can kind of curve the roots so it looks like he's jumping for joy."

"A jumping tooth. Now, why didn't I think of that?" Connie said straight-faced.

"I like it! Just think what a cute cake it'll be for a dentist."

Connie scrunched up her mouth. "I hate to tell you, Angie, but I don't think there is such a thing."

Chapter 5

Finally, all this time of waiting and anxiety was coming to an end.

Paavo lifted his dress-shirt collar and slid his necktie over it. *Just a few more hours*, he told himself.

Before starting the knot, he reached into his pocket one more time to make sure the jewelry box was still in there, a handkerchief stuffed on top of it to prevent it from slipping out.

After reaching his decision at work the other day, he'd gone to see Yosh's brother, who owned a jewelry shop. He knew Tadeo, or Tad, as he liked to be called, would give him a fine ring at a good price. Even at a discount, he was appalled by how expensive diamond rings were. Still, he couldn't give Angie anything cheap.

Tad had suggested a ring that was a little unusual and shown him a Siberian blue diamond solitaire, marquise cut, in a six-prong white gold Tiffany setting. It was only a half-carat, but was the most beautiful engagement ring Paavo had ever seen. He bought it and had been praying ever since that she'd like it.

Touching it made his heartbeat quicken and caused a

dryness in his throat that not even a hard swallow could alleviate. He wanted to get this over with. Last night, once again, he hadn't slept a wink, but this time he spent the night thinking about tonight's dinner with Angie and asking the Big Question. At six A.M., he'd given up and gone in to work. Luckily, no case sprang up to get in the way of his plans. Yosh, who knew what Paavo was about to do, had twitted him about it all day.

The ends of his tie in hand, he watched himself in the bathroom mirror as he crossed one length over the other to begin a Windsor knot.

If it had been up to him, he'd simply say, "Angie, want to go to Reno?" They could buy a license in Reno and be done with it in ten minutes. No waiting period, no tests, no relatives, wedding showers, bachelor parties, or gift registrations. No hurt feeling over bridal party choices, no rehearsals, no decisions on church, day, time, reception, honeymoon, or clothes to wear to any of them. All in all, a very reasonable way to get hitched.

He let go of the tie. Why was he doing this? He pulled the skewed knot apart and started over.

The truth was, Angie wouldn't want to elope. She and her mother would be in seventh heaven planning her wedding. They'd probably come up with the biggest bash in San Francisco since a major movie star married the high-society publisher of the now defunct *San Francisco Examiner.* He wondered if that was an omen.

The temptation to take the ring back to the jeweler and forget about it nearly overwhelmed him.

He looked at his tie. The back side was half as long again as the front. He pulled it apart and pressed a cold washcloth against his forehead. *Get over it,* he ordered himself. *You've faced gun-toting crazed killers. You can ask one little woman to marry you and cope with her mother's wedding plans.*

He drew in his breath and began the knot again.

He would order crêpes suzette for dessert, and when Angie's eyes were on the flames, he'd put the ring on her dessert plate. The waiters would be told that as soon as she noticed, they were to disappear and not return until he gave the nod that she'd said yes.

Of course, if she said no, he wouldn't want dessert anyway.

The knot ended up so lopsided that no matter how much he pulled and tugged, it wouldn't straighten out. He yanked it off his neck.

No need to worry so much. She wouldn't say no. She couldn't . . . though she had once before, he reminded himself. Still, that was months ago.

Things were different now.

Yet Angie was nothing if not unpredictable.

She wanted him to propose. No doubt about it. This nervousness was part of the ritual, nothing more. Other men survived it and he would, too.

Somehow.

As he worked on the knot once more, out of the corner of his eye he noticed that his cat had joined him. Hercules sat on the bathroom floor, his tail curled around him, whiskers twitching, as he looked up at Paavo.

Paavo was sure the cat was laughing at him.

* * *

Angie and Connie stopped talking when they heard a knock on the door. A loud knock. A cop kind of knock.

"That can't be Paavo," Angie said as she got up. "He's never on time for a simple dinner date. It practically takes an Act of Congress to have him show up when he's supposed to for an important function."

She opened the door. It was him.

"What are you doing here?" she asked, and peeked around him to check the hallway. "Is anything wrong?"

"Why do you always think there's something wrong when I come to see you?" He walked in and noticed Connie at the table with papers spread all over. They exchanged greetings, then he turned back to Angie. "We're supposed to go to dinner now."

"I know, but you're on time." He was wearing one of his nicest sport jackets, a Ralph Lauren she'd bought for him at Saks. His shirt was new, and his tie had a crisp, full Windsor Knot. What was going on?

"I made reservations for us at Les Fleurs," he said.

"Les Fleurs?" Her antennae went on full alert. He hadn't indicated tonight was in any way special, and that was a very expensive place.

"You've always liked it there" was his only response.

"Yes, but . . . you're never on time," she insisted.

He frowned. "What's that supposed to mean?"

"It's true. I didn't expect you to show up this early. You say seven o'clock and you're never here before eight-thirty or nine. Not ever."

"Why are we arguing? Is that what you plan to wear?"

She had on slacks and a silk sweater. As one who

loved to dress up and used any opportunity to do so, she would never wear anything so casual to an elegant restaurant. She wasn't sure how to answer.

"What's going on?" he asked, his brow creased.

"I invited Connie to come over after work to help me with a dentist's cake."

His jaw seemed to tighten, and she had no idea why.

"How close are you to being done?" he asked.

"An hour, maybe."

"An hour?"

This grilling was irritating her. He made it sound as if she was in the wrong here. "Well, considering that you've never been on time before, I didn't think it would be a problem. I've got my new business to consider after all."

She watched him shut his mouth, an act of self-censorship. Oh, he always meant to be on time—he'd assured her of that often enough—but last minute issues cropped up. Most were life-or-death issues, not cakes. And that, she supposed, made a difference.

"Hey, you two," Connie said, joining them. Her eyes were wide as she took in Paavo's clothes and his expression and noted his choice of a restaurant. "Why don't I leave? You're okay with the tooth thing, Angie. Go out with Paavo."

Angie was irritated. Obviously neither of them gave any importance to her need to be sure that everything was as close to perfect as possible in her new cake business. Well, she would show them. Both of them. "I need you here, Connie. This is very important to me. To my business."

"I've had a long day," Connie pleaded. "I haven't

been sleeping well lately. I don't see how I can help you anymore."

"But you've got to! You are helping, believe me. Just . . . go back to the dining room table, okay? I'll be right there."

Connie and Paavo exchanged a strange glance, then Connie shrugged and did as she was told. Angie's gaze leaped in confusion from one to the other.

"I'll call the restaurant and tell them we'll be late," Paavo said.

Angie cheered up at those words and went to join Connie. "Just relax a while," she called to Paavo as he reached for the phone. "I'll be ready to go in no time."

Baron Severus's basement seemed different tonight, Zoe thought as she entered The Crypt Macabre a little after eleven. She wore a tight-fitting, studded black leather jacket and slacks and black patent Doc Martens. The bouncer had given her a leering smile and when she handed him ten dollars didn't even question her being there. She guessed that meant she now belonged.

Candles lit the room, and the soft, haunting sound of Peruvian wind instruments played in the background. Costumed Goths in black or deeply colored garments, either ultra-sleek leather and vinyl or flowing and romantic velvets and brocades, moved in and out of the shadows. She did the same, making her way across the dark room, searching for the Baron.

A hand took hold of her arm. "The ice princess returns."

She spun around to see the same tall man who'd been so obnoxious to her. "And you, the Frog Prince."

"You've cut me to my slimy green quick," he said good-naturedly.

"Good. You can hop away and lick your wounds." Their eyes caught a moment before she jerked her arm free.

"Why so unfriendly?" he asked, hurrying after her.

Tonight he wore a deep-red poet's shirt with flowing sleeves, a black velvet vest, black slacks, and boots. *If he had a sword,* she thought, *he'd look like a swashbuckler. And if he'd wash that red crap off his eyes and get some sun, he might even be halfway decent-looking.* "Don't you have something else to do? Like kill yourself?"

She reached the far wall but hadn't yet seen the Baron anywhere. She regretted having dashed out so suddenly the first time she'd visited, but coming face to face with the man—or monster—of her nightmares had shaken her so much she had to leave. She assumed she'd have plenty of other chances to see him and learn about him and the people around him, since this was his club.

"He's not here yet." Rysk folded his arms, his mouth down-turned. "All the babes zero in on him. He's a cool dude. I'd hate him if he wasn't."

"Like he'd care, I'm sure." She backed up to the wall and faced the crowd. As much as she should be alone to find a way to get close to the Baron, Rysk's nearness made her a little bolder, a little more self-assured.

"Forget about him." Rysk put his hand against the wall beside her head and leaned closer. "For one thing, you're not his type."

She was forced to make eye contact again. His eyes were hazel, deep and intense. "Oh? What is his type?"

He smirked. "Gorgeous. And rich."

She whirled away from him, her cheeks fiery. "Thanks loads! Why don't you go play shooting gallery? You can be the duck."

"Don't worry about it." He followed close, his breath tickling her ear as he said, "You're gorgeous enough for me."

"Stuff it!"

Rysk laughed, but before he had a chance to reply, a teenager ran up to them. He was dressed in the Goth-as-vampire costume—a white ruffled shirt and black-with-red-lining opera cape. The gold ring through his right eyebrow and circle of bleached blond hair looking like a raw pancake on the very top of his head spoiled the overall effect, however. "Where's the Baron?" His face was drenched in perspiration.

Before they could answer, he turned and plunged toward a large man who vaguely resembled a huge white sponge. His brown hair was so short it was mere stubble, and his ears protruded, as did his two front teeth. If not for his white skin, black lipstick and black fingernail polish, he would have looked like the boring, overweight neighbor who spends every weekend drenched in sweat, mowing his lawn.

"I've got to see the Baron," the teen said. "I've got to give him this." He held up a paper bag. The man took it and looked inside.

"Who are they?" Zoe whispered.

"The big one is the Baron's assistant, Wilbur Fieldren. I don't know who the kid is." They followed as Fieldren led the boy to the back of the club and knocked on a door. The Baron came out, followed by the spacey

Mina Harker. He and the boy spoke together, the boy animated and shaking as if badly frightened.

Finally the Baron patted his shoulder and walked to the center of the room. Tonight his hair wasn't slicked back but fell in clean, thick waves to his shoulders. He wore a traditionally cut black suit and with it a blue silk shirt with a round, buttoned collar but no tie. He was the antithesis of the young, motley crowd before him, yet he commanded their complete attention.

The only time Zoe had ever heard a group of people fall silent so quickly was in a church, and even there she could usually hear a baby crying or a toddler whining during the service.

"My friends," the Baron began. Piercing brown eyes gazed out at the crowd, capturing people one by one with their intensity. "I'm sorry to interrupt your time of play, your time to feel free of the torments and troubles of the world outside, but I bring you grave news. Terrible news that you must pay close attention to. It is a matter of life . . . and death."

A buzz began in the room, followed by shushing sounds.

"Look carefully." He nodded, and the boy held up a thick white candle and a small glass bottle filled with clear liquid. "This candle and this flask filled with holy water were left at the door of my young friend's home."

Audible gasps filled the room. "A religious fanatic has targeted us. I suppose"—he gave a toothy smile—"whoever did this thought we would sizzle when we touched the water and would burn from the flame of the candle. We're only missing a Bible and the tolling bell of the sacrament to have the complete paraphernalia of the so-called exorcist—the symbols of excommunication. They snuff the candle, muffle the bell, and slam shut the book when they cast us from their feeble churches."

The crowd laughed nervously.

"I wish it was a laughing matter," the Baron said solemnly. Zoe felt his rumbling, stentorian voice deep in the pit of her stomach and experienced the pull of his seductive manner, of the power that radiated from him to the others, drawing her into his fold.

"The madman hunts those he regards as evil. He believes in vampires and witches and"—he paused—"in demons."

Every vestige of party-going had disappeared, and the people stared in stunned silence.

He bowed his head, as if all their worry was borne on his shoulders. "The sad part is that this man is dangerous. He believes people who feel alive at night, who live as we do, who like our music, our way of . . . escaping . . . the ugliness and bitterness of this world, are possessed. He will seek us out. He will try to harm us, to drive evil from our souls. He thinks that we, who live for the night, must be destroyed."

All together, the crowd moved closer to the Baron, as if seeking his protection.

He gazed sadly at them. "You may need to fight for your very lives if he accosts you."

"What does he look like?" a young woman asked.

"My friend here saw him. Travis, what can you tell these people?"

Zoe took a step forward, her hands unconsciously clenched. She didn't see the sharp look Rysk sent her.

"I'm not sure," Travis said. "He's a white guy, kinda ugly." The group softly laughed, and the boy chuckled self-consciously. "He wore a hat, an old man's hat, like from the thirties or something. He was kinda old. Fifties or sixties, maybe. He was pretty skinny, maybe six feet tall. I don't remember his face—just his eyes. He knows me, man, and it kinda freaked me out." Travis glanced up at the Baron. "That's all I know."

"That's helpful, my friend." The Baron patted the boy's shoulder and then stepped toward the people, his arms outstretched as if he would shelter them all.

"The man's name"—the Baron waited to be sure he had everyone's complete attention—"his name is Mason Markowitz. Remember that, for it may save your lives. I am his prime target, my friends, but he hates all of us." His voice boomed. "He thinks our kind are outcasts, freaks, and monsters! He wants to take away our freedom, make us cower like the nine-to-five slaves in the rat race they call modern life!"

Cries of "No!" and "He can't do that!" echoed through the room.

"We won't let him!" the Baron roared. The crowd cheered, ready to do his bidding. Rather than incite them further, as Zoe expected he would, he dropped his pitch almost to a whisper. "Markowitz is crazy and therefore dangerous. Together our love, our strength, will shield us." He grew louder. "Together we will be victorious over everyone who wishes us harm!"

People cheered.

"If he tries, we will crush him!"

Shouts of "Yes! Yes!" were deafening. As they quieted, Zoe's voice rang out. "What do we do if he comes after us?"

The Baron stood very still, and the full force of his eyes struck her like a body blow. Silence reigned, the room mesmerized by what might follow.

"Come to me if you see him," he said, and she felt as if he was speaking to her alone. "Come to me if he is near. Come to me if you are afraid." Slowly, carefully, and loudly he enunciated his last words. "I will not let him harm you!"

The room erupted, and the entire crowd surged toward the Baron. Hands, men's and women's, stretched out to touch him, to thank him for caring for them, for loving and protecting them. As the music began, a raucous Sisters of Mercy tune, he smiled and seemed to grow even larger in stature. He touched and hugged and patted his people, relishing this love fest as they danced wildly around him.

Zoe backed away, scarcely able to believe what she had witnessed. She'd thought tales of the Baron were bizarre and exaggerated, some out-and-out lies. Now she wondered if she was the one who had been naïve.

Chapter 6

A hand shook his shoulder. With a start, Paavo opened his eyes and blinked, momentarily confused. Angie's living room . . . her couch . . . her. He sat up and saw that she'd draped a blanket over him. "I must have dozed."

"Six hours' worth," she said, and smiled.

"Six . . ." He looked at his watch. "Midnight?"

"I hated waking you. You were sleeping so soundly, I thought you must be very tired."

He rubbed his eyes. Angie was in her nightgown and fluffy pink robe. No candlelight dinner for them tonight.

"Did you get everything taken care of with Connie?" he asked, blinking and trying to get his brain to function.

"Yes. Now I just have to make sure it works. I'll get up early tomorrow—probably seven or so. That way, if the cake we planned turns into a disaster, I'll have time to try something else."

He shook his head and yawned. "This business of yours is amazing. I had no idea so much time went into baking cakes."

She grinned. "Do you want to stay?"

The idea was tempting, but she looked tired, and he realized that getting a seven A.M. wake-up call was not a normal part of Angie's routine. One benefit of not having a regular nine-to-five job—the other being a wealthy and generous father to support her—was that she could sleep in while trying to come up with something innovative, exciting, and lucrative to do with her life. Until this cake business turned up, her poor choices in career planning had resulted in lots of beauty sleep.

The standing joke around Homicide was Angie's inability to figure out what she wanted to do with her life—other than marry him, that is. He had a sneaky suspicion they even had a pool going as to when—or if—he'd marry her, but no one would confess to it.

If he ever found a way to act on his decision, wouldn't they be surprised? Tonight was not the night, though. And particularly not after he'd just fallen asleep on her couch and she'd worked all evening on her new business. No, he needed to do this thing properly.

"I'll head for home," he said, "let you get some rest. Seven will be here before you know it."

"I'm sorry about the way the evening turned out," she said, slipping into his arms.

"It's not your fault I fell asleep." He kissed her, more of a to-be-continued than a good-bye kiss. "How about tomorrow night?" he asked as he opened the door.

"I have to take my tooth cake to the party and set it up. It starts at eight, so I'll be there at seven. Connie promised to go with me, and afterward we're going to dinner."

He nodded. "It's good you're not going out alone right now. I'll call you."

"Okay."

As he walked toward the elevator, he wondered when he'd next get a chance to pop the question.

He walked into Homicide a little after six A.M. Having fallen asleep at Angie's and ruining his plans, he'd spent the rest of the night lying awake.

Ironically, whenever he had pondered his future, which wasn't often, he had never imagined himself married. Instead, he envisioned a life that was short and lived as a loner. Now that image had changed, or so he hoped.

Maybe that was the reason this sudden derailing of his plans bothered him so much. He was combating a lifetime of karma. The life he was leading and a rapid conclusion to it wasn't enough for him. He wanted more. It was as if the brass ring was almost within reach and he was straining for it but it was still just beyond his fingertips. He shook the image away.

He and Angie would go out soon, he'd propose, she'd consent, and everything would be fine.

He turned to the current batch of cases on his desk, each more boring than the one before it. *Focus,* he told himself. They weren't really dull. It was just that he had something so much bigger on his mind—something about life, not death.

Calderon's desk caught his eye, and he remembered how, as he'd listened to the discussion of Lucy White-feather's murder, some aspect of it nagged at him, almost as if he were hearing it for a second time, not the first.

That brought to mind the first time he met Angie. He'd been investigating a murder that occurred near her apartment when she received a ticking package. She'd put it in the dishwasher. A strange thing to do, but it had saved her life when the package exploded. That should have told him something about her. Warned him? No, intrigued him. As his murder investigation and the threats against Angie's life intertwined, he soon came to see beyond the rich, pampered, and beautiful woman he'd thought she was, to the warm, loyal, generous—and, yes, beautiful—person he'd fallen in love with.

Nothing about the way she thought or acted was as he'd learned to expect from his own life experience; nothing was as harsh or cruel or selfish. She was just . . .

He forced himself back to his notes concerning a gunshot victim. The perp had been arrested, and a plea-bargain was in the works. Case closed, except for writing out a long, tedious report.

He could just imagine how Angie would tussle with an attorney at a plea-bargaining. The guy wouldn't know what hit him, sort of like the time she hit *him* smack in the face with a ham sandwich. He grinned. Much as he'd tried to appear angry, inside he was laughing hard.

He shook the image away. *Concentrate!* But the memory of how she'd washed the mustard and mayonnaise from the sandwich off his face . . . and how they'd ended up in the shower together . . . and . . .

"Good Christ!" he muttered, shaking his head. The bureau was empty, and he stood up and paced, trying to shake off these distractions. The other inspectors hadn't arrived yet, and once they did, they'd soon head out to interview witnesses, track down leads, testify (or, more likely, sit around a courtroom waiting to testify), while he was supposed to finish up paperwork.

The unfortunate part was that even though he had no difficult murders to solve at the moment, it wasn't because people had decided to love their neighbors. They still killed each other but weren't bright about it, leaving a trail of witnesses and evidence that practically begged the police to find them. Dumb killer; easy arrest; case closed.

He shut the folder of photos from a murder scene and again slid Angie's picture from his top drawer. She had given it to him shortly after visiting Homicide and noticing that other inspectors had pictures of wives, kids, friends, or even a beloved pet on their desks, while his was empty. It was just one of the numerous small presents she'd given him. Generous to a fault, loving . . .

Stop this! He was driving himself crazy. He glanced once more at the photo, remembering how Angie, graciously and with dedication, had visited his stepfather, Aulis, each day while he was in the hospital and continued until he was safely back on his feet. Aulis had been brutally attacked when his apartment was broken into. Angie had stood by Aulis and Paavo's side through that entire ordeal.

Finally, he shoved the photo back in the drawer and slammed it shut.

He had to do something work-related or he would go nuts. Turning to his computer, he began to search through old records and computer files of unsolved murders, looking for one with a similar modus

operandi to the Whitefeather case. He first keyed in
murders that had candles at the murder scene. Big mistake. The number of murders and the strange uses candles had been put to was overwhelming. He narrowed
the search by adding the words votive and ritual.

It worked.

A month ago a body had been found in an empty lot
near Sausalito's yacht harbor. The woman had been
strangled. A paper bag filled with votive candles was at
the side of her naked body, leading to speculation
about some sort of ritual involved with the killing. The
case got very little publicity for two reasons—the
woman was a street person and most of Sausalito's income comes from tourists. No one wanted to rock that
particular boat by advertising anything as distasteful as
a grisly murder.

Too bad.

When Paavo entered the Sausalito Police Department,
just over the Golden Gate Bridge from San Francisco,
and told the desk sergeant who he was and why he was
calling, he was directed to Trent Bowdin.

Sergeant Bowdin was in his late twenties, about six-
four, with a blond crew cut, wide blue eyes, and a mis-
sionarylike squeaky clean demeanor that made him
appear completely out of his element handling a murder case. Sausalito was the kind of town where the
worst crimes were souvenir rip-offs, pickpockets, and
druggies. Bowdin probably charmed the tourists, especially the female ones.

As soon as he realized Paavo was interested in the
case, he drove him to the spot where the body had been
found. Bowdin knew San Francisco's police depart-

ment was organized differently from many cities. All homicides were handled by officers in the Bureau of Inspection, not by cops in the precinct stations. Homicide was a specialty, the inspectors in the bureau specially trained.

Bowdin had been floundering and wanted to pick Paavo's brain. That was okay. Paavo wasn't using it for any cases at the moment anyway.

The body had been found in a vacant lot near the water between the tourist areas to the south and the marina further north. The lot had been excavated and, once the review process was completed and permits granted, a bank of townhouses would be built there.

"She was lying right out there," Bowdin said. "Candles—the short ones like you see in church—next to her. We figured they were going to be used in a ritual but for some reason the killer got chased off."

As Paavo studied the scene, he buttoned up his jacket and raised the collar. Cold air from the bay was cutting through him right to the bone. He couldn't stop shivering and was surprised Bowdin wasn't reacting the same way.

Warehouses, a restaurant, a couple of businesses, and other lots being readied for construction were nearby, but no homes. It was the sort of area that would be completely empty in the middle of the night.

Bowdin admitted that he had no suspects yet. The only lead was an old man who had been seen hanging around the area. "One of the shopkeepers said they thought his name was Mac or Marx or something like that," Bowdin said. "But we haven't been able to find him. He was probably some old drifter."

"Could be, but if people noticed him enough to mention him to you, there was something unusual about the guy."

"That's what we thought. We haven't given up on him altogether. Only other lead was a shoe print. A clear one."

Paavo glanced at him, interested.

"A Kmart sneaker. Turns out one of the M.E.'s team wore the same shoe. He swore he never stepped in that exact spot, but who knows?"

"True." It sounded like another dead end. Few would admit to stomping over a crime scene. Trained investigators and medics should know better, but those in Sausalito might well have been out of practice.

Bowdin gave a nervous laugh. "I'll let you know something, police force to police force. We're keeping it out of the press, of course."

"Agreed." Paavo had no problem with keeping any information from the media.

"It was very strange, and we really can't explain it at all. Maybe it was just a coincidence, you know, but we stored the body in a mortuary—our morgue is small and filled, and we knew we'd have to keep the body on ice a long time pending the outcome of the investigation."

"Yes . . ." Paavo encouraged him.

"The woman's body was stolen."

That was the last thing he expected to hear. "Was it recovered?"

"No. We can't figure out what happened. All we know is it's gone. Disappeared. We're trying to reconstruct who had access, how whoever did it managed to get inside. That's another weird thing. No break-in.

The easiest explanation is that the corpse got up and walked out. That's a joke, of course."

Bowdin didn't laugh, and neither did Paavo. "You said the candles were still in a bag beside the body, right?"

"Correct."

"Do you think the killer might have taken the body back to complete the ritual?"

The sergeant was silent a long time. "What makes you say that? Sounds like you've got a case in the city we should know about. Is that what brought you here?"

Paavo told him about the Whitefeather murder.

"If it's the same situation as we've got, why haven't we found the body displayed with the candles all around her? Why has he kept her?" Bowdin asked.

Paavo had no answer. "The report shows the victim's name is Mina Harker." As soon as he said it aloud, something about the name seemed to resonate, something in the far reaches of his memory, but it didn't want to move forward. "How did you find that out? Fingerprints?"

"A missing person's report fit Harker to a T, even down to a heart-shaped tattoo on the right tricep and a chipped front tooth," Bowdin said. "The problem was, when we went to talk to the girl who filed the report, she was gone. Judging from the Gate 5 address she gave, she was another transient."

"What was her name?" Paavo asked.

"It's in the file. I'll call it in to you."

"Thanks. Can you tell me anything else about Harker?"

"We've found nothing more," Bowdin replied. "She

was young—seventeen, eighteen, or so. She looked like any runaway living on the streets. We put out a report on her but came up empty. Not even a birth certificate. It wouldn't be the first time a runaway changed her name. She was blond, blue-eyed, five feet seven, and her fingerprints weren't on record. Last time I checked, there were about a hundred thousand runaways who fit her general description."

"I'm not surprised," Paavo said. He was about to end the conversation when another question struck him. "Can you tell me one more thing?"

"Sure."

"Was her heart cut out?"

"Where the hell did you hear that?" The sergeant looked stricken. "God damn it! We were trying to keep that detail under wraps. It was our way to make sure we had the right perp, once we found him."

Chapter 7

 "I'm exhausted, Angie," Connie whispered out of the side of her mouth as she sliced another piece of the latest Comical Cake and served it to a guest. They were in a modern redwood and glass building overlooking the Sandpoint Golf Course, an exclusive private club. A group of golfers surrounded them, admiring the cake Angie had created for the club's tenth anniversary.

It was a sheet cake—actually, four sheet cakes cobbled together to recreate a golf course, complete with hills, sand traps, water hazards, and bunkers. Along the lower edge of the cake, Angie had drawn a cartoon strip. The first pane showed a golfer hurling his golf club and jumping up and down in fury after hitting his ball into a pond. The next pane showed him looking up in bewilderment at his club caught on a tree limb. The last pane showed the chagrined golfer climbing up the tree. At the bottom were the words, "Golf—evolution in reverse."

"I can't take another minute of this," Connie continued. A dab of frosting stuck to her finger, and she wiped it onto the full apron she wore over her ruffled mauve blouse and hip-hugging purple skirt. At Angie's prompting, she'd taken extra care with her clothes and hair, but so far the rich male partygoers were more interested in cake.

"You're doing just fine," Angie murmured, scarcely paying attention. Her mind was on Paavo.

He'd called from Sausalito and asked if she'd be free for dinner tonight, possibly to meet him there for dinner on the bay. She couldn't make it, since she'd already agreed to stay at the golf club and serve. He seemed surprisingly disappointed, as if he was quite anxious to talk to her. She wished she had some idea of what it could be about. Lately, whenever they tried to get together, something would come up, and it usually had to do with her business, not his. That was a complete turnabout from the past.

It bothered her that he wouldn't simply tell her whatever it was he wanted to say. Why couldn't he? That's what was so troubling. It wasn't as if they had no time together at all.

A part of her wanted to believe he didn't actually have anything special to relay. Perhaps he simply wanted to be alone with her because he enjoyed her company. Maybe any special motive was all in her mind. Or maybe . . .

All in all, there were too many maybes in this relationship.

Now, instead of going to dinner with Paavo and discovering what was troubling him, she was stuck here with a constantly complaining Connie.

"I've used muscles I didn't know I had," Connie whined. "In fact, I never knew cake decorating was so strenuous."

"Think of how strong your hands will become from squeezing the pastry bags and the muscles you'll build on your arms from carrying around huge amounts of cake mix, blending a variety of colors of icing, even holding the bags still so you can make proper designs. It's better than most exercises."

"Only if I want huge shoulder and back muscles on skinny legs atrophying from standing still. I'll end up shaped like Charlie the Tuna. What about the way my feet hurt from hours of standing? And my back from bending over the cakes? And my neck from hunching—"

"Stop! We'll serve a few more pieces, and then we'll be out of here."

"Your cakes are very clever," an elderly woman in a beige lacy Chanel suit said to both Angie and Connie. "I believe my club might be interested in having the two of you make some cakes for us."

Connie smiled at the woman, but before she could even say hello, Angie began her rapid-fire speech about the benefits of buying a Comical Cake. Connie abruptly turned away. Angie was on her way to roping in another customer. For someone so successful at talking people into buying her products, Connie didn't understand why for so long her friend had been unsuccessful at actually running a business.

Stan walked up to her. Ever since he'd decided he was a "partner" in Angie's enterprise, he would pop up unexpectedly at parties, usually in time to take leftovers back to his apartment. If he happened to arrive too early, such as this afternoon, he'd spend his time "supervising."

"Why don't you grab a knife and help me serve?" Connie said.

"I'm a silent partner." Stan waited until Connie had dished up three pieces of cake then took one for himself. "It's pretty nice of you to help this way," he said, just before filling his mouth with a bite.

Connie glared at him, then glanced at Angie, who was still talking with the member of the blue-haired set. Didn't she ever take a breath? She certainly didn't bother to see how Connie was doing. For all Angie knew, she could have dropped dead face down in the frosting.

As if Angie would care. It was as if she'd ceased to exist for anything but slapping cake slices onto dishes. Her so-called friend had everything going for her—a successful business, a good family, and a man who loved her and surely wanted to marry her. What did Angie care about her or their friendship? Nothing.

"Do you close your gift shop while you're helping Angie?" Stan asked. "I heard it doesn't do all that much business."

Connie whirled at him. "Where did you hear that?" As if she didn't know.

"Oh . . . well, um, I'm sure I misunderstood. You're a real sport about this, that's what I meant to say."

With each word he spoke, Connie became more furious. "A sport?"

"Yes. Oh, that man wants a piece of cake."

Connie served the customer and sent him off with a pasted-on smile. Then she frowned. "Angie."

Angie didn't even look her way as she wrote down the phone number of the woman she was talking with.

"Angie!" Connie said again.

"One minute, Connie," Angie replied, still not facing her.

"It's not that she's ignoring you, Connie," Stan said out of the side of his mouth. "She's busy."

"Busy like a fox. Seems to me she's having a good time chatting with these partygoers while I do all the work."

"It's her job."

"I think she's taking advantage of my good nature." She put down the cake knife.

"Don't be so uptight," Stan continued around a mouthful of cake. "It's okay."

"I doubt it." Hands on hips, she glared at Angie's back.

"I'm outta here," Stan said, grabbing a glass of punch in one hand and another piece of cake in the other. "The last place I want to be is in the middle of a cat fight."

Connie ignored him. "Angie," she called sweetly.

Angie wasn't paying the least bit of attention to her.

"Angie!" Her voice was a little more strident. "I need to talk to you."

"In a minute," Angie said quickly.

Connie grew more irritated. "Angie, I mean it!"

"Excuse me," Angie said sweetly to the woman she'd been talking with. She grabbed Connie's arm and dragged her a few steps away from the cake being served. "What is it? I was talking to a potential customer—a potentially huge customer!"

"I'm feeling used." Connie folded her arms. "You aren't giving me proper recognition for the work I'm doing."

Angie stared at her. "Have you been sampling too much champagne?"

"I haven't had any." Connie blinked away tears.

"Maybe that's your problem. Of course I value you. Now, get back to serving the cake." Angie's eyes were already wandering back to the old biddy.

"You don't value me enough or you wouldn't talk to me that way. I know what's going to happen. I can see it now."

"See what now?"

"Nothing."

"I give up." Angie waved her arms in exasperation. "I couldn't do this without you! I swear it. Now, will you please leave me alone? The woman I was with runs a huge nonprofit organization. If I can get them to use my cakes for a charity function, I'd be set for life!"

"Leave you alone?" Connie's cheeks grew fiery red. "Is that what you want?"

"Yes!" She added, sotto voce, "For a little while."

"Fine. How about for a *long* while!" She took off her apron, shoved it in Angie's hands, and marched out of the room.

Horror-struck, Angie casually folded up the apron, tucked it under her arm, and wearing a huge smile, sauntered back to the woman.

"I'm sorry, Miss Amalfi," her potential client said. "I was thinking about this a bit more, and I don't think a comical cake quite fits in with our concern about the rain forest. Thank you for your time."

With that, she walked away.

Angie stood there, contemplating hara-kiri with a spatula, when Stan walked up. "I just saw Connie leave in a huff. I don't know what's wrong with that woman," he said.

"Me neither," Angie replied, blood in her eyes.

"Well, I guess there's one thing I can do to help," Stan said.

"There is?"

"Here you go!" He handed her the cake server.

Surrounded by brightly burning candles and incense, he stood before the altar with his eyes shut, his hands clasped and pressed against his breastbone. The filth was all around him. Vomit. Excrement. Urine. Blood. The desire to destroy raged within him. To kill, to stomp out the whores and harlots with their lies and their phony smiles.

Only his Queen stood above the others, perfect and divine. He'd followed her today, watched her with her cakes, serving others, working to ingratiate herself with the swine.

Soon, my Queen, they will all bow to you!

He quaked with the need to act. Taking deep breaths, he waited until he was filled with visions of darkness and of hell. Only then did he turn to the Book to read a favorite passage.

You, Mortal, shall not be alone, for a Queen awaits you, and she will reign with you as Consort and Mistress. Her Dark Ladies, the Four chosen as Night's Concubines, will do her bidding. As your Power is perfected, all will tremble, Queen and Concubines, in Your Presence as you lead them from Darkness to Deepest Night. Perfection is summoned from the Undead Pentagram: the Five that you have called to you.

From the Four Corners of the Earth, they will come to you, bringing you Power and Strength and Secrets of their Lands. Your Queen alone must be of the True West, a Place of Gold.

"Good morning, Connie," Angie said as she burst into Everyone's Fancy. As usual, the shop was empty. "We've got to talk."

She headed straight for the back room, where Connie had a small office crammed tight with a desk, table, two chairs, shelves, and many boxes of stored merchandise. She placed two nonfat lattes and the white-and-green Victoria pastry box on the table. Inside were scones, fritters, and the custard napoleons that Connie particularly loved.

"What's all that?" Connie asked blandly. She picked up her feather duster and, still out in the shop, began flicking it over the knickknacks near the office door, as if she couldn't care less about Angie or the box of goodies.

"Could you take a moment to come in here and talk to me?" Angie called.

Connie sighed heavily. "I guess I can do that." She dragged her desk chair to the table across from Angie.

"Coffee?" Angie gave Connie a latte and then lifted a napoleon out of the box for her.

"Thank you for the coffee." Connie slid the pastry back, her lips pursed. "I'm dieting."

Connie was always dieting, but that hadn't stopped her before.

Angie wasn't one to beat around the bush. "I was wondering about yesterday and why you were so upset."

"Why shouldn't I be? You schmooze while I stand around working, and I'm the one with a store to run."

"But I've got to find customers," Angie explained logically.

"You and me both!" Connie shouted. "I've got bills to pay tomorrow, I have no idea what's happening with my inventory, and you expect me to serve cake? The heck with that. Let them eat bread!" With that, she stood up, marched out into the shop, and began furiously dusting once again.

Angie hurried after her.

"These people see how cute your cakes are, and it helps your business grow," Connie continued, a cloud of dust wafting around her head, "but it isn't doing my business any good at all. I can't do it anymore."

"It's only been a couple of weeks."

"That's two weeks too many."

"But Connie, I need your help." Angie was on one side of a display table, Connie on the other. "That's why I came here. Please, we can work it out, can't we?"

"I just wasn't cut out for this, Angie. I'll lose all my customers if I stay away from the shop."

Angie looked around. "What customers?"

Connie's mouth dropped open, and she put down the duster. "Well! So that's how you feel!" She headed for the sales counter and the too-silent cash register.

Angie pressed her hand to her mouth. "I didn't mean it that way! Really. I'm sorry! I just meant that—"

"Oh, no!" Connie jumped back. "How did that get here?"

Angie hurried to her side. A dead mouse lay on the counter behind Connie's collection of porcelain angels. "You have mice?" she asked.

"No, I don't! I never have before. I don't know!" Suddenly, angry tears filled her eyes.

"Connie, tell me what's wrong? Please tell me." Worried, she reached for Connie's hands but was rebuffed.

"Nothing! I told you! Will you just leave!"

"Why?"

"First you insult me, then you ask why?"

"All I meant was that people will come to your store when they need a cute gift or a treat for themselves whether you're here or not."

"So I'm not needed here either, is that what you're saying?" Connie was so angry she could scarcely spit out her words.

"For cryin' out loud!" Angie gathered up her pastry and bustled toward the door. "There's simply no talking to you!"

Connie folded her arms and stood at the door like a cigar store Indian. "You've got that right."

Chapter 8

"Looks like we got a friggin' serial killer on our hands," Calderon said as he wandered through aging steel desks, file cabinets, stacks of folders, books, and papers to drop a sheaf of faxes onto Benson's desk. "These are from the Sausalito P.D."

Paavo stood up and looked over Benson's shoulder. "It's the same M.O., then?" he asked as Benson began reading through the material.

"Sure is," Calderon replied. "Good work, Paavo. It was a help, a big help. Makes it even easier to catch the SOB. We're going over to Sausalito, checking out the crime scene, maybe even having some fish for lunch. Let's go, Benson."

Benson shoved the boring police reports into a folder, glad to leave them for first-hand viewing and discussion. The two inspectors swaggered out the door.

Paavo dropped back into his chair and watched them go. What he wouldn't give for an interesting case right now. The temptation to sneak a glance at the Sausalito file was great.

"Well, did you do the dirty deed yet?" Yosh asked.

Paavo jerked himself upright and then glanced around to see if the inspectors and secretary still in the room were listening. He shook his head. "Not yet," he answered softly.

"Why not?" Yosh's voice carried like a megaphone.

Rebecca Mayfield lifted her head from her computer and glanced their way. She smiled at Paavo. He smiled back and lowered his voice even more. "She's been too busy."

"Too busy? Is that a joke? What does she have to be busy about? You don't have a big case for her to stick her nose into."

Paavo tried to whisper his response. "She bakes cakes."

Yosh burst into laughter. He now definitely had everyone's attention, including that of Lieutenant Hollins, who had entered the bureau to talk to Bill Sutter. "So she's pushed you aside for Duncan Hines, huh? What a gal!"

"No, that's not it," Paavo said, glaring at the others until they turned back to their work.

Just then, the sound of high heels on the outer office's scruffy linoleum floor was heard. Very high heels. Angie appeared in the doorway, an almost otherworld vision against the drabness of Homicide in a smart rose tweed suit over a trim and petite body, four-inch high heels, lipstick, and matching long, manicured fingernails. She was carrying a bakery box.

"Here's your chance," Yosh said. "Not an oven or Mixmaster in sight. Go for it, pal."

Paavo hurried toward her. She said hello to the others in the room, all of whom she'd met since dating

Paavo. "What are you doing here?" he asked. "It's still morning."

"I was up early. I'm sorry to bother you, but I needed to talk." She saw that everyone was watching, so she gave them all a half-hearted smile. She handed Paavo the pastries. "Do you think your friends would like these?"

She hadn't finished the question when Benecia, the lieutenant's secretary, offered to help. Paavo handed her the box.

Oohs and aahs and thank-yous followed as Paavo led Angie to his desk.

"Are you terribly busy?" she asked.

Paavo pushed the paperwork to one side. "This can wait. Nothing more is going to come of it."

"What is it?"

He wondered if she was stalling. It wasn't like her to want to know about homicides. "Drug overdose," he answered. "Seems there's some heavy-duty stuff going around. The guy was one of those Goth types."

"That's the long, black trench coat set, right? Columbine and all? I don't know much about them."

"I don't either yet. What I've learned doesn't make a lot of sense. They say there's too much hatred and violence in the world and that most people ignore it so they revel in it. They seem to believe the dark parts of the soul are beautiful—things like sorrow, fear, pain, and especially death."

"It sounds sick."

"I agree. Let's forget about them." He studied her a moment, noticing the dark smudges under her eyes and a pinched look to her face that hadn't been there a couple of days ago. The uneasiness he'd been feeling came back to him along with the morose thoughts of never being able to propose.

Had she figured out what he wanted to ask her? Was she here to tell him not to bother? His stomach twisted, and he broke out in a cold sweat. "Something's wrong," he managed to say with a modicum of calm. "Do you want to tell me about it?" Inside, some raving lunatic was screaming that he didn't want to hear it.

She took a deep breath then blurted, "Connie hates me."

Connie? This was about Connie? Relief hit him so hard he was almost giddy. "I'm sure she doesn't. You're her best friend."

"She does." Angie placed her hand on his. "She wouldn't even eat a napoleon with me!" Dejected, she gazed at him with woeful eyes.

He could feel the silent chuckles of every eaves-dropping inspector in the bureau. He stood and shrugged on his sport jacket. "Let's go." As they walked out the door he glanced back at the others. "Break time."

They went to Zeno's restaurant around the corner. Police inspectors, assistant DAs, and even judges could be found there at all hours of the day.

Paavo ordered coffee, bagels, and cream cheese. "Now, tell me about you and Connie," he said as they settled into a small, dark nook.

She presented her sad story in heartrending fashion.

"Maybe you're being hard on her," he said after their food arrived. "She does have a business to run."

"Hard? I wasn't. I tried to explain—"

"You hurt her feelings."

She was stunned. "I didn't mean to! I was only trying to help." Elbow on the table, she propped her chin in her hand. "People just don't understand me."

"People?" He gazed at her. "This sort of thing hasn't happened to you before, has it?"

"Only once." She straightened. "My sister Frannie wouldn't talk to me for months when she and her boyfriend were having troubles and I told her I thought she'd be better off dropping a loser like him. He *is* a loser, too."

"Is that the guy she married?"

"Yes, but this was before they were engaged. I thought she'd want to hear my opinion. I was wrong."

He didn't reply. He'd seen homicides resulting from one person's desire to inflict on another their opinion on matters of the heart. "Sounds like you learned a lesson."

"I suppose." She smeared cheese on a piece of bagel. "Although I still don't see why my cousin Richie got mad at me when I gave him a copy of a good diet."

"Oh? And how would you feel if someone did that to you?"

"This was different. He'd gotten so fat his health was at risk."

"Don't you think he knows that?"

"I was just trying to give some reinforcement to him to slim down. He didn't let me explain."

"I see."

"Then," Angie began, but when she caught Paavo's eye, she clamped her lips together.

"Then?" he nudged.

"I don't—"

"Come on."

She sighed. "It has to do with my old friend Nona Farraday."

"The restaurant reviewer?"

"That's right. On occasion, I'd make a suggestion about a review, especially if she had something wrong. Like once, she confused *roulades*, which are beef rolls, with *rouleaux,* which are cream rolls. I would have died of embarrassment if it had been me. I called her and told her she should demand an immediate revision of her magazine article. Instead of doing that, she got mad—at me! She told me to keep my nose out of her business. Can you imagine?"

"Well . . ."

"I give up. I'm misunderstood. I'm the victim here! I was just trying to be helpful, to help Connie, help Nona, help Richie, help all those near and dear to me, and what happens? They get mad at me. Nobody appreciates me, Paavo. Nobody!"

It was on the tip of his tongue to tell her how much he appreciated her, and then some. Instead, he studied her. Despite the dark, romantic corner, the quiet atmosphere, the soft jazz playing in the corner, the timing was all wrong. This was definitely not the occasion to bring up the cause of his sleepless nights.

He took a sip of coffee. "You're all worked up, but you must be missing something," he said. "There's nothing wrong with you as a friend. Okay, you're too outspoken at times, but your friends and relatives know you; they know that's what you're about. Frannie and your cousin Richie still love you, Nona Farraday still talks to you about restaurants, and I'm sure Connie has a reason for acting the way she is that has nothing to do with hating you."

"But she does! It's my fault. I've been so busy with my business, I haven't paid enough attention to those around me."

"I can't argue that," he said, wondering if this might not, after all, be the opening he needed. "I've been trying to talk to you for days."

"See what I mean? That settles it. I'm going to turn over a new leaf. I'm going to talk to my sisters."

He hoped he hadn't heard right. "Your sisters?" Angie had four older sisters. Nice women, but founts of enlightenment they were not. In fact, he wondered what new notions they might put into her head.

"They can help me," Angie said. "I'll ask them what it takes to be a friend."

He rubbed his chin. "I don't know about that. Well, maybe Bianca, but . . ."

"But what?"

"I'm sure you can think of a way to take care of this yourself. Go to Connie. Try to work it out."

"I've already tried that. Connie's the source of my problem. My sisters are older and wiser. I'm sure they'll have lots of advice for me. That'll settle it, I'm sure. Yes. I feel much better now." She glanced at her watch and jumped to her feet. "My God, I had no idea it was so late. I've got an appointment with a new customer, and then I've got to get home and bake. I've got a special cake—a huge wedding cake—to deliver to Fugazzi Hall tomorrow!"

He dropped some money onto the table and followed Angie out the door. So much for paying more attention to those around her.

Angie didn't like the appearance of the house of her latest customer. What should have been a beautiful Victorian home—with a turret, no less—in a good neighborhood looked like it had been taken over by a devotee of grunge. It was a shame.

Nevertheless, anyone who could afford a home this size could certainly afford a Comical Cake. She stepped up to the front door and rang the bell.

After a while, she rang it again and then knocked.

Finally, she heard footsteps in the hall. The door was opened by a hefty man with very short brown hair, wearing a floor-length black silk bathrobe and black slippers. His eyes were dark-rimmed, as if he'd just woken up.

"Baron Severus?" She extended her hand. "I'm Angie Amalfi."

His puffy eyes opened wider. "Miss Amalfi, whatever are you doing here so early?" He took her hand and shook it. To her surprise, his fingernails were round and high and painted black. They looked like black parrot seeds. She didn't give in to the desire to wipe her hand against her green wool Jil Sanders dress.

"I thought we had an appointment," she said. "Am I early?"

"Er . . . yes, about twelve hours. You see, when the Baron said he wanted to meet you at twelve o'clock, he meant at midnight. Not"—he shuddered—"noon."

"Midnight? Oh, dear. And you are?"

"I'm his assistant, Wilbur Fieldren. Oh, my, whatever shall we do? The Baron is most anxious to meet you, but right now . . . Come in, come in. Excuse my dress, or lack of. We're all late sleepers here."

The house was an assault of mahogany Victorian antiques, with heavy drapery and table scarves in dark reds and greens. Fieldren led her down a hall lined with overlapping Persian carpets, with sideboards and armoires filling every available inch of wall space and crammed with figurines and knick-knacks. Multicolored Tiffany-style lamps with low-watt bulbs dimly lit the way, and she found herself clutching Fieldren's arm more tightly than she would have liked so as not to stumble on the carpet or bump into a piece of furniture.

The study was also stuffed with furniture and had a strange, almost medicinal smell to it. Two brown leather chairs were against one wall, a window behind them, but the heavy purple brocade drapes were closed, so no sunlight entered the room. A small drum table sat between the chairs. He led her to one and she sat.

Small round candles burning on wrought-iron candlesticks emitted the offensive odor, almost like camphor. She wondered if the house had some kind of bugs he was trying to get rid of. It was all she could do not to wrinkle her nose. "Those are interesting candles," she said, hoping the assistant would take it as a cue to extinguish them.

Instead, he took a deep breath. "The Baron finds the scent most stimulating. Don't you?"

She was appalled, but he was a potential client. "Very."

"Now, about the Baron's club," he began. He told her

that there was dancing and there was liquor for those over age twenty-one but mostly it was filled with young people who liked to dress up in dark, mysterious, romantic ways, as if they were little Lord Byrons and such. The owner being a baron lent it an air of validity.

The club sounded very strange. Angie couldn't quite imagine it and also wondered how much scrutiny this so-called baron's pedigree could stand up to. She kept her mouth shut and nodded.

"Why don't you bring us a cake to see how the Baron likes it? Many of the members here have a sweet tooth, as I do, I'm afraid." He smiled and patted his generous stomach. Angie's own stomach turned at the sight of his fingernails, not to mention his suggestion that she bring them a cake to try. What nerve!

"You'll come at night—after midnight is best—so the Baron will be sure to meet you and have time to devote to you alone."

"Of course." She stood. "I'm rather busy at the moment, I'm afraid. I'll call you when I have more time so we can talk about the type of cake you'd like and my cake prices."

"Of course."

Saying good-bye quickly, she hurried to the door.

"We look forward to you coming back soon!" he called after her.

Once outside, she let the warmth of the bright sunlight fill her and took a deep, cleansing breath. *I'll be back,* she thought, *when hell freezes over.*

He skulked toward the street, eyes searching for prey, his mind elsewhere, wrapped around the one above all

others who would be his, the one he would love for all
eternity.

To have someone to love—didn't all beings, great
and small, want that? He'd never given it much consid-
eration in the past but had merely gone his way, doing
what he must, what he'd learned he must. And then his
heart had changed, and he felt the first pangs of love.
True love.

He heard a noise behind him.

Slouching into the shadows, he found an opening
between two buildings and eased into it, listening. The
footfalls were distinct yet soft, as if someone was pur-
posefully trying to remain hidden.

A leap brought him to the bottom of a fire escape,
and he pulled himself up onto it, then scurried to the
roof as quietly as he could. He waited. Before long, a
man appeared below. He was tall but gaunt, his shoulders stooped as if from age and the weight of worry. In
the lamplight, the man's face was drawn, his cheeks
sunken, his hair long and white, yet his eyes were res-
olute as he vigilantly searched the darkness for neither
man nor beast.

Mason Markowitz.

He watched as Markowitz sprinkled holy water on
the grounds of St. Michael's Church. *The fool,* he
thought. *Why put holy water on a deconsecrated
church?* It would do no good. The church belonged
to him and his people. This clown was wasting his
time.

He remembered how frightened Travis Walters had
been by this crazy old man. Of course, Walters was just
a boy and a nervous sort at that, so afraid of his own

shadow that if anyone said boo, he would run crying to his mother. Or the police.

What if Travis went to the police and told them everything?

His eyes zeroed in on the old man, and an idea came to mind. A devilishly clever idea. He was well pleased.

Chapter 9

"Bianca, it's so terrible." Angie reached for one of her sister's butter cookies. It was late morning. She'd gotten up early, baked and decorated the wedding cake, and decided to make an emergency visit to her eldest sister before the time came to deliver it. "I desperately need your help." She bit into the cookie and chewed woefully.

"What's wrong, Angie?" Bianca poured them each some coffee before joining her at the kitchen table. She was the most down to earth of Angie's four sisters. With a husband and two children, she was content to raise her family and do a number of things the old way that their mother, Serefina, had taught them. Even Serefina from time to time grew irritated by Bianca's lack of adventure and her innate conservatism toward just about everything.

"Paavo said . . ." Angie felt tears well up in her eyes.

Bianca placed her hand on Angie's arm. "Paavo? I thought everything was fine between you two, even better than ever after all he'd been through with his family. What's wrong?"

"No. I mean yes. I mean he's not the problem. It's

what he said about me." Her wails stopped her from being able to say more.

"Stop crying and tell me!" Bianca ordered. It was just like a big sister to have no tact.

"He said I'm too outspoken! I need to learn how to be a friend!"

Bianca raised her eyebrows. "He just wants to be friends now?"

Angie shook her head. "Connie got mad at me, and as I was trying to explain to him all about what happened between us, I mentioned a couple of others who also got a little tad irritated from time to time. He said I needed to talk to someone like you."

"Oh?" Bianca sat a little straighter in her chair. Obviously, she took this as a compliment. "I suppose I've had more years of experience in being a friend to people than you have." She stroked the front of her neck as if trying to smooth out some wrinkles.

"So what's the secret?" Angie wiped her tears, then took the compact from her purse to make sure her mascara wasn't all over her face.

Bianca thought a moment. "Be nice and be honest."

"Oh, puh-lease! I don't want platitudes. I want details. You have lots of old friends, right?"

"Well, I would have friends if I wasn't so busy." Bianca sighed and grabbed a cookie for herself. "I have to cook and wash and run the house and take care of the kids and listen to family."

"Family—"

"That's what I said. Always family!" She waved the cookie. "All of you take so much time, I just don't have any left for myself."

"You don't?" Angie was shocked. Bianca complaining?

"It's not that I'm complaining. I love my family." She dunked the cookie into her coffee and watched it as she spoke. "And you should come first. But sometimes— sometimes I'd like to be able to see people and do things just for me, you know?"

"Yes, I never dreamed—"

"Why should you? Why should you think about your big sister? My hopes, my dreams, my way of having fun? I've always been here for you, for John, for the boys, for our other sisters, our cousins, their kids. Sometimes I feel as if all of you just keep taking more and more pieces of me until there's just nothing left for my own use." As she lifted out her cookie, the part that had been in the coffee broke off and sank to the bottom of the cup. She put the remainder on her plate.

To Angie's horror, tears filled her sister's eyes. "Bianca, I'm sorry."

"Don't be sorry. It's not you. I'm just feeling sorry for myself, I guess. And to think that you, who has everything, are feeling bad. I just don't know what to do anymore. I can't make everybody happy all the time."

"No one expects you to!" Angie said, patting Bianca's hand.

"Yes, everyone does. That's just the problem."

"I didn't mean to upset you."

"No. You didn't. No one ever does." She dried her eyes and tucked her wet tissue in the pocket of her apron. "It's all right. I'm used to it."

Angie didn't know what to say. "Well," she murmured after a long silence. "Thanks anyway."

"Ah, I've just thought of something." Bianca rushed off, and in a moment she was back with a cassette tape in her hand. "You should listen to this. It's old, but it might help."

"I don't have a tape player in my car. Only a CD player."

"Oh . . . well, you can borrow my portable one if you'd like. Just be sure to bring it back."

"Great." Angie looked down at the tape, and her face fell. It was Dale Carnegie's *How to Win Friends and Influence People*.

Mason Markowitz huddled in the shadows and watched the dark-haired woman park a Mercedes-Benz coupe outside Fugazzi Hall, a reception hall and night club in the North Beach district. On his large bony frame his skin sagged, as if he'd recently lost a lot of weight. He wore a baggy, wrinkled brown suit with a belt whose buckle bore a new, tighter hole. On his head sat a battered brown fedora.

She got out of the car, walked around to the passenger seat, and opened the door, then lifted out a bright-red wedding cake. The cake rested on the edge of the car as she scanned the area, as if searching for someone or something.

The cake tottered, in danger of sliding off its base before the little brunette righted it. It was so huge it could have weighed as much as she did. She was quite pretty—beautiful, in fact, with a healthy vibrancy about her. Even across the street he could feel her attraction, feel the strong life force within her.

He had to talk to her. How skittish would she be if he

approached her? Perhaps as a customer? He could always ask about her cake business. It had been a long time since he'd eaten cake. Three years, in fact. They didn't serve cakes where he'd been spending his time.

If he could get inside Fugazzi Hall, he could talk to her there, but it was probably a private party.

He needed to make contact soon. Things were growing worse much more rapidly than he'd expected. Time was speeding up. *Ars Diabolus* told of grave changes in the future. The future, he found, was now.

She continued to stand there waiting for someone or something. It was his chance. He hurried across the street toward her. "I need to talk to you."

She seemed alarmed at his appearance. He should have realized that, with a classy woman like her. His hair, he knew, was so long it hung in wild tufts of white below his hat, and the remnants of two weeks of meals stained his shirt and tie.

"I'm sorry, I'm in a hurry," she said, trying to pick up the cake.

"It's terribly important!" he yelled.

"Go away, or I'll call the police." He noticed she gripped the cake's wooden base tighter, as if ready to bop him with it if need be.

Across the street, a tall, dark-haired man got out of a city-issue car. The man had ice-blue eyes and a hard, chiseled face. Perhaps she didn't have to call the police; it seemed one was here.

"Oh—sorry, you're not the person I thought you were. Sorry!" he said again as he backed up. The woman looked at him quizzically as he scooted around a nearby delivery truck so the cop wouldn't see him.

Markowitz knew he'd failed this time. She wouldn't talk to him now. It was all right, though. He had another idea.

Paavo walked up to her just in time to prevent the cake from slipping off the board she'd put it on. "Are you all right?" he asked. "You look upset."

"Me, upset? Why should I be? Connie ran out on me, Stan's never around when I need him, and you're late!"

"Just a little."

"Enough that perverts approach me on the street!"

He looked around. "You mean that old man? Where did he go?"

"Oh, forget it. He was just another street person wanting a handout. Let's go inside."

By the time they'd entered the hall she was feeling guilty for having snapped at him. After struggling to carry the big cake down in the elevator and into her car, she'd called him and asked if he could help her get it into Fugazzi Hall. She hadn't wanted to disturb his Saturday for her business, but she was desperate. He hadn't complained but instead had come right over. And what thanks did she give him?

Her guilt grew as he not only carried the cake into the hall for her, but helped set it up and then stayed to serve it.

As much as she appreciated his thoughtfulness, she quickly concluded that would be the last time she let him serve. The number of women who flocked to the cake, asking him for seconds, and in a few cases thirds, made her blood boil. More than half of them stood around and made small talk about cakes and baking—as if he cared—as they nibbled at her creation, scarcely tasting it.

A couple of them threw one piece away just so they could chat with Paavo while he gave them another. She was furious.

Once she and Craig Claiborne finished this Fugazzi Hall stint, they would go to her apartment and order a pizza. She was far too tired to cook. Maybe afterward, a nice soothing soak in a tub filled with Dior's Poison bath gel—and Paavo—might be exactly what was needed before worrying about tomorrow's cake or about finding someone to help her with her business.

Julie Sung waved good-bye and hurried away from the others. Coworkers, perhaps? Who else would be in this desolate area at this hour? The others went to a parking lot, and she crossed the street to a bus stop. As she passed under the streetlamp, he saw her face, her beautiful face, and the words of *Ars Diabolus* heartened him.

She appeared almost happy, he thought. Well, she should be. Tonight she would achieve immortality. Too bad she didn't know it.

Once, just once, he'd like to be able to tell one of his consorts what awaited her and not have her scream and try to get away. He was used to that reaction now. The first time, it had caught him by surprise, and he'd had to kill her quickly to shut her up.

Now he knew to expect it.

That was why he carried a syringe filled with sodium pentothal.

The street was empty except for the woman. In the distance, he saw the approaching bus. He'd have to act quickly.

As he walked to the bus stop, he tripped. Arms flailing wildly, he stumbled toward her. Amusement filled her face, and she put her hands out to help steady him, even though he was easily twice her size.

Her expression turned to alarm as he grabbed her arm with one hand while with the other he plunged a needle through her light wool jacket to her skin and emptied the syringe.

"What are you—"

He pulled her close, her head crushed against his broad chest, muffling her cries. In seconds, the sodium pentothal did its work, and she slumped. With her tucked firmly against his side, he led her to his car and placed her in the passenger seat. He gently brushed her long, black hair back off her face. She was so very beautiful, so very exotic. He fastened the seat belt around her, placed a kiss on her forehead, then got into the driver's seat. A quick check all around told him no one was watching, and he drove away.

In the back seat were candles, rope, a knife, and a heavy plastic bag.

Chapter 10

The next evening, Angie had a spring in her step as she walked out of the restaurant where she'd delivered a cake to a couple celebrating their fortieth wedding anniversary. This one was small—just a simple cake in the shape of a big nose with a bird, colored cobalt-blue, sitting on top of it. Around the edges of the nose were the words "May the bird of happiness fly up your . . ."

Apparently, for many years the couple had gotten a chuckle out of a song with those lyrics. It wasn't one Angie was familiar with—thank goodness.

Except for Connie running out and leaving her high and dry, she was getting the hang of this cake business pretty well. She even liked it. Her customers were usually festive and good-natured. What surprised her was that they were often also quite nervous waiting for a gala to begin, even those who entertained regularly. About half of her setup time was spent calming down her customers.

She loved the psychological aspect of the job. Maybe she should have gone into psychology instead of cooking. The thought of being a psychologist, using her keen insight to help soothe troubled souls, was a heartening one.

Now, if only she could figure out why Connie had ditched her and her business, she'd be even happier.

She needed Connie's help. Stan and nothing were the same thing, and she didn't want Paavo involved. He was far too busy with his own job anyway. For the first time in her life she had a business that was poised to take off. She had to be sure not to blow this opportunity.

As she neared her Mercedes, the old man who had approached her outside Fugazzi Hall came up to her again. She backed up. "Who are you?" she yelled, looking around for help. "What do you want?"

"There's great danger," he said.

"From you?" she cried. Her breathing quickened, and thoughts of the ritual killing sprang into her head. She didn't know if she should try to outrun him, despite her Cole-Haan platform shoes, or stay and stare him down, like she'd been told to do with a mad dog.

Self-defense classes cautioned her not to show fear. That was easy to do in a gym with an instructor and a bunch of determined women, but not so simple out here on the sidewalk, facing a deranged man.

He moved even closer. She was ready to turn and run when a young woman stepped out of the shadows. "You're messing with the wrong chick this time, old man," the woman yelled. Her voice was loud and sharp, and her words spoken fast. "Get the hell out of here if you want to see another birthday."

He looked from one to the other, then turned and hurried down the street.

Angie stared at the woman in shock before she remembered her manners. "Thank you," Angie murmured finally.

"Damned creeps going around bothering women. This girl's had enough of it." The woman's face turned pale, and her breathing seemed suddenly labored.

"You did good," Angie said, studying her with increasing concern.

She swayed a bit and stumbled toward Angie's car, then turned and leaned against the fender, bending forward at the waist. "Whoa, I guess my blood's gone supersonic on me. I got to rest a minute." She was about Angie's age with shoulder-length dyed black hair. She wore a cheap beige jacket with a hood, and army-navy-surplus blue jeans covered long, thin legs and slim hips. Her shoes were inexpensive white sneakers.

"What's wrong?" Angie asked, lightly touching her shoulders.

The woman tried to stand, but dizziness must have overtaken her, because she slumped back against the car once more. "God, I hate this," she murmured, rubbing her stomach.

"Does your stomach hurt?"

"Not. It's just . . ." The woman put her hand to her temple and studied Angie a long moment. "I felt dizzy. That's all. I'll go after it passes."

"Maybe an adrenalin rush, as you said?" Angie suggested.

The woman seemed to smirk at the words. "Maybe. Or, I'm just a little hungry."

"Hungry? Is that it? There's a restaurant on the corner. Let me help you."

She shook her head. "Girl, I could eat for a month on what they'd want for a leg of chicken."

"Do you need some money?" Angie asked softly.

The woman didn't respond for a long while. "I don't like saying yes to a question like that, if you get my meaning. On the other hand, I can hardly see from Big Macs parading in my eyes."

"Here." Angie reached into her purse and pulled out a ten. Normally, she ignored beggars. She'd heard too many stories about a person trying to help someone and ending up robbed or worse, but something about this woman touched her, along with the way she had helped her.

"I'll pay you back," the stranger said, making sure the money was pushed deep into her pocket. "I'm not broke because I want to be; I had a job but lost it."

Angie nodded. She'd heard that one before.

"You know what I was? A pastry chef. Nobody wants pastry chefs anymore. Too many fast-food places and grocers mass-producing sweets, and the old places priced themselves right out of business."

Angie couldn't believe her ears. Her prayers were answered. "You're kidding."

"Honest Zoe Vane doesn't kid. No way."

Know your Queen, Mortal, by her connection to the Earth, Fire, Ice, and the Heavens.

Through the Heavens, you shall know her. Beware the Moon in Void of Course, for only in its Fullness, in the House of Aquarius, shall you rise to the Power that is yours. Strong forces are aligned to stop you, and your Struggles will be fierce.

The God of Hades must be in retreat, or no power will be forthcoming.

At such alignment, Mortal, shall your transformation to Dark Lord be complete. The Queen and her Consorts will be yours.

Time was speeding, hurtling him through the continuum toward eternity. He was high, higher than he'd ever been. Mission three accomplished, and not only for his Queen, but also to rid the world of his enemy. He could have danced for joy. If only she were here to dance with him.

He turned to his astrological tables. The Book was very specific. The moon went through the various houses constantly, and the reference to Hades meant the planet Pluto, but what of this requirement that the full moon be in Aquarius at the same time as Pluto was in retrograde?

That sounded somewhat rare. Did he have to worry that he would be an old man before the moon and planets were aligned properly for his Queen?

He studied the planetary charts. Pluto had gone from stationary to retrograde a month earlier. Could it be? The date was just before the voice had directed him to his Queen's first consort.

Excitement bubbled within him.

Pluto would remain in retrograde for four more months. A lunar calendar presented the cycles of the moon during this period. When he found the next full moon, he stared at the chart, awed and shaken and, yes, humbled by what he was seeing.

This very month, this exact month, the full moon would occur in the house of Aquarius at the same time as Pluto was in retrograde, precisely as demanded by the thousand-year-old text.

Sweat broke out on his forehead. Could this conjuncture be one that happened regularly and he'd never realized it? He continued to search for the same three elements to conjoin during the year and then went on to the next year and the next. All three did not occur again simultaneously until the year 2014.

There was much work to be done, and forces, as the Book warned, were trying to stop him. He must eliminate them, all of them. Could he meet the challenge?

He remembered the Book's warning—beware the moon in void of course.

The moon was void of course on that day until 11:03 P.M. After that time, it entered the sign of Aquarius. He glanced at the date, and a chill crept down his back before he erupted into a loud laugh.

How very literary, he thought. *How very perfect.*

The date was Friday, March 15: The Ides of March.

Chapter 11

 Angie sat on the sofa in ivory lounging pajamas and matching mules, her feet up, the morning *Chronicle* on her lap, and a wake-up cup of coffee on the end table. From the picture window, a million-dollar view of the bay stretched from Oakland and the Bay Bridge in the east, to the Golden Gate in the west.

She was startled to read that there had been another murder in the city. A woman had been strangled, a Korean woman named Julie Sung. She was only twenty-one years old and had been last seen heading for a bus stop in the south of Market area.

Her body was found in an alley, just as the last woman's had been.

The newspaper alluded to it as being another "ritualistic" murder scene. Angie stopped reading. She'd been having trouble sleeping lately, and the story alone was enough to give her nightmares. She didn't want any gory details.

At the sound of a soft tapping at her door, she looked through her peephole to see Zoe Vane in the doorway. In a momentary flash of enthusiasm, she'd given Zoe her business card, but later, her more rational self decided she would never hear from her again. Zoe's employment story had to have been made up. Angie had always heard there was a shortage of good pastry chefs. The woman had surely laughed all the way to the nearest bar or crack dealer, waving Angie's ten bucks as she went.

Her irritation flared. Had she seemed such a soft touch that Zoe was here to ask for even more money? She yanked the door open hard, ready to run her off.

"Here you go," Zoe said, her hand outstretched. "Your change." She handed Angie three dollar bills, two quarters, and a dime. "I bought myself some big old sacks of dried beans, rice, lettuce, and Tabasco. I'll be eating real good."

Stunned, Angie gazed from the money in her hand to Zoe. "What about that Big Mac?"

Zoe smiled, making her narrow face and sad, dark eyes light up. "Fast food's bad for you," she said simply. She'd pulled her hair back in a braid and wore a white shirt and blue jeans; her beige jacket was in her hand. She acted much tougher than she really was.

Angie's throat tightened, and she handed the money back. "It's for you. Won't you come in?"

Zoe's eyes widened as she entered the fancy apartment with the delicate antiques, the small Cézanne watercolor over the state-of-the-art entertainment system, the beautiful view.

"Since I'm here," Zoe said hesitantly, "I wondered if you could use a little help?"

"I believe I could," Angie said.

Zoe reached into her back jeans pocket and pulled

out a piece of white paper. Unfolding it, she said, "You probably know some of these guys."

Angie gazed at the list of several top chefs in the city. "These are your references?" she gasped.

Zoe shrugged.

"And they can vouch for you?" Angie asked incredulously.

"Maybe one or two forgot me, but I hope some remember. You can call and ask them about Honest Zoe Vane. See what they tell you."

Zoe looked a lot healthier today, although her skin was still too pale against such black hair.

Angie made a quick decision. Refolding the list, she placed it on the coffee table. "I'll call them another time. I'm sure everything will be just fine. In fact, if you're ready to start work, I have to bake a cake this morning for a surprise party for a"—she coughed delicately—"proctologist. It's obviously the type of profession people love to joke about. This is the third request I've received in as many weeks. The other two I refused, but since *this* one wanted a cake in the shape of a rubber glove, I accepted."

Zoe grinned. "I'll bake a cake into any shape you want. Now, you sure you don't want to contact the people on that list first? Because I don't want to get no grief about Chef So-and-so says this or that later on."

"I'm comfortable with you," Angie said with grave sincerity.

Zoe gazed at her a moment, then dropped her eyes. "You're a nice person." Her voice was quiet.

Given the way her so-called friend had been treating her, those words buoyed Angie's spirits. "Let me show you what I need you to do. You can get started while I dress. You might not think of me as so nice once I put you to work. I'm pretty fussy."

In the kitchen, cake pans in a variety of shapes were stacked on the counter.

Zoe stood in the doorway. "That's how you make your cakes?"

"The trick, you'll find, is in the decoration. How's your handwriting, by the way?"

"My teachers told me I should become a doctor."

"Oh, dear. Well, I learned from Sister Mary Ignatius, so it looks like that'll continue to be my job."

"Excuse me, is Homicide in there?" a nervous teenager who'd been pacing the Hall of Justice corridor asked Paavo as he reached the door to Room 450. The boy had dyed the top of his hair blond and wore a gold ring in one eyebrow, baggy jeans, and a T-shirt. He looked like a refugee from MTV.

"This is it," Paavo said. "I'm Inspector Smith. Can I help you?"

The boy turned his head from side to side. "I need to talk to someone. I . . . I think I saw . . ." He swallowed, then ran his tongue over his lips. "It's about Julie Sung."

Sung was Calderon and Benson's latest murder victim. The two had finally headed for home for some sleep after being up forty-eight hours working the case.

"You can talk to me," Paavo said, not wanting to tell the kid to come back later or even to wait. Nervous witnesses tended to get cold feet, which often led to a bout of forgetfulness.

Paavo led the boy to his desk and gave him a seat. "Can I get you coffee or a Coke?"

The teen shook his head.

"What's your name?"

He had to clear his throat before he could speak. "Travis Walters."

"Travis, thanks for coming down here to talk to us," Paavo said, trying to make him feel more at ease. He didn't look like the type who would normally give the police the time of day. Paavo quickly took down his address and phone number. "Were you a friend of Julie's?"

"Yeah, kind of. She was nice." His eyes widened as the shock of her recent murder hit him again. "That's why—" He stopped, suddenly unsure.

"It's all right," Paavo urged, his voice calm and soothing. "Go on."

The teen was so thin and pale a stiff breeze could have blown him away. "I'm worried," he whispered.

"Why?" Paavo would have liked to turn on a tape recorder, but the kid was already having a hard time talking, and the chance of him freezing up was high.

"I was with a friend. He drives, I don't. We thought we'd go by and, like, you know, pick up Julie after work. She worked late—I guess you know that, too. We thought she'd be at the bus stop, but we didn't see her. Instead, we saw an old man. He was, like, just standing there staring, standing where she should have been. I think . . . I think he might have had something to do with her murder."

"An old man?" Paavo tensed. Bowdin had talked about an old panhandler hanging around the Sausalito crime scene—Mac or Marx. There were lots of homeless old people in the Bay Area. It might not mean a thing. "Why do you think he might have been involved?"

The boy's blue eyes were stark. "I've seen him following me. He hates us—people who live like we do. Rave, the whole scene. He even came to my house and left some holy water and a candle. The guy's a freak, and I've heard he's dangerous."

"Do you know his name?"

"Yeah. It's Markowitz. Mason Markowitz."

"You're sure of that?"

Walters suddenly seemed to grow panicky and gave a quick nod.

"Good, that's very helpful," Paavo said encouragingly. He didn't want to lose Walters, and a lot depended on the answer to the next question. "How did you learn his name?"

Walters chewed his bottom lip thoughtfully. A sheen of sweat beaded on his forehead. "I just heard it. I'm not sure where." He stood up. "Look, it's just an idea. I mean, like, I didn't see this guy kill her or anything, but if he was involved, and if he's hanging around my house, I want some protection."

"Don't worry," Paavo said, also standing. "Inspector Calderon or Inspector Benson will be in touch with you very soon."

"They'll take care of my protection?"

"They'll do everything they can. Try to think of anything else that might help them. Oh, by the way, where did you know Julie from?"

He backed up, his eyes darting. "From school. I got to go now." He turned and hurried out the door.

His last answer was a lie, and Paavo wondered why he chose not to answer that particular question truthfully. Where had Travis and Julie met that the boy wouldn't want to say?

He quickly wrote out a report of Walters's interview, along with the teen's address and phone number. Two copies went to Calderon and Benson, and one he kept for himself.

Neither lead inspector had yet returned to the bureau. Paavo opened the Sausalito report to see what had been written about Mac or Marx. Scanning it, he found nothing more than he'd been told, but something unrelated caught his eye—the answer to another of his questions.

The friend of Mina Harker who had filed the missing person's report had given her first name only. The name was Lucy.

"Frannie," Angie said, her head swivelling from side to side following her sister's pacing as she rocked and patted her baby, trying to get him to stop crying. "I need to talk to you about friends." She'd left her endless stream of cakes to pay a visit to her sister's small city home. Now that she had hired a helper, she had a little time in her life once again. Time to think about Connie and Paavo and others around her.

Seth Junior's head bobbed on Frannie's shoulder, his face beet-red and contorted from crying. She was the sister closest to Angie in age. She was the tallest of them and had a bulimic's thinness, even during her pregnancy. Her hair was light brown, chin length, and permed into ringlets. Angie would have preferred an inch-long surfer clip to that mess. Frannie's blue denim housedress hung shapeless, and the Birkenstocks looked ready to fall off. "Which friends did you want to talk about?" She rubbed the baby's back, hoping a loud belch would stop his distress.

"Not any one in particular, just in general," Angie explained. She made a funny face at her nephew and nearly had her eardrums explode with his next cry. "How do you keep your friends?"

"What are you talking about?" Frannie had to shout to be heard.

"You must have someone to talk to, don't you?" Angie shouted back.

Frannie turned the baby sideways in her arms and rocked him from side to side, which he hated even more than being on her shoulder. His tone was strident. She rocked harder. "Of course, when I so choose, which isn't often." She flopped into a chair and began bouncing her son on her lap to see if that would stop him. It didn't. "I'm self-contained, a fine-tuned machine. I don't dawdle."

"How can you be that way with a baby?" Angie tried to hide how appalled she was.

"He'll learn. I have no patience with a brat."

"Don't you want company?"

The baby's cry turned earsplitting. "No, I don't," Frannie shrieked. "Before little Seth, I was busy with my new job, then my new husband, then my new apartment, then my new car. When I got pregnant, I was always sick. The last thing I want is other people telling me their woes. As if I care!" Her eyes narrowed. "Why are you asking me this?"

Angie trailed after her into the kitchen, where Frannie warmed a bottle of formula. Angie didn't bother to give her any of the gory details. To say that Frannie was a bit self-centered and lacking compassion was like saying the moon was round. "I'm having trouble with a friend, and I wanted to talk to someone about it."

"You? You have no business having trouble with anyone. You need to be choosier about who you associate with and talk to, the way I am." The bottle warmed, she crammed the nipple into the baby's mouth. "I can't believe you, Angie. You just don't know how to deal with people. They'll bleed you dry if you let them."

Angie bit her tongue. "That's why I'm asking."

"Precision and organization, those are the keys."

I'm out of here. She got up to leave when Frannie suddenly handed her little Seth, who promptly spit a mouthful of formula onto her favorite Dolce & Gabbana dress.

"Before you go," Frannie called from the bedroom, "I've got a book you need. It should help you straighten up and fly right."

With little Seth hanging over her arm, Angie dabbed at her dress with a clean diaper. "What book is it?"

Frannie could have written the book in the time it took her to find it, but eventually she returned and handed it to Angie. *Time Management.*

Paavo drove to Lucy Whitefeather's address, a flat in a three-story building in the Ingleside district. She had been living at home when she was killed.

Ruth Whitefeather answered. The ravages of losing a daughter showed in her lined and haggard face.

He introduced himself, gave his condolences, made small talk about the investigation—the police doing all they could, and so on—and then held up a picture of Mina Harker. He didn't hand it to her. It was a death photo, and many people were squeamish about even touching such a thing. Ruth Whitefeather was one of them. Her whole body jerked as she realized why the eyes were shut.

"Have you ever seen this woman?" he asked. "I'm trying to find out if she and Lucy knew each other. Her name was Mina Harker."

"She's dead, too?" Ruth asked, horrified yet unable to avert her gaze.

He nodded. "We think the same man killed them both."

Ruth's eyes filled with tears. "I'm sorry. I've never seen her. Not many of Lucy's friends came to the house. Maybe her boyfriend knows this girl. He's a good man. Hard-working, with no . . . airs. I'll give you Earl's address."

Paavo tried Earl Pierson's home phone and when no one answered, he drove to Pierson's work address. C&Y Pipe Fitters was in the southeast part of the city, an area where an increasing number of industrial buildings was being converted into yuppie offices and lofts. Pierson was back in the shop, and Paavo waited at the front desk for him.

Tall, barrel-chested, with a scar over his right eye, he greeted Paavo with a string of expletives. "Why are you here?" he demanded. "Another woman was just killed, and you waste time asking me more questions? I told those other two assholes I don't know nothing about it. Lucy's killer is out there, not here!"

"I know that," Paavo said. "I'm here to ask about this woman." He showed Pierson the Harker photo.

He calmed down immediately. "Is she another victim?"

"She was killed in Sausalito about a month ago. A woman named Lucy reported her missing."

His gaze lifted to Paavo's at the name of the town. "Sausalito, yeah. She went there a few times."

"Do you think Lucy knew Mina Harker?"

His head rolled from side to side. "I don't know. Maybe. Lucy and me, we had troubles. She was going to school, to college. Look at me—a pipe fitter. We split up for a while. She got into some bad shit. Evil, she called it. One night, about two weeks ago, she came back to me, crying. She said she was sorry. She wanted us to be together again."

"Did she tell you where she'd been? Who she'd been seeing?"

He shook his head. "She didn't want to say, and I didn't want to ask." The big man's eyes turned inward and hollow. "She was back with me again. That's all that mattered."

Paavo left. There was nothing more to say.

His last stop was a long shot, but worth the trip if it panned out. He went back to Sausalito and was directed to Officer Kimura, who handled most of the town's missing person reports, including the one on Harker.

Paavo introduced himself. "The Harker report was given to you by a woman named Lucy," he said.

Kimura nodded. "She wouldn't give her last name. Young, pretty. Brown skin, brown eyes, long, black hair."

"Is this her?" Paavo handed him a photo of Lucy Whitefeather. To aid in the investigation, her mother had given Paavo one of Lucy's high school graduation photos. It hadn't even had time to yellow with age.

Kimura didn't need to study it. "She's a little older, a lot more 'cool'-looking now—but that's her." He handed back the photo. "So, you found her for us."

"Not exactly," Paavo said.

Chapter 12

"We've got the name of the killer," Calderon said as he strutted into the bureau.

Paavo stood at the coffee pot, filled his cup, then faced Calderon. Only moments earlier he'd walked in and noticed the Travis Walters report untouched on Calderon's and Benson's desks.

Yosh, who'd been writing the conclusion to an investigation on a multimillionaire who'd died on his honeymoon while jogging with a wife forty years his junior, shoved aside his paperwork, put down his pen, and swiveled in his chair to face Calderon.

"He left fingerprints at the scene," Calderon said smugly. He sat at his desk, feet up, and stretched his arms high as if to get the kinks out after a hard day's work.

He knew he and Benson had the only interesting case in Homicide at the moment and that it was driving the other inspectors nuts. He played up every news flash with all the drama of a Shakespearean tragedy.

"His name's Mason Markowitz, and he's an interesting case, if you believe in spirits." He paused dramatically. "Markowitz was, from all we're hearing, just a normal guy, an insurance agent in a small town in Illinois until about three years ago, when he was in an auto accident."

Paavo moved closer, eager to hear more. Bo Benson sat on the edge of his desk, enjoying Calderon's verbal swagger. "It wasn't even much of an accident, but Markowitz hit his head against the windshield and was knocked unconscious. He stayed that way for two months. The doctors couldn't say why he was in a coma. His injuries didn't seem that bad. When he woke up, he was a changed man."

Calderon stopped, looking like the cat who ate the canary.

"I give up," Yosh said. "What was changed?"

"He claimed he could see people on the other side."

"Other side? You mean dead?" Paavo asked.

"I saw that movie," Yosh said skeptically. "But wasn't it about a little kid?"

"Markowitz didn't say he could see dead people. He said he could see *devilish* people."

Paavo and Yosh exchanged glances. "What the hell does that mean?" Yosh asked.

"What am I talking here? Swahili? It means what I just said. Markowitz thinks he can recognize when people aren't people at all but are really demons and devils and witches and warlocks."

"Sounds like the Salem witch trials or something." Yosh picked his pen up and began flicking the top so that the ballpoint bounded in and out.

"I know. It's like all that garbage I never paid attention to in Catechism classes," Calderon said, starting to grow annoyed with Yosh's dismissive attitude. "Anyway, this guy thought it was his duty to expose evil, to warn good people about staying away from the bad ones, but now it looks like he's gone a step further. Now if he thinks some people are evil, he just kills them."

"You're saying he's some kind of killer-exorcist?" Yosh flipped his pen onto his papers. "Are you kidding us?"

"I wish we were," Bo interrupted. "Markowitz apparently hunts demons, vampires, werewolves. He goes after all of them and roots out or kills the evil entities."

"A night stalker," Paavo said.

"Exactly. The shrinks who worked with him swore he wasn't dangerous, that all he was doing was seeking monsters. So even though his wife—now ex-wife—had him put in a mental institution several times when he headed for a big city to hunt evil, he'd always be let go after a seventy-two-hour hold."

"Claiming he could see demons wasn't a good enough reason to hold him longer?" Yosh asked.

"If it was, the loony bins would be all filled up." Calderon, unable to keep quiet, answered for Bo. "His old lady couldn't handle worrying about him and what he might do to other people or to her and fighting with authorities who refused to lock him away until he got over his crazy ideas. She left him and moved to Florida."

"Are you guys saying he killed three women because he thought they were demons?" Paavo asked.

"Who knows what a guy like that would think?" Calderon replied. "It doesn't matter, anyway. We know who he is. We'll nail his ass in no time now."

"We figured the candles were his idea of how to cleanse their bodies or something," Bo said. "Maybe he cut out the hearts instead of driving a stake through them."

"Isn't that just for vampires?" Yosh asked.

"Shit! How the hell are we supposed to know about all that crap!" Calderon bellowed. "It's just mumbo jumbo. The guy's a frickin' murderer. I don't care why, and I don't care how."

"What about the fingerprints?" Paavo asked. "Where did you find them?"

Calderon grinned. "He messed up big time. Everything else had no prints. He must have used gloves. But we found a tiny bottle under Julie Sung's body. It had water in it. Once we learned about Markowitz, I suspected it might have been holy water, but there was no way to tell. Anyhow, there were two sets of prints on it. One came up clean—maybe whoever sold the flask or that of a priest, who knows? And the others were his."

"Interesting," Paavo murmured. He quickly told them about the connection he had discovered between Lucy Whitefeather and Mina Harker and about the visit from Travis Walters.

"Whoa-ho-ho!" Calderon shouted, and high-fived Paavo. "Fingerprints and an eyewitness. We got him now, bro!"

Before Paavo went to Angie's apartment that evening, he called to make sure Connie wasn't at the apartment and that they'd be on time for his reservation at Les Fleurs.

She was dressed beautifully in a shimmering royal-blue low-cut dress that shone silver as she walked. It showed off a nice amount of cleavage and clung to every delicious curve. He was sure the dress had some fancy designer label, but he couldn't have cared less about such things. The look was what mattered, and this one made his hands itch from wanting to touch it—and the body it covered.

She handed him the keys to her new Mercedes. One of these days he'd have to buy himself a new car. The ancient Austin Healey he drove was held together with bailing wire, the seats were nothing but lumpy cotton stuffing, and Yosh claimed it'd stop altogether if he ever forgot to feed the mice on the treadmill under the hood. On the other hand, the city issued a car for him to drive at work, and nothing he bought could compare to Angie's, so why bother?

He'd loved the Ferrari that had been destroyed not long ago. While this car wasn't as eye-catching, it had class to spare.

His mood was good, and despite his nervousness, this dinner was exactly what he'd been waiting for.

Once seated, he ordered for them both an appetizer of calamari stuffed with salmon, a salad of warm spinach with smoked duck breast, followed by filet mignon *en croute*, mixed vegetables, and crêpes suzette for dessert, with a different wine for each course. It was one of the most elegant meals he'd ever eaten.

They made small talk through the dinner, with Angie chatting about her business as well as her talks with Bianca and Frannie, her concerns about Connie, and the new helper she'd hired. As they waited for the crêpes suzette, Angie went to the ladies' room.

He expected she was also going to check her telephone messages. Being a businesswoman agreed with her. Although tired, she seemed happier and more self-satisfied than she'd been in quite some time.

The waiter came out and asked if monsieur was ready to have the crêpes suzette served. He wasn't. The restaurant made a wonderful presentation of the flambé dessert at the table, and he wanted Angie to be with him, especially since he'd arranged again to surprise her with the engagement ring.

For the umpteenth time, he reached into his pocket to be sure it was still there. It was. Fifteen minutes had gone by since Angie had left. She should return any moment, and then . . .

After another five minutes, he beckoned a waitress to check on her in the women's room. She might be sick.

The waitress came by and announced, "Mademoiselle is on her cell phone. She said she will join you in another minute."

He nodded, glancing at his watch once more.

The waiter came by again five minutes later, and Paavo waved him away.

Twenty additional minutes passed before Angie returned.

"I'm so sorry. I didn't mean to take so long," she said, fairly bursting with enthusiasm. "I had a couple of messages, one for an appointment with the owner of a dot-com company." She leaned forward in her chair. "He throws a little party for the staff every month, business is apparently quite good, and he would like me to provide interesting novelty desserts on an ongoing basis. It could mean a lot for my business." Her face positively glowed. Unfortunately, it wasn't for the food. Or him.

"I see."

"I'm so excited! I've got to get ready for tomorrow's meeting. I'd like to bring some ideas. It's a lingerie business, and should be a lot of fun—" When her eyes met his, she stopped talking. "Oh, dear! I'd forgotten all about dessert."

"Yes," he said through gritted teeth. "Do you want it now? The waiter has been hovering over our table. I think he'd like to serve us and get us out of here."

She barely glanced at the waiter. "I'm so stuffed, Paavo. I love crêpes suzette, but I think I'll pass. I'm mulling over so many ideas for lingerie cakes, I can't think of anything else."

"I see."

"I guess you don't really want to hear about it."

He didn't reply.

"Well, shall we leave?" she suggested brightly.

"As you wish."

Though he thought he had hidden his dismay and frustration, she must have sensed his unhappiness. Maybe it was his curt responses. "I'm sorry," she said. "On second thought, let's stay. Dessert would be nice."

With that, he sighed. She couldn't read his mind about wanting to propose, and he certainly didn't want his engagement to come at a time when her mind was filled with cakes that looked like bras, panties, and camisoles. He could wait. "It's okay. Your business is doing well. That's good, Angie. I'll ask for the check."

"You're sure?" Her brow was wrinkled with concern.

He grinned, despite himself. "I'm sure."

"It was a wonderful dinner. Absolutely lovely— almost as if this were a special occasion or something." She peered at him curiously.

"It was time for a good meal, that's all. To celebrate your business success," he added.

The smile she gave him was worth tonight's disappointment. There would be another chance. "I do love you so very much, Inspector Smith."

"I'm glad to hear it, Miss Amalfi."

Chapter 13

A pale young man dressed in baggy black pants, a black Siouxsie and the Banshees T-shirt, black spiked hair, black eyeliner, and three silver studs in one ear walked up to Angie and Zoe as they handed out pieces of cake at an Elks Club meeting. The cake was an elk's head complete with antlers created by a judicious use of cake, frosting, and toothpicks.

"Where's the punch bowl?" He carried a large sack of ice on his shoulders. To say he looked out of place in this meeting hall was an understatement.

"This is a nice place." Zoe folded her arms. "What's trash doing in here?"

Angie, who'd been ready to answer, stared at Zoe in astonishment.

"If you mean me," the fellow said, eying her frilly blue apron with a smirk, "I'm delivering ice. What does it look like?" He shifted the ice to rest it on one hip.

"Go deliver it someplace else," Zoe ordered. "This is the cake area, in case you haven't noticed."

121

"You're doing your job, I can't do mine?" he asked petulantly.

"If it is your job!"

"Hold it." Angie's head swiveled from one to the other. The tension was so thick she could almost taste it. "What's going on here?"

"This creep seems to have lost his way." Zoe flicked her thumb at him.

"Don't listen to her." He put the ice at his feet, surprisingly at ease despite the venom Zoe was hurling at him.

Zoe's eyes narrowed to anger. "How did you end up here? Are you following me?"

"Don't you wish, sweetheart." The man grinned, a straight, shiny-toothed smile that reached his eyes, quite at odds with his otherwise dark, punkish looks. "I will admit, though, when I saw you with a beautiful woman, I decided I'd come here to look for the punch bowl instead of asking one of the fat old dudes who runs this place."

He turned to Angie and extended his hand. "My name's Rysk, with a *Y*."

"Angie Amalfi." She shook his hand. He was much stronger than she'd expected. "Rysk is an interesting name. Are you one?"

"Nope. I'm as dependable as they come."

"Don't listen to him," Zoe warned, hands on hips.

"Looks like my friend here's hustled you for a job." Rysk said. "What's the matter, Zoe? Afraid I'll cut in on the action?"

Angie was all ears and eyes watching these two, and she was interested to meet someone who might shed some light on Zoe. Where could Zoe have met Rysk?

The bristling hostility between them intrigued her. She wanted to know more about them both.

"I don't know which I'm more pissed off at," Zoe said. "You calling me a friend or your delusion that Angie would want to hire you for anything!"

Rysk turned to Angie. "I saw you two lugging around those cakes. I can do that for you easy. What if you dropped one? I'd save you time and worry. I'll work for only ten bucks an hour, and I'm an independent contractor, so you don't have to worry about payroll taxes or anything."

She knew what he meant. He wanted to get paid under the table.

Nearly spitting, Zoe glared at Rysk. "Nobody needs to pay someone to carry a cake. I carried all kinds of cakes when I worked for Cocolat. They aren't exactly heavy as stones, you know."

Rysk ignored her. "I could use part-time work," he said. "And if Zoe ever stopped being so angry, she'd tell you I can be trusted."

"Right, about as far as you can throw him," Zoe commented before Angie could reply. "Ignore him, Angie. He's bad news."

"Don't listen to her, Angie. She hardly knows me . . . yet." He winked at Zoe, and as she sputtered in outrage, he gave Angie a boyish grin.

Amused, Angie wondered just what was going on between these two and how she'd ended up in the middle of it. On the other hand, it was getting more and more difficult for her to deliver cakes, especially big ones, and at the same time to take new orders and prepare the ones already scheduled.

"Give me your phone number and a couple of references and I'll keep you in mind," she said. "Now you'd better take that ice to the table at our right before it all melts."

The web was being woven tighter. Alone, in the dead of night, a crescent moon overhead, he felt at peace. He had moved another step closer.

First Mina. Dear, sweet Mina. She'd trusted him, let him choose a special name for her. As he got to know her better and realized why the conjunction between them was so strong, his path, his life, became clear.

He could have cried for himself, for his loneliness as a child, when others called him a monster, a freak, and a lunatic. In time, he began to understand who and what he truly was. As he learned to accept the forces of darkness, to revel in their blasphemy and his own contentment, others stopped regarding him strangely and instead looked up to him.

He'd never forget the day Lucy came to him. Dear Lucy. He had almost laughed aloud. Mina and Lucy, both his for the taking. That was when all doubt left his mind.

Joy filled him, and for a moment he was tempted to reveal to *her*, the one who would be his Queen, who he was and all that he planned. But that would be unfocused and dangerous. She wasn't ready yet to give him the answer he deserved.

There was much more to do and little time. The Ides of March. Only ten more days.

But first, he had a couple more loose ends to take care of. He picked up the phone.

Chapter 14

 Yosh shut his notebook and put it in his breast pocket. "Well, I'm convinced. It looks like suicide to me."

Paavo didn't reply. He felt bone-chilling cold and for some reason was finding it hard to breathe, as if the air had been drained of oxygen. Yosh felt none of that, and Paavo wondered if he'd caught a flu bug. He hadn't felt this cold and miserable since he'd been in Sausalito.

They stood in an alley off Sansome Street, peering up at the three-story-high walkway that linked two financial district office buildings. That morning, they'd gotten a call from the patrol officer on the scene that a young man had fallen from it onto the street below and been killed.

When they arrived at the scene, Paavo was saddened and dismayed to discover that he recognized the victim—Travis Walters. The boy had practically begged for protection, and all Paavo had done was to make a report. Walters had been frightened and nervous, but he hadn't seemed at all suicidal, and yet . . .

Paavo studied the bridge between the buildings.

What had happened here in the early hours of the morning? All of its windows were sealed. To fall from it, Walters had to have gone to the floor above, lowered himself to the top of the structure, crawled to the middle, and then either jumped or fallen . . . or was pushed.

Walters was dressed in a black opera cape with red lining, loose, black slacks, and a white ruffled shirt. On his cape was a patch with Germanic lettering that said NOSFERATU RULES.

"What's Nosferatu?" Yosh had asked. "Some rock group?"

"It's the name of a vampire," Paavo had responded. At his partner's look, he explained, "Angie likes old classics. We went to see it. It was pretty grotesque. The guy was rotten, not your friendly old Bela Lugosi type."

They had carefully checked for any sign that the boy had been forced onto the top of the bridge. Crime scene investigators had dusted for prints other than his on both the window he'd pried open and the fourth-floor ledge he'd climbed onto before lowering himself to the bridge.

Eyeballing it, only one clear set of prints was found. The CSI would have better information after running their tests.

Officer Varney, who had called in the homicide report and secured the crime scene, walked over to Paavo. "I just remembered something." He hesitated. "It's probably nothing, and finding the body must have pushed it right out of my mind."

"What is it?" Paavo asked.

"Well, this alley is part of my normal patrol. Not to drive into, but to pass by two, three, or more times each night, depending on what's going on."

Paavo nodded; he knew the routine.

"The time before, an old man was in the alley. A street bum. You know the type."

"What did he look like?"

"Tall, shaggy white hair, skinny. I rolled down my window and called him, told him to get on home. He never even glanced my way. It must have been because of him that I paid close attention to the alley on my next drive by. That must have been what caused me to decide to investigate what looked like a mound of old, dark clothes on the ground. I just don't know."

Mason Markowitz, Paavo thought, heartsick that he hadn't taken Walters's fears more seriously. He shivered.

"Are you all right, Inspector?" Varney asked, alarmed by Paavo's expression.

He didn't answer but instead asked, "Had you ever seen the old man before this morning?"

Varney shook his head. "Never."

Mason Markowitz slowly walked away from the grisly scene. He shook his head that someone so young could have gone so bad. The boy had been a demon in the making. He had evil attached to his soul.

Markowitz expected to die fighting the dark forces. Already demons had found him and assailed him, but like a modern-day gladiator, he would not give up the fight.

Everything had been stripped from him but self-doubt. He had nothing more to lose.

As Markowitz walked the streets to his apartment, lost in his morbid thoughts, he had no idea he was being followed.

"He wouldn't listen to me," Geraldine Walters said, trying to control her tears. She lit another cigarette. Her hair was short, straight, and dirty blond, her face tanned and lined with dryness, the area above her upper lip yellow-tinged from tobacco.

Yosh handed her yet another tissue. He and Paavo sat in the living room of the two-bedroom apartment. The furniture was cheap—bottom-of-the-line Sears or Penney. Stacks of *TV Guide* were the only visible reading material.

The dead boy's mother was coping with the news better than Paavo had imagined she would—almost as if she'd expected it.

Travis Walters had been seventeen years old. He'd been thrown out of public high school and was enrolled in an alternative school for troubled youths. He rarely bothered to go, preferring to sleep most of the day. A loner, he had no school friends, and his relationship with his divorced parents was sullen and hostile.

At home, he'd spent all of his time shut in his room, a sanctum his mother never entered.

"I'd make him go to visit his father," she said. "I'd tell his father to do something with him, but he couldn't. Travis seemed to hate us, hate everything we ever tried to do for him. All he wanted to do was play video games and listen to that crappy music. I told him to stop it, to clean up himself and his room, to stop wearing black. You know what he said to me?"

Paavo and Yosh shook their heads. They sat quietly with the woman and let her speak, let her pour out her anger and resentment and deep, deep hurt.

"He said he was a vampire. A vampire! The damned fool idiot. I wanted to wring his neck. Or laugh." Her tears turned to sobs. "Instead, I slapped him. Nothing, nothing got through to him. Nothing. And now . . ."

The two detectives waited until she gained some control.

"Had he ever been in trouble with the law?" Paavo asked.

"Never."

"No record of any kind? Tickets?"

"Not even got a parking ticket. He had no license. I didn't want him to drive until he showed he was more responsible." She shut her eyes and shook her head.

Paavo again waited. "Do you know where he spent his evenings or who his friends were, Mrs. Walters?"

She stared at the wet tissue as if it might hold answers that had eluded her for years. "I suppose I should, shouldn't I? In his room, he had his own computer, TV, stereo, Nintendo—everything he could want. Why wasn't he happy?"

"Did he talk about the places he went?"

She sucked hard on the cigarette, then crushed it. "He'd talk about a club sometimes. A place he and his friends hung out. I had the impression, though, that it wasn't a club at all, but someone's home. Maybe some kid's garage or something. I just don't know. There was one kid who would come by the house. Fred . . . I don't remember his last name."

"Would you find his phone number for us, Mrs. Walters?" Yosh asked politely.

"I'll try. Travis might have had it memorized. He's . . . he was . . . very private."

"Did he ever mention an old man watching him? Or the name Mason Markowitz?"

She seemed puzzled by the question. "No. Why? What's this about?"

"What about a flask of holy water?"

"Holy water?" Her expression told him he could have been speaking in tongues.

Just then the doorbell rang.

"That must be my husband. I mean my ex. Travis's dad. Excuse me." She hurried to the door.

"I'm Inspector Calderon." The voice carried into the house. "And this is my partner, Inspector Benson. We'd like to talk to Travis Walters."

Geraldine Walters glanced in confusion back to Paavo and Yosh, then spun on Calderon. "Is this a joke? Get out of here! All of you!" She screamed at Paavo and Yosh as well. "Get out!"

Calderon gawked in confusion at Paavo and Yosh and quickly yanked a photo out of a folder he carried. "Wait, Mrs. Walters. We just need to ask if Travis—or you—recognizes this picture. His name is Mason Markowitz."

She slammed the door on them all.

Paavo's blood turned cold. He recognized the old man in the photo. He was the panhandler who'd approached Angie outside Fugazzi Hall.

"I can't talk now, Paavo. I'm sorry." Angie clutched the phone tight. "I've got a kitchen filled with flies. Flies! I don't believe this!"

"Flies? Are you all right?" he asked.

"I'm fine—if you can call an infestation fine. I've got to go before they destroy all my work. Oh, my God! One is headed for the living room. I'm sorry! Bye!"

She immediately put down the phone and picked up the bedsheet she'd pulled from the linen closet.

Unfolding it and holding the ends, her arms wide, she crept into the kitchen, step by quiet step, careful not to tread on the part that dragged on the floor. She'd never tried to sneak up on a mass of flies before.

Late the night before, a man had phoned requesting a cake of a devil's head. He wanted it to be realistic, and he was willing to pay her well. She thought her best bet for creating such a cake would be to find a devil's mask in a costume shop and copy it.

As she called around the city, she discovered how popular they were. Most were already rented. If the devil looked like Richard Nixon, her task would have been easy. Lots of those masks were available. Apparently older men had finally gotten tired of yelling "I am not a crook" at parties.

When she finally located the proper sort of mask in the Mission District, she asked the shop to hold it for her. The store was dark and dusty, and the devil, demon, and witch masks were almost too realistic to suit her. They were the stuff of nightmares, which she seemed to have far too many of lately. The shop and its owner, a woman with long, green-tinged hair and matching teeth, gave her cold chills.

Red devil mask complete with horns in hand, she had hurried back to her apartment. There was just enough time to pick up the cake she'd decorated for a bowling league tournament banquet and deliver it. It wasn't easy to bake a spherical cake or to decorate it, until she realized she could hold it by the finger holes while slathering blue marble frosting all around. When finished, she had put it on a little toothpick stand to keep it from rolling. It was one of her finer achievements.

She had dashed through her apartment to the kitchen to get the cake, stopped in the doorway, and shrieked.

Her cake was covered with flies. How had they entered a twelfth-story apartment? The doors were all shut, and the windows rarely opened. If she ever went out and left any windows open, the wind up here would blow her belongings from one side of the apartment to the other.

The sheet, she hoped, would now get rid of most of the little beasties. She inched closer, not wanting to disturb them as they munched and pranced on her once beautiful frosting. They'd ruined one cake, and the last thing she wanted was to have them fly all over her apartment, hide, and then attack another cake. Finally close enough, she raised her arms and heaved the sheet over both cake and flies. Quickly grabbing the edges, she swirled it so that the flies couldn't escape. A few did, but she'd deal with them soon enough.

Rolling the whole mess together, she carried it to the garbage chute.

"Mrs. Calamatti, are you down there?" she called, sticking her head inside the chute. She didn't want to bean the old lady with her cake, even though it probably wouldn't do much damage, considering the state of her neighbor's mind. The woman spent most of her time poking through the garbage, looking for treasures. Not that she needed the money. She had plenty of it, but couldn't remember she did. The Depression was much more real to her than the new millennium.

When Mrs. Calamatti didn't respond, Angie dropped the cake, then went on a search-and-destroy mission through her apartment, meticulously checking all doors and windows. How had those flies gotten in? A couple of them could have been in a sack of groceries, she supposed, though that didn't seem very likely. Or maybe one very pregnant fly had somehow snuck indoors and multiplied, and then the whole family had hidden until they had a Comical Cake to attack.

How long was the lifespan of a fly anyway?

No, that didn't make sense. At the moment, she had no time to ponder the great fly mystery. She had another bowling ball to create. She got on the phone with Stan and asked him to put his oven at 350 degrees. The only way to get through this on time was to bake a lot of cakes at once and pancake them together into a ball. Somehow she'd manage.

Comical Cakes had never failed anyone yet.

Chapter 15

"You mentioned that Travis spent a lot of time on the Internet," Paavo said. He'd hoped that Mrs. Walters would be able to provide some help. "I'd like to take a look at the computer, if I might. His friends don't know or won't say much about how he spent his time. It might give me answers."

Geraldine Walters looked as if she hadn't slept at all last night. He hadn't gotten much sleep either. Yesterday, he'd checked school records and talked to the boy's teachers, attended the teen's autopsy and run searches for any prior offenses, and just before dawn had gone back to Sansome Alley and talked to people who worked night shifts to see if anyone had noticed Travis or an old man.

Nothing new resulted, which brought him here this morning.

"Come on in." She led him to Travis's bedroom and switched on the lights. "There it is. You can take it, if you'd like. I don't think I could ever touch it."

"That shouldn't be necessary." He stepped into the bedroom and stopped short, as if he'd hit a wall. The smell of damp earth and decay turned his stomach. Morbid was the only word Paavo could think of to describe the room.

"I wouldn't let him paint the walls black," Mrs. Walters said, oblivious to the stench. "He did this instead."

Every inch of open space, including the ceiling and the windows, was covered with posters from *The Crow, The Lost Boys, Vampyre, The Hunger,* the bands Alien Sex Fiend, Bauhaus, Nine Inch Nails, and other venues also filled with blood, death and dying, that he neither recognized nor wanted to. It was a room made for nightmares.

He turned on the computer. All password protection had been overridden. Walters had either trusted his mother or had nothing to hide or . . .

"Do you know how to use a computer, Mrs. Walters?" Paavo asked.

"I haven't gotten into them yet," she said.

So that was it. Walters hadn't needed to trust.

Geraldine left Paavo alone as he read through the e-mails and perused the history file of Internet visits.

Most of the e-mails were between Travis and a Fred Limore. They showed Walters to be a lonely boy living in a delusion of a world filled with evil, a boy expressing a dangerous interest in satanic cults, crypts, the causes of the murders at Columbine, and the demons behind the Son of Sam.

It was sickening but also very sad reading.

Suddenly, Paavo sat up and reread an e-mail to Fred in which Travis feared he was in danger. The e-mail had been written a week earlier.

There were no more e-mails after that.

* * *

Paavo knocked on the door. He wouldn't want to admit he'd spent the drive over here to Fredrick Limore's home thinking about flies, but he had.

What in the world had Angie been talking about yesterday? Had some customer wanted her to make a cake that looked like a swarm of flies? That must have been it. As long as she was nowhere near Markowitz, he was comfortable.

Cautiously, the front door opened and a dark-brown eye appeared. Paavo flashed his badge. "Are you Fredrick Limore?"

The young man pulled the door wide enough for Paavo to see most of his face, pale, with sleepy eyes. He had on a loose gray sweatshirt and brown cords. "Yeah, that's me." His words were heavy and slurred.

"Did you know Travis Walters?"

"Yeah." Limore's voice turned soft. "I heard he bought it."

"I'd like to ask you a few questions."

He stiffened. "I don't know nothing."

"You might know more than you think. First, how old are you?"

"Eighteen. Why?"

"In that case, your parents don't need to be here while we talk. Can I come in?"

"You have a search warrant?"

Paavo stared coldly at him. "I'm not here to search, just to ask a few questions. You can handle this however you like, but we will talk."

The teenager opened the door wide to let Paavo enter. "My mom's at work. So's my dad."

Paavo entered the upper-middle-class home. The spotless living room was furnished in yellow gingham with ruffles and frills galore and yet had a strangely staged feel to it, as if, despite the hominess of the decor, there was little warmth in this household.

He began by taking down basic information about Limore, who he soon found out worked as a bicycle messenger. "Tell me about Walters," Paavo said. "Had he talked about killing himself?"

Limore had hopped onto the sofa, legs crossed under him. "It's not unheard of these days."

"So he talked about it?"

"We all do, man. Life isn't worth much, you know. Not the way things are." Limore brushed a lock of purple hair aside. It was the only long lock of hair on his head. The rest was about a half-inch long, was dyed black, and had a fuzzy look to it. His bare feet were almost as black as his hair. His hands were equally filthy, with dirt under the nails. Paavo couldn't help but wonder what a woman who would furnish her home this way thought of her son's appearance.

"Many people think life is bad but don't kill themselves," Paavo stated. "What do you think drove him to it?"

"I don't know. Maybe he was scared," Limore offered.

"Scared of what?"

"That he'd be found out."

"Tell me."

"He was . . . a vampire." Limore stopped talking, obviously waiting for Paavo's reaction to this revelation.

"I thought vampires were supposed to live forever and that they killed others, not themselves," Paavo said with as little color in his voice—neither emotion nor cynicism—as he could muster. No one had ever told him how much of an actor he would need to be in his job.

"Yeah, but it's a crappy life," Limore said.

"Are you one as well?" Paavo asked.

Limore smirked. "If I was, I sure wouldn't admit it to a cop. A lot of the Goths are, though. It's part of our way."

Just last week Paavo had a case in which a Goth male had overdosed. If Walters was involved with drugs, delusions and paranoia could easily have followed. The tests from the autopsy would tell him a lot. "What is the Goth way?" he asked.

Limore suddenly backed off. "I don't know. I mean, we're just a group of guys, a few girls. We hang out, that's all."

"Except that one of your friends might have killed himself."

"He was wigged out, man. Probably got some bad . . . uh . . . liquor."

"Where do you and your friends meet?"

"Nowhere special. We go to each other's places, that's all."

"Tell me some of their names."

"I can't do that, man. I can't rat on my friends to the cops. They'd never talk to me again."

"Look, a man's dead. We want to find out why. We want to make sure he wasn't given an assist off that building, understand?"

"Well, if he was, it wouldn't have been from any of us." Limore abruptly broke off his words.

"Yes?" Paavo asked.

"I did hear there's some weird old dude in town. He's some kind of vampire slayer or something. We were warned to watch out for him. I thought it was just a kind of joke, you know. Just some rumor going around about a killer to make things a little exciting for us, make things a little different. It gets kind of dull sometimes. Life sucks, then you die, you know?"

Paavo waited.

Limore began to play with his thumbnail. "But what if it's not a rumor?" he said quietly. "What if it's true and a vampire killer found Travis? That could be what happened!"

Paavo knew the kid was acting. He was willing to go along up to a point. "Do you know his name?"

"No."

"Have you ever heard of Mason Markowitz?"

"No."

Paavo drew in his breath. "If you believe one friend was a vampire, what about the others? Aren't you all in danger?"

"Holy shit, man, we're in for it! I'm really scared."

"Knock it off, Limore."

The kid stared at him. Paavo returned the look, and before long Limore dropped his eyes.

"What's really going on?" Paavo said. "This isn't a game anymore."

Limore continued to worry the thumbnail, as if looking for guidance on how much he should or shouldn't tell. Finally, he shrugged. "The hell with it. The closest me and Walters came to being vampires was eating raw meat from Albertson's. We once got our hands on a bottle of human blood from a blood bank and tried to drink it. Do you know what that shit tastes like?"

"So why would Walters kill himself?"

"Hell, man, I don't know!"

"Where did you hear about this vampire killer?"

"I'm not sure. A bunch of people were talking about him."

"What else did you hear?"

"He left some holy water outside Walters's house. That's all I know, I swear it."

"Where is it now?"

"Hell, he probably threw it away. I would have."

"Walters said he knew Julie Sung. You, too?"

"She was Travis's friend, not mine."

"Didn't you drive Travis to the bus stop to pick her up the night she was killed?"

Limore paled. "We just drove by. We didn't do anything. We never even saw her."

"You saw an old man there."

"No. There was no one. The bus stop was empty."

"Are you sure?"

Limore shrugged. "I didn't see anyone, that's all I can tell you."

"I'd like a list of people who knew both you and Travis."

"I can't do that, man," Limore whined.

"You just said there might be some guy who thinks he's a vampire slayer out looking for them. It might not be playacting this time, Limore. They might all be in danger—or even dead. One of them might know something to stop whoever is behind this. You owe it to them to tell me."

"I should call them first."

"Do you want to call them from the police station?"

Chapter 16

The house had been built in the twenties, and that might have been the last time it'd been painted. Paavo and Yosh could see why Officer Crossen had referred to it as a den. The entryway was so dank and sunless it looked like a cave.

The inside had been divided into a number of small apartments.

"Brr, this is creepsville," Yosh said, his jowls shaking, as he and Paavo followed Crossen into the house. The door off the entry was open, and inside a tiny, middle-aged Hispanic woman sat on a floral wingback armchair facing a tabletop television.

She turned off the set as the policemen entered the room. Standing ramrod-straight, she faced them.

"This is Mrs. Garcia, the landlady," Crossen said. "She's been quite helpful. A couple of nights ago we got an anonymous tip about cruelty to animals going on in one of her apartments. This was our first chance to check it out, and she agreed to let us into the room to look around—right, Mrs. Garcia?"

The landlady nodded, her eyes frightened.

"The room belongs to an old guy named Milt Mason. He's not home. We didn't have to touch anything, just checked what was in the open. That's when I called Homicide. I pay attention to the cases you guys are working."

Paavo knew it wasn't within the landlady's rights to go into a man's rented room, but enough landlords did it for him not to make an issue of it, especially not if she had found the evidence Crossen implied she had. Paavo only wanted to make sure nothing would compromise the case. As long as he was following the landlady's bidding, it wasn't a problem.

Mrs. Garcia led them to the second floor, which had four bedrooms and a shared bathroom. She unlocked the second door on the right and pushed it open.

A hawk, stuffed and mounted with his wings spread wide, stood on a bookshelf just inside the door.

"Quoth the raven?" Yosh asked. "Why do I feel as if I just walked into a Halloween setup?"

"This is no play," Paavo said.

Large and small candles formed a circle on the floor. Others stood on the bookshelf, windowsill, and dresser top. Clippings from vampirelike and supposed satanic cult slayings throughout the country hung by thumbtacks on the walls.

A pillow with a grimy pillowcase and a rumpled blanket lay on the floor. Although the wall held a Murphy bed, a table butting up against it overflowed with papers and pharmacy bottles.

"Look at this," Yosh said. "Lithium. Thorazine. Isn't that used for schizophrenia? The guy shouldn't be able to walk, let alone kill people."

The landlady gasped and ran out of the door.

On a table were newspaper stories about the two San

Francisco ritual murders plus a small clipping about Mina Harker's murder in Sausalito.

"I thought this place was creepy," Yosh murmured. "It's just gone into high camp."

Paavo walked to the bureau and studied a tray of bathroom supplies. The toothbrush was damp, as was a glob of shaving soap that clung to a Gillette razor.

"Someone was here not long ago," Paavo said, touching the toothbrush. He opened the closet door. Instead of a pole for hanging clothes, it had shelves. "Take a look, Yosh. There's nothing campy about this."

Row after row of bats, each with a tiny wooden dowel stuck into its midsection, had been pinned onto wooden boards and lined up on the shelves. From the blood on the boards, it appeared the bats had been alive when they were caught and pinned there.

"That's gross," Yosh said with a shudder. "I don't like bats, but they deserve better than to fall into the hands of the Marquis de Sade."

Paavo studied the displays. "Time to call Calderon and Benson. Looks like we found their night stalker."

When Calderon and Benson arrived, search warrants in hand, Paavo and Yosh left Milt Mason's apartment, positive that when this was over, they'd learn that Milt Mason and Mason Markowitz were one and the same.

As he and Yosh stepped onto the sidewalk, the same cold chill that Paavo had felt at the scene of Travis Walters's suicide struck him, and his breath grew short. He looked around, having the eerie sense of being watched, but no one was there.

The sooner Benson and Calderon found Markowitz, the better he would like it. Just the idea of Markowitz having been near Angie made him nervous. And the more he learned about Markowitz, the eerier the whole situation became.

Angie drove into the Haight-Ashbury district. The sun was down, the streets dark, and she struggled to stay awake. She was so tired, she ached in places she had never even known existed. The red devil cake rested snugly in the passenger seat of the Mercedes. She had barely finished it in time—a couple of flies she'd missed the day before had led her on a merry chase.

The district had a high crime rate and was the part of the city most into witches and warlocks. No wonder this was where a devil cake was wanted. If demons and their minions had a favorite city, it was surely San Francisco. Still, a job was a job, and Comical Cakes never disappointed.

What had her especially upset was that she'd had to break another date with Paavo to create this cake and deliver it on time as well as the more routine cakes she and Zoe had handled today—another baby shower and a promotion in a lawyer's office. For that one she'd been asked to design a smiling barracuda. Oooh-kay.

As much as she wanted to see Paavo later, she was so exhausted she could scarcely think. It wouldn't be fair to him to ask him to spend an evening with someone in imminent danger of loud snoring. Instead, she'd soak in a tub with the Guerlain's Samsara bath gel she'd just bought and then crawl into bed.

Maybe she needed to contact that fellow named Rysk and have him take over the deliveries after all. Doing it all was getting to be a bit much. Zoe spoke terribly about him, yet Angie had noticed a look in her eye when she gazed at him that wasn't hate-filled in the least, and he'd been out-and-out flirtatious with Zoe. Well, she'd give it more thought when she was less exhausted.

Whether she hired Rysk or not, she definitely would lease a minivan to help with deliveries. A two-door Mercedes was too awkward to use; it couldn't carry more than a couple of delicate, oversized cakes per trip.

An arrow pointed to a walkway with the street number she sought—a dimly lit walkway that led to the end of the building.

Steeling herself, she inched along in the dark until she came to a door. She knocked.

A thin little man opened it. His nose was hawklike, his thick glasses grossly magnified his eyes, and his face was crisscrossed with lines. "Who are you?" he asked, hugging the door.

"I'm from Comical Cakes," Angie said. "I brought the cake you ordered."

"Me?"

"Yes. Here it is." To the man's astonishment, she elbowed the door wider and put the cake in his arms.

He gaped at the box he held. "A cake?"

"That'll be—" She stopped herself. Looking at the man's home, at the man himself, she couldn't imagine why he had ordered such an expensive cake from her. She couldn't charge what they'd agreed to on the phone. "Thirty dollars."

"Thirty dollars for a cake?" he shrieked with outrage.

"Hey, you ordered it. I worked hard on it, too. Now, if I could have my money."

"I don't think so." He pushed the cake into her arms.

"I'm sure it's exactly what you wanted." She shoved it back at him. "It's a great cake."

"I doubt it," he replied, giving it to her again and holding his arms out at his sides so she couldn't return it.

"Won't you even look at it?" she asked.

"I'm busy, lady. Go away! I don't know nothing about you or your cake."

"What are you talking about?" She marched past him right into the apartment, placed the cake on the coffee table, and lifted the box lid. "You can at least look at it. Isn't it exactly what you said it should be? I kept my part of the bargain, and you need to keep yours! At a big discount, besides!"

He peered into the box. The red devil cake leered back at him. His eyes widened and he screamed. "You are evil!" he yelled.

"Me? You're the one who ordered it!"

"Get out!" He lunged toward a chest of drawers. She was afraid he was going after a gun and began backpedaling. "All right, I'm going!" she cried, stumbling over her feet in her attempt to get away from him.

"Evil one!" he yelled, brandishing a crucifix at her.

"It's just a cake."

He raised his fist, and she turned and ran. As she lurched down the dark pathway, something hit her back and hair before she reached the sidewalk and turned toward her car. Luckily, the man didn't follow her out to the street. She jumped into the car and locked the doors.

Tentatively, she touched the back of her head to see what he'd hit her with. At first she thought she was bleeding, and then she realized the red coloring wasn't blood.

It was frosting.

Paavo turned off the lamp on the nightstand, pulled the quilted comforter over his shoulders, then, careful not to disturb Hercules, who was curled up asleep at the foot of the bed, rolled onto his left side and shut his eyes. Taking a deep breath, he waited for sleep to envelop him.

He'd called Angie earlier, wanting to see her tonight. He could understand her being exhausted from baking all day plus having to go out and deliver some cake this evening. Damn, but he was sick to death of being understanding. Still, he didn't want to pop the question when she was too tired to keep her eyes open.

Soon things should settle down, and she'd be available again. She couldn't keep up this pace forever, could she? Of course, she'd never had such a successful business before. Was this her future?

He didn't want to think about that. He didn't want to think about anything but going to sleep, which hadn't been easy to do for well over a week now.

Instead, his mind turned to the material on Mason Markowitz he'd read earlier, which had been collected by Calderon and Benson. Markowitz had arrest records and psychiatric holds from five other jurisdictions, and in every one he'd been convinced he was going after demons or vampires, stopping them, and breaking up their "nests" before they hurt anyone.

Each time before, the police had arrested Markowitz for disturbing the peace or on similar charges based on the crazy ideas he spouted. Always he'd been let go because the cases were weak. He'd never been connected to any crime, although strange deaths and missing persons had featured in each of the locales he'd visited.

That's what made this case different. Markowitz's fingerprints had been found at a murder scene.

It was odd that a man could be careful to leave no clues on or around three victims and then forget a flask of holy water.

Of course, no one ever accused most criminals of being Mensa candidates. That was why they were caught. The smart ones gave the cops fits.

Paavo rolled over, reminding himself it wasn't his case.

Travis Walters was his case, and Walters had believed in much the same stuff as Markowitz.

Fred Limore had eventually coughed up the names of two other friends, but they'd had even less information about the deceased than Limore. All three implied Travis's beliefs had caused him to take his own life. None would admit to having known Julie Sung or would name any place where Walters hung out. They made it sound as if he'd led the life of a hermit, yet he'd gotten Markowitz's name from someone. Who that was just might be the key to this whole investigation—both his and Calderon's.

More and more Paavo's instincts told him Walters hadn't killed himself, but how another person could have caused him to go out onto that bridge and jump, leaving no prints or evidence of having been there, was another mystery.

He flopped onto his stomach, putting the pillow over his head. Hercules mewled in annoyance.

Every bit of evidence pointed to suicide, whether he

wanted to believe it or not. Geraldine Walters didn't believe it either, but then he'd never known any parent who could believe their child took his own life.

He sat up in bed and switched on the lamp. Hercules bounded onto the floor and stalked out of the room, his tail flicking with indignation.

Paavo couldn't explain what it was about the Markowitz evidence or Walters's suicide that bothered him; all he knew was that something did. Twelve years of experience rarely lied.

He had to get some sleep. He went into the kitchen and pulled the day's newspaper out of the trash bin. If he couldn't see Angie, he could at least read about the people she associated with. Back in bed, he sat propped up against his pillows and opened the paper to the society page, the answer to an insomniac's prayers.

He was just dozing off when the doorbell buzzed.

Grabbing his .38 revolver, he walked to the door and checked the peephole.

Angie stood on the front porch, pale and wide-eyed. And there were strange red blobs on her hair.

When he opened the door, she threw herself into his arms.

Chapter 17

"This has been the suckiest day of my entire life," Angie muttered as she snuggled closer to Paavo on the couch. Her hair was damp from a quick shower, and she was wrapped in his big blue terry robe. "The thought of those toads in my apartment still gives me cold chills. They were so ugly! And when I walked in, I'm sure I felt one slither over my foot before I turned on the light." She began to shiver again.

"Take it easy," he said for at least the twentieth time. "Toads don't hurt you." He stroked her soothingly on the back.

"Toads give you warts, don't they? What if I get warts on my feet? What if they leave wart germs on my clothes? Who's doing this to me?"

"We'll find out, Angie," he said, trying to calm her.

At least he agreed that someone had to have done this on purpose. Flies might have gotten in through some action on her part, but not toads.

She had no idea how many there were. She'd told him all about how, after fleeing that crazy devil mask guy

150

who'd thrown the cake at her, she'd jumped into her car, and it wouldn't start. Her wonderful new Mercedes-Benz sat there deader than last year's top fashions. Luckily, its GPS service immediately recognized that the car was disabled and called for help. It would have been nice if the tow truck had shown up half as fast.

Afraid that her so-called customer might sneak up on her, she'd got out of her car and run a half-block to a house with an enormous plant container on each side of the doorway. She'd hunkered down behind one of them, spider-plant fronds jabbing her head and tickling her nose, and kept an eye out for the truck. The plant, or at least that particular one, was named spider for more than its shape.

When help finally arrived, the mechanic eventually realized the problem was with the duplicate key she was using. Its poorly-cut edge not only could jab a finger, it also caused the key to fit improperly. He filed it smooth.

Back at her apartment, when she turned on the light, she noticed something that resembled a little brown log on her coffee table. Then it moved.

Another hung from the drapes. Two scurried toward the kitchen. As she realized what the strange tickle she'd felt on her foot had been, she screamed and ran out of there.

"I want to meet that new helper you hired," Paavo said. "She's got to be behind this. Maybe the flies, too."

"But why? I'm her source of income."

"None of this was happening before she came to work for you," Paavo replied.

"It can't be her. It just can't!" Angie didn't think she could cope if she had to go back to handling her business all by herself.

"Did you see any signs of a break-in?" he asked.

"Who would know, with those toads jumping all over the place? I hope that animal control company looks under the pillows on the sofa and under the bed-covers and all. I really don't want any more surprises like that."

He held her closer. "I'm sure they will." While she showered, he had called a twenty-four-hour service that promised to report first thing in the morning.

"Toads! What's my apartment turning into? The plagues of Egypt or something?"

"Stay here a few days," he said, tilting her chin up with his finger, forcing her to look at him, and brushing her lips with his. "I'd like that. You can stay even longer if you want."

"I can't. I've got to get back to my business." He dropped his hand. She clasped hers together tightly. "I've got cakes to bake and deliver, and I won't let this stop me." She shuddered. "I just hope they haven't crawled into the cake flour—or the oven. I don't think the smell of burning toad would do wonders for my mood or my food!"

"I'll help you check the place out," he offered with affection.

Whoever was doing this was trying to squash her and her business. No way would she let them. She squared her shoulders, a militant light in her dark eyes. "I'll handle it."

He straightened then, his arms flung across the back

of the sofa. "Just be careful, okay? Whatever's going on, I don't like it."

"Me neither. It's not as if anyone I know is mad at me, or—" Just then, a light bulb went on in her head. There was someone. She shut her mouth.

"What is it?"

"Nothing."

He gave her a look that told her he didn't believe her.

"I need to think about this a bit," she said, and then yawned.

"You can go in and lie down on the bed." He leaned forward on the sofa, not touching her, elbows on thighs. "I'll sit out here awhile, give you time to relax, maybe get to sleep."

She looked at him, and for the first time in days really saw him. He'd been loving, supportive, and helpful, and instead of thanking him, she'd railed against reptiles and carried on about cakes. What kind of awful, self-centered, type A workaholic was she turning into?

She placed her hand on his back and languorously rubbed it. "I'm so sorry about the way I've been acting. Today. Yesterday. The day before. I don't know what's wrong with me or even where all my time goes anymore."

"It's okay. You're doing something you want to do."

"I guess so. But I want to be with you, too." Her voice dropped to a whisper. "More than anything else."

Wordlessly, he glanced over his shoulder at her. Sky-blue eyes, eyes that made his heart spin, caught hers and held.

"I don't know what I should do—not even what I

want to do," she said, her voice taking on a sudden huskiness. "But I'm not happy with what this cake business is doing to us."

"Angie, it's all right." He turned toward her. "You're doing what you have to."

Her arms tightened around him, and she pressed her nose, her cheek, to his hair. Her eyes squeezed shut. "It's not all right," she whispered intensely. "I don't mean to ignore you; I don't want to. I'll do better. I'll do it all! I promise you."

"Hush," he said.

She lifted her head. Their gazes met, and then their lips.

Mason Markowitz bolted upright, a cold sweat on his forehead. Wide-eyed, he surveyed his surroundings under the Folsom Street freeway. The candles had long since gone out, and the sky was beginning to gray with dawn.

She had come to him once again in a dream. Alone, she walked beside an ocean, smiling and happy. The sun shone down on her so bright it wrapped her in a hazy glow, her features indistinct.

The other one with long, black hair, the one he had failed, suddenly stood in front of him. She opened her mouth, and blood gushed from it, pooling around his feet; then, alive, it crawled onto his ankles, up his legs.

He scooted off the old newspapers with a shout and crouched, looking all around him. The air stirred; he could almost hear the flapping of Baalberith's cape of wings, almost see the horned and taloned beast hovering over him, laughing, laughing, laughing.

He pinched himself hard. *Please let me still be*

asleep, he prayed. But he wasn't. He fell to his knees, his hands clasped over his head. The lord of the flies and his minions must not prevail. He must stop the ascension of the Dark Queen.

He prayed for the strength to do that which he must.

Chapter 18

The pest exterminators were already waiting outside her apartment when Angie arrived to let them in. She explained that she didn't want the toads killed, just gathered up and moved somewhere else. Some toad-loving place, not a big-city apartment building.

They eyed her as if she were crazy. Maybe they were right. As she waited in the hall, the lead serviceman made a quick run through the apartment, then came out to assure her the toads were harmless and that there weren't hundreds of them but twenty at most.

She didn't care what the number was as long as no squishy reptile greeted her when she came home later that day.

Where would anyone have found a bunch of toads anyway? Did pet shops carry them? She had no idea. If not, did that mean someone knew about a toad hangout, and they went there and set traps or something? Toads were little-boy things, not the sort of creatures she or her sisters had had anything to do with as children.

It was all too weird.

She called Zoe and told her not to show up until

noon and then put in a call to Rysk; she left a message. She needed all the help she could get.

Next she phoned her sister Caterina. Cat was a woman who always wore elegant clothes and loved spas, massages, week-long visits to health farms, personal trainers, tennis coaches, and beauty makeovers. She lived in a bay-front home in Tiburon, a pricey town just across the Golden Gate.

Angie reached her on her cell phone. To her surprise, Cat was in the city, heading for the Furniture Mart, a wholesale outlet on Market Street. She invited Angie to join her.

Cat aspired to be an interior decorator. She'd been aspiring for about ten years now. As far as Angie knew, the only house she'd ever decorated was her own, over and over, and still hadn't gotten it right. Tubular chairs and plastic sofas didn't look good, no matter how expensive they were.

Angie hurried to the Mart, eager to see it, as it wasn't open to the public. Cat met her at the door.

"Well, little sis, what brings you here?" Cat asked as they entered a room containing rows of sofas. They were arranged by style, with none of the accents of a furniture store. Cat forged ahead, as if cataloguing the sofas in her head, then headed for a sea of armchairs.

It wasn't my good judgment, Angie was tempted to say when her sister didn't even look back at her. She had to rush to keep up. "I wanted to ask your advice," she called.

"Advice?" Cat skidded to a halt, as if no one had ever asked for her advice before. They certainly hadn't done so on home decoration. "Don't tell me you're finally going to move those dreadful old antiques out of your apartment. I've prayed for this day, Angie. I truly have! Let's go to the lamps. I know a darling wrought iron that would look wonderful in your place. I've got so many ideas to share with you!"

Angie bit her tongue. Cat and her friends were big on sharing. She dashed after her sister. "Wait. That isn't it. It has to do with . . . friendship."

"Friendship? What do you mean? Maybe a nice loveseat? Something in a leopard print—that would make a statement to your friends."

As Cat zigzagged through floor lamps, Angie tried again. "You seem to have a number of friends—"

"Oh! Why, yes, I do. I'm glad you noticed. I have a zillion friends. Why, we send out over five hundred Christmas cards every year." She fluffed her platinum hair. Angie hated the color. "To keep friends, every time you get a chance, immediately make sure you do lunch. It works like a dream!"

"Lunch?"

"I try to go out at least twice a week, and with a different friend each time. Never go with the same person twice, Angie, it's a waste of—Ah! Here we are. I wonder if we want two of them for an even more dramatic statement."

As she pondered some truly ugly loveseats, Angie said, "That's not what I meant."

"No? I know—sectionals. You can put a big sectional in the corner."

"No, no! I was wondering if you've ever had a friend turn on you. Start to, almost literally, dish you dirt?"

Cat's mouth dropped. "One of your friends is doing that to you?"

"I think she's trying to destroy my business!"

"What?" Cat grasped Angie's hand and dragged her to a turquoise and purple chaise longue near the door. "Who is this backstabber?"

"I . . . I suspect it's Connie. God, it makes me so upset!"

"She's jealous," Cat stated.

"I can't believe that," Angie countered.

Cat arched an eyebrow. "I've met Connie. We've spoken, *mano a mano*, so to speak. I know what I'm talking about."

"Oh, my." Angie stared at her.

Cat nodded knowingly. "You came to me because I know how to handle people. Trust me in this. She's envious."

"Do you think?"

"Why else would she be trying to destroy you and all you've worked so hard for?"

"I don't know." Angie's voice was tiny.

"She's hateful!" Cat announced.

"Maybe you're right!"

"Are you an Amalfi or not?" Cat demanded.

"I am—"

"Then stop being such a wimp!" Cat pointed at her. "You need to get even! This very minute. Fight her! Make her rue the day she ever messed with you. Don't let this harridan screw you one second longer!"

Angie pounded her fist into her palm. "Who needs her anyway?"

"Damned sure you don't. Let her know you're tough. Nobody messes with an Amalfi!"

"I'll do it!" Angie leaped to her feet, ready to dash out the door to do battle.

"I'll come with you to the parking lot," Cat said.

"I've got something you need in my glove compartment. I don't know why someone gave it to me, but it'll do you good."

"Oh?" As they rushed through the Mart, Angie wondered what it could be.

Cat reached into her car, rummaged around, and then pulled out a little paperback. *How to Manage Your Anger in Ten Easy Lessons.*

The cake, a tryout for the lingerie company job, looked like a giant blue lace garter. The master decorator and her apprentice regarded the frothy monstrosity with mixed awe and morbid fascination. Angie nearly dropped the pastry bag she was using to make rosettes in the frosting when the doorbell chimed. No one ever used her bell. It was tiny and low and seemed to be nothing more than a knot in the wood of the doorframe.

Rysk stood in the doorway, smiling at her. "You called?"

"Yes, but you didn't have to come by today. We don't have any deliveries ready, and—"

"We?" His eyes lit up as he asked a bit too eagerly, "Is Zoe here?"

Angie smiled, stepping aside. "Yes. She's helping me. Come on in."

"Er, sure. Why not?" The mask of insouciance and bland uninterest was back on his slim face. He walked slowly through the living room, taking in every detail, then the kitchen.

"Hey, Zoe."

Zoe glanced at him. Her mouth wrinkled as she went back to cleaning up from the last cake. "Look at what the cat dragged in." Sponge in hand, she gazed at

Angie. "Flies, toads, and now snakes. What's your apartment turning into, a zoo?"

"I've asked Rysk to work for me. To deliver cakes."

She snorted. "He's lucky to find his way to the john. It's your money, girl. If you want to throw it away on that loser, don't say I didn't warn you."

Angie had basically ignored Zoe's warnings about Rysk since she was in need of his help, but now she realized Zoe was making a very good point. "I did ask for references," she said, facing him.

"Yes, well . . ." He hesitated.

"And I want to know your real name and where you live and that you have a driver's license and insurance. You will be driving a minivan for me, once I lease it, that is."

He opened his wallet and gave her his driver's license.

"You'd better check his references well, Angie," Zoe cautioned. "Fifty bucks on the street could get him a DL that says he's Leonardo DiCaprio." Tossing the sponge in the sink, she stood with her arm pressed to Angie's shoulder and peered down at Rysk's identification.

"I wonder how well she checked out yours, Vane," he sneered.

"Edward Bowie," Angie read.

"Edward?" Zoe snickered. "Somehow I don't see you as an Edward."

He eased back, arms folded, so that most of his weight rested on one leg. "Guess that's how I got the nickname."

"You live in the Mission district," Angie read. "By yourself?"

"It's cheap. And I don't have a roommate." He cast her a shrewd look.

"Any moving violations?"

"Just parking tickets . . . for the last three years, anyway."

"About those references," she began, when she heard a knock on the door. Paavo's knock.

She should have realized he'd come over today to check out Zoe. Last night, he'd been convinced Zoe was the cause of all her problems.

Zoe was close-mouthed and private. Even though they'd worked together for five days now, she was still as much a mystery to Angie as when they first met.

One thing that wasn't a mystery, though, was why Zoe couldn't find another job as a pastry chef. After five minutes in the kitchen with her, Angie had realized Zoe knew nothing more about pastry than what was written on the back of a Betty Crocker piecrust box. Although her lies had been disappointing, Angie had to admit that if she'd been in Zoe's predicament, with no place to live and no food, she'd have lied, too. That was the one reason she hadn't fired her on the spot. As they worked together, she saw that Zoe worked hard, learned fast, and had a great eye for whimsical decorating.

Angie liked Zoe and refused to believe she had been behind any of the strange goings-on.

"Zoe, Rysk," Angie said as she led Paavo into the kitchen. "I'd like you to meet my friend, my very special friend, Paavo Smith." She often forgot how big and intimidating he could be. One glance at Zoe's and Rysk's expressions reminded her.

A glance back at Paavo told her what *he* was seeing as he inspected her helpers—pale, emaciated, sooty dyed hair, weird makeup, and strange clothes on both.

She gulped, then forced a big smile. "Paavo, I'd like

you to meet Zoe Vane and Edward Bowie, who goes by the name Rysk."

Paavo was shaking their hands when Angie added, "Paavo is a homicide inspector."

Rysk's eyes darted a moment toward Zoe. "Ah . . . interesting work," he said.

"Yes, it is," Paavo responded, giving each a long, piercing look.

"Nice to meet you," Zoe said quickly, then to Angie, "I can handle everything here if you'd like to visit with your friend. It's no sweat, girl."

Paavo didn't give Angie a chance to reply. "Are you new to the city?" he asked Zoe.

"Chicago," she answered with all the friendliness of someone hooked to a lie detector.

"What brought you here?"

She concentrated on washing a cake pan. "Earthquakes, fires, floods, power brownouts, gangs. All the things that make life worth living." She glanced at him. "What'd you expect? Oh, yeah, and it's a pretty city."

"An expensive city," he added.

"Chicago's no walk in the park either. Why, do you know about a cheap vacancy?" Angie could see a glint of fire in her eye at all these questions.

"No. I'm just glad you haven't had to join the ranks of our homeless."

At Zoe's pursed lips, Angie jumped in. "Rysk is here to talk about a job delivering cakes for me."

"Really? Business is even better than you've indicated," Paavo said.

"Well . . ." Angie murmured.

The full force of Paavo's cold gaze turned on Rysk. "Interesting name," he said.

"I guess." Rysk was wearing one of his more outrageous outfits—a black turtleneck, red vinyl vest, and purple velvet trousers. Green coloring showed on the spikes above his forehead, and all three earring studs sparkled. At least he'd gone easy on the eyeliner.

Paavo's eyes narrowed. "Have you been in the city long?"

"All my life." Rysk raised his chin.

"Me, too," Paavo said. "Mission High. You?"

"Washington."

That in itself told Angie a lot. Washington High was in a middle-class, family-oriented section of the city. Paavo's own high school was in a much tougher neighborhood.

"What were you doing before you started working for Angie?" he asked.

Rysk put his hands on his hips. "Hey, Angie, your boyfriend sure is a cop. I haven't been grilled like this since I worked at a hamburger joint and put my hand on a burner by mistake."

"You're not used to it?" Paavo asked, pointedly eying the hair and clothes.

Rysk stiffened. "This is a live-and-let-live kind of town."

"Doing what?"

Rysk shook his head. "You don't give up, do you? Okay. I worked at a dot-com company. Lots of guys like me did. Unfortunately, after the initial start-up flurry, the whole thing went belly-up." He shrugged. "Easy come, easy go. Something else will show up eventually. I'm working on my own web site in my spare time."

"About what?" Paavo asked.

"It's a strategy game site—people play for free, and the advertisers will cover my costs. The game's called Destination, but it won't be a fantasy setting. Instead, it'll be set in different periods of American history." He rocked back and forth enthusiastically, and Angie saw the glance of interest Zoe slanted at him.

"It sounds like Ultima," Angie said brightly.

Rysk regarded her with growing kinship. "Yeah, a bit, but it's not medieval. It's like Doom and Civilization combined. There'll be classes and levels. The ultimate will be god level. That's for real hard-core gamers."

Angie nodded, interested. "But god level isn't as much fun as the lower levels. There are no restrictions." She was unaware of admiring looks from her two new assistants. Paavo was staring at her as if she'd just sprouted horns.

"You're a gamer?" Zoe asked, astonished. "I've logged in over a hundred hours real time and have never reached god level."

"Well, I've played a few games online. Age of Empires is one of my favorites."

"All right!" she murmured. Rysk, too.

"You did time somewhere, didn't you?" Paavo asked Rysk unexpectedly, bringing the conversation back to jarring reality. Angie had once heard that if a person was an ex-con, he was supposed to admit it to a police officer when asked.

Rysk stared back at him, his expression blank. "No."

This was going too far, Angie decided. "I, uh, think I should talk to Rysk and then let him go on his way," she said, trying to hustle Paavo out of there. She wanted Zoe to like Rysk, not think he was a jail graduate.

"How about you both write down your social security numbers," Paavo said to Zoe and Rysk as he tore a sheet from his notebook and put it on the table with a pen. "I'll check them for you, Angie. It'll save you time."

So infuriated by his audacity that she was speechless, Angie just stared at him, her cheeks burning.

He would have needed a bag over his head to have missed her outrage. "I *know* you always check out people you hire," he said, trying to appease her. "You're busy. I'm being helpful."

Angie was trying to remember the last time she'd hired anyone.

"It's all right, Angie," Zoe said, jotting her number down. "I, at least, have nothing to hide." She handed the pen to Rysk, eying his reaction.

He weighed the pen a moment. "Me neither." He scrawled some numbers on the paper.

Angie took the paper and brusquely stuffed it into Paavo's hand.

"I'll leave you to your business, Angie," Paavo said, tucking the sheet into his breast pocket. He glanced at Rysk and Zoe. "Nice to have met you both." No one smiled.

"I'll be back in just a moment," Angie said as she followed Paavo out of her apartment to the elevator. He pressed the call button. "That was a horrible thing to do to me—and them! How could you?"

Paavo faced her, his jaw firm. "Get rid of them."

"What are you talking about?"

"They're hiding something."

"They're such a cute couple, how can you say that? They seemed truthful to me," Angie cried.

"That's what worries me."

Chapter 19

Paavo had to wait overnight for the results of his identity checks to come in. An Illinois driver's license showed a Zoe Vane, age twenty-five, living in Chicago. He had her photo faxed to him. It was the same woman.

The Chicago P.D. checked to see if she had any kind of record. She came up clean in both city and state. He stared at the fax photo and wondered at the sadness on her face.

While it was hard to tell if she was lying, according to Angie she was beyond private, keeping everything bottled up inside, which meant it might burst out into . . . what? She troubled him. She was up to something, and it had nothing to do with baking cakes.

Rysk was a puzzle. Searching Department of Motor Vehicles, local, state, and federal records had turned up nothing at all on Edward Bowie, although he did show up on social security's database as a self-employed programmer. Social security records were easy to tamper with, however.

Paavo usually read people pretty quickly, but there

was something impenetrable about that guy, and it troubled him.

He was clearly older than he seemed and older than most Goths. Paavo would have placed his age around twenty-seven or twenty-eight. He'd seen guys like that before, the baby-faced ones who kept a youthful appearance as long as they didn't become dissipated. Put teenage-style clothes on them, cut their hair a certain way, and they could fool most people.

Edward Bowie was one of that type.

Along with age came wisdom. He wasn't the cool, mellow, relaxed dude he pretended to be, but whether that wisdom caused him to be dangerous was another question.

He and Zoe were into the Goth look, as Travis Walters had been. He needed to find out more about that subculture and just how dangerous it might be.

Walters's autopsy came back as he was searching Bowie's records. Walters had such a mixture of drugs in his system, if he hadn't jumped from the bridge, his brain might have burst anyway. Whether Travis took the drugs by choice or was forced was another matter. The coroner reported that paranoia and suggestibility would have been a likely result. Walters might have been psychologically driven to jump off that building rather than physically.

Whatever had happened, the death-and-demon-worshipping Goth world was riddled with drugs. The autopsy report further convinced Paavo that Angie should have nothing to do with people in that subculture.

The problem was to convince her of it.

* * *

"Edward Bowie doesn't exist," Paavo announced as soon as Angie picked up the phone.

"That's hard to believe, considering I hired him yesterday and he'll start delivering cakes for me today," she said with more than a little sarcasm.

"His driver's license is a phony."

"Or the DMV records just might be wrong. Everyone knows they're a mess. He's a nice guy, Paavo. A little mixed up in the way he dresses and does his hair, but that's not a crime. I like him. I want him here, and he's given me no reason to stop paying him to help out."

"You're not being reasonable—"

"No. *You're* the one who's not reasonable. I've got work to do. Zoe is in the kitchen waiting for me."

"Watch them both."

"Trust me on this, Paavo."

"I worry about you."

"I know. I love you." With that, they agreed to meet soon, and Angie hung up.

As she headed from the living room to the kitchen, she was startled to see Zoe in the small hallway between the bedroom and den.

"What are you doing here?" she asked, approaching her.

"Just looking for the john," Zoe said.

"It's off the bedroom. You used it yesterday."

"That's right. I forgot."

After Zoe disappeared into the bedroom, Angie walked to the door of the den. Why was Zoe back there?

She studied her desk and even opened a couple of drawers. Paavo was causing her to be overly suspicious, that's all. Her eye caught the Rolodex by the phone. It was on the *Y*s.

She never would have turned it there. She didn't know and hadn't done business with any *Y*s lately. She twirled the hundreds of names of people she'd worked with and had known over the years. Although she might feel as if she didn't have many friends, she couldn't say the same about acquaintances.

If Zoe had been looking at the Rolodex, what could she possibly have been looking for?

Zoe was already back in the kitchen when Angie returned. "Did you go to the den?" she asked.

"The den? No. Well, I looked in and saw the bathroom wasn't connected to it, if that counts. Look, if something's in your craw about the den, just speak out. I don't want any bad feelings here. If I did wrong, say so."

"No. Just curious. It's nothing."

Zoe gave her a sidelong glance. "If you're going to be suspicious of anyone, it should be Rysk. He's the one who's a mystery."

Why the sudden outburst? Angie wondered. "He's a nice person."

"That's easy to pretend . . . for a little while. Just watch your back."

"Why don't you like Rysk?" Angie asked.

Zoe shrugged. "It's not that I don't like him. He's a puzzle." She had an odd expression on her face. Could she have been looking in the Rolodex for more information about Rysk? His phone number perhaps?

That was possible . . . and Angie could understand Zoe not wanting to admit it to her.

They were putting the finishing touches to a cake that looked like a computer when Rysk showed up. They'd made the monitor into a face sticking out its tongue. The cake had been requested by a computer tech support group.

He entered the kitchen. "Hey, cool. I've had computers do that to me."

"Haven't we all?" Angie said with a chuckle.

Zoe glanced at him, then at Angie. "While you're boxing these, I'll run down to the market and get another pound of butter. We're almost out."

"Get two. We'll use it." She handed Zoe some money. The Hyde Street Market was just a couple of blocks away.

"I don't think she likes me," Rysk said at the sound of the front door shutting.

"What's with you two?" Angie asked.

"I guess I got off on the wrong foot when we first met."

"Where did you meet?"

He grinned. "At a dance. She's a good-looking woman."

Ah! How interesting! Before she had a chance to pursue it, Rysk picked up two of the cakes and carried them to the van. Angie had finished packing the third and had begun the fourth when he returned.

"This box isn't sturdy enough for the computer cake," she said. "I'm going to look for something to strengthen it in the den."

She walked into the den and immediately realized that if she doubled the boxes—one inside the other—that would do it. She whirled around and returned to the kitchen to find Rysk on the floor and scrambling to his feet. He bumped his head on the underside of the kitchen table as he did so. Zoe's backpack lay open. She'd left it under a chair beside Rysk.

"What are you doing?" Angie asked.

"I thought I saw a big glob of frosting," he said, rubbing his head. "I wanted to clean it up before it was ground into your hardwood floor."

"Really?" She pulled the chair aside but didn't see anything.

"It was just a shadow, I guess," Rysk said.

She looked at him quizzically.

"You got what you need for the last box?" he asked.

"Yes. Why is Zoe's backpack open?"

"Is it?" He reached down and zipped it shut. "Guess she left it that way. Say . . . you don't think . . ." His gaze shifted between her and the backpack. "Look, Angie, if you're going to be suspicious of anybody, it should be Zoe. She's the one who's a mystery."

Hadn't she just had this conversation?

"She's a nice person," she said.

"That's easy to pretend . . . for a little while. Just watch your back."

Déjà-vu.

"Why don't you like Zoe?" she asked.

Rysk shrugged. "It's not that I don't like her. I do. She's a puzzle, though. An intriguing puzzle."

Angie studied the almost wistful expression on Rysk's face. Could he have been looking in the backpack for information about Zoe? Her address or phone number?

It was all becoming, as Alice said in Wonderland, curiouser and curiouser.

Before she had a chance to ask him more, Zoe returned with the butter, Rysk left with the deliveries, and the cake-baking marathon began again.

* * *

Mason Markowitz stood in the nighttime shadows and gazed at the luxury apartment building. He'd walked the streets since the infernal armies of Baalberith had invaded his sanctuary and swarmed over his possessions, corrupting them with their paws and hooves and tails.

He needed the woman. He would wait here for her for all eternity, if necessary. And then he'd stop her.

His head pounded. That must be why the vision was so unclear this time. He rubbed his temples, trying to see, trying to know.

No matter. The answer would soon be his.

Chapter 20

The white angel food cake came perfectly out of the oven. In less than an hour, it would be transformed into an angelically smiling bunny. A newly pregnant woman's husband had called to order a cake of a dead rabbit. He wasn't pleased when Angie told him that rabbits were no longer used in pregnancy tests and didn't have to die to prove that a woman was knocked up.

Eventually, Angie talked him into substituting a cheerful rabbit holding a test tube. He didn't think that was very comical, but she refused to make a cake that looked like Bugs Bunny wearing a toe-tag. No one else, she was sure, would do such a thing either. Besides, who would want to eat it?

He relented. Angie almost gave in to the urge to slip in a note giving his wife condolences for being married to such a jerk. The longer she worked with the public, the more she wondered about these people and their sick senses of humor.

Anyway, the cake she envisioned would be cute and highly edible.

"I can handle this if you want to get out for a while

to see your cop or a girlfriend," Zoe offered.

"Thanks. I don't think so. Visiting my sisters is quite enough for now."

"You have sisters?" Zoe asked.

"Four. No brothers."

"That must have been fun when you were growing up," Zoe said, her voice suddenly wistful. "Do they all look like you?"

"Kind of, except for one who dyes her hair platinum."

"A blond?" Zoe looked interested. "Do you two get together often?"

"Once in a blue moon, I'm afraid, except for holidays. She's older and married. All my sisters are. Do you have any brothers or sisters?"

To her surprise, Zoe's eyes reddened, and she hastily lowered her head. "A sister. She's only seventeen," Zoe said.

"Is she back in Chicago?" Angie asked, wondering if the cause of Zoe's tears was homesickness.

"No." Firmly, Zoe shook her head, squaring her shoulders. "She's out on her own. Our mom died, and our father remarried, and his new wife—well, we both went out on our own at an early age."

"I see," Angie said, not sure that she did, but feeling bad that she'd upset Zoe and not wanting to cause her any more heartache.

"You're lucky to have family around you," Zoe said. "And I imagine you have a lot of girlfriends to have fun with as well. You're a lucky person."

"I don't know about that," Angie said ruefully, her mind going to Connie. She couldn't discuss her. The subject was too hurtful.

"Really?" Zoe said. "Do you—"

She was interrupted by Stan's shave-and-a-haircut knock on the door.

"Hi. The luscious smell of freshly baked cake wafted across the hall from your place to mine," Stan said. "I took it as an invitation."

"Come in. We'll have some cake left over when we cut out the rabbit ears."

"Rabbit ears? Are you making a TV cake? I thought everyone used cable now. Or satellite dishes."

Zoe glanced up as they entered the kitchen and laughed. "Now, that's funny," she said.

Stan joined her in laughter, then glanced at Angie. "Why?"

Angie didn't bother to explain but made introductions.

As she peered at the two of them, a new idea popped into her head. "Stan used to help me with these cakes," she said. "He's quite good at it, but his job at the bank takes up too much of his time." *That'd be the day.* "He's an assistant vice president, almost, so he isn't able to be here much."

Stan gawked at her. "But you threw me—"

Angie kicked him.

"A vice president," Zoe said, measuring water into the mixing bowl. "That's impressive."

"Almost," Angie replied. "He lives alone and comes over here to help me get rid of leftovers."

"Does he?" Zoe glanced up at him as she stirred the white icing.

"I like being of help." Stan puffed out his narrow chest.

"Are you saying you're a man who likes to bake?" Zoe asked playfully, adding a little more water. "I didn't know there was such a thing."

"I like to eat," he answered.

She laughed.

Zoe's ability to laugh at Stan's awful jokes was a definite plus, Angie thought. Last evening, while getting ready to go to dinner with Nona Farraday, she'd spent a fair amount of time thinking about Zoe and Rysk and their strange interplay, but she had reached no conclusions.

Her dinner with Nona had been fun. They'd been rivals back when Angie wrote restaurant reviews. Since she'd given that up and she and Nona did have a lot in common, she'd decided they should be friends, and called.

Nona seemed happy to get together with her, but as they talked, Angie was bitten by the review bug all over again.

So much for palling around with Nona. They made better rivals than friends anyway.

"Stan can help us decorate the cake," Angie said. "He's quite artistic."

"I am?" Stan looked stunned.

Angie nudged him closer to Zoe. "You help Zoe with the icing while I cut the cake into shape. We need lots of pink and blue."

"I'll get rid of the pieces you don't need," he offered. "This is great, Angie. I'm glad you've finally found someone who actually wants to be helpful."

"What do you mean?" Angie asked.

"Connie hated helping out. I thought you two were friends," Stan said. "Was I ever wrong!"

The room began to swirl as blood rushed to Angie's head. This was too much. Even Stan knew Connie didn't really like her! How gullible she'd been. She didn't know whether to laugh or cry.

"Who's Connie?" Zoe asked.

"No one I wish to talk about," Angie announced curtly. "Let's finish this cake."

"I love helping," Stan said to Zoe. "And I love cake with thick frosting."

Angie's doorbell caused her to leave them. Rysk was right on time to pick up cakes for delivery. She had asked him to leave off his earrings, eye makeup, and colored hairspray, and wear clothes a little less off-putting to her customers. He showed up in blue jeans, a Nike T-shirt, and brown leather bomber jacket, with his hair combed to the side instead of sticking straight up. To Angie's amazement, he was actually good-looking.

"I picked up the Windstar for you this morning," Angie said. "It's parked across the street."

"The white one?" he asked.

"That's it. The keys are right there on the table by the door. Let's go into the kitchen to get the cakes and addresses. You have four deliveries today. By the way, Zoe's here, and so is my wonderful neighbor, Stan."

"Oh?" Rysk walked into the kitchen to see Zoe smearing some icing onto a bite of cake.

"Hey, Zoe," Rysk said.

She frowned at him and popped the cake into Stan's mouth. Stan's gaze was lustful, but Angie suspected it was more for the dessert than the woman. Rysk's smile vanished.

"This is my neighbor, Stan Bonnette," Angie said. "Stan, meet Rysk."

The two men shook hands while eying each other like two stallions each guarding their position.

"So, you're Angie's driver," Stan said after swallowing.

"That's me." Rysk hooked his thumbs in the belt loops of his jeans. "And I'll help doing other things if she wants."

"Not if she's got half a brain," Zoe murmured, returning to the bunny cake and smoothing a circle of pink frosting.

Stan lifted an eyebrow at that. "Angie's a great gal," he said. "We've worked together on all kinds of projects. I'm sure Zoe is a great asset, too." He flashed her a big smile.

"But for how long?" Rysk asked, his glare never leaving Zoe's face.

"I enjoy working here," she responded, avoiding eye contact with Rysk. "Making these cakes is fun, not work. And who can complain about working in cool digs like this, with good food for lunch each day, coffee, whatever?"

"Can I come back to help again, Angie?" Stan asked.

"You lost your chance, fellow," she answered.

"You might want to rethink that," Zoe said softly, angling her head toward Rysk while giving Angie a worried look.

"Have you filled up your cookie jar yet?" Stan asked, oblivious to the sudden tension in the room.

"It's still empty," Angie replied as she tagged the cake boxes for Rysk's deliveries.

"Angie!" Stan wailed.

"Help is coming your way, my good man," Zoe said. "I promised Angie I'd bake up some of my specialty, coconut bittersweet-chocolate cookies. I've eaten so much of her food, I owe her a real treat, and believe me that's what they'll be."

"They sound exquisite," Stan was all but orgasmic. "I'll help. Do you want to start now?"

"Exquisite?" Rysk mouthed to Angie. She shrugged.

"I've got to finish putting this cake together," Zoe said.

"I'll help," Stan replied. "Two hands are better than one, and the sooner we get done with this rabbit, the sooner we can get to real baking. Angie, this is a woman after my own heart."

Angie laughed, but she noticed that Rysk didn't seem to find Stan's carryings-on in the least bit amusing.

Zoe was concentrating on blending the coloring into the icing. Stan was drooling over the cake, and Rysk was watching Zoe.

Pure desire was in his eyes. Yes! She knew it. Any two people who argued as much as they did had to be in love—or they'd have killed each other by now.

Now, what to do about it?

"Miss Vane," the deep voice called from behind her.

Zoe's bones chilled. Slowly turning, she faced the Baron. His eyes held hers firmly as he glided closer. "Baron," she whispered.

Tonight The Crypt Macabre was filled with the usual night crowd, but she'd noticed extra security by the doors.

"I regret we haven't had a chance to get to know each other better." He held out his hand, and she gave him hers. Everything inside her clamored to run from him, but it seemed her turn had finally come to have the Baron's attention bestowed upon her. She had to be sure not to mess it up.

"It's been a drag on me, too," she said, working to maintain a jaunty, hip demeanor. "But you always have chicks lined up around you ten deep. I can't even get close."

He chuckled. "You can get as close as you like anytime, Miss Vane."

She smiled. "The name's Zoe."

"Zoe." The name curled around his tongue. "I've watched you for some time. I could feel your eyes on me. You have powerful eyes . . . Zoe."

"Not me." She was unable to stop herself from taking a step backward. "I'm just old reliable Zoe. Nothing special."

"You sell yourself short." He tucked her arm in his and, holding it close, led her to a small bar. "I like your dress and this necklace." As he lifted the amethyst, his fingers brushed her neck. He moved his head closer, as if to study it. Her breath stopped. The room seemed to sway, and visions of him kissing her throat filled her head. Or . . . her heart pounded . . . was he biting into it, like some vampire?

"Your order, miss?"

Startled, she opened her eyes to see the bartender looking at her expectantly. He was pouring a scotch and soda for the Baron.

She ran sweaty palms over the short, tight, black satin shift the Baron had complimented. He was regarding her with a knowing smile that unsettled her even more than her strange vision had. "Gin and tonic, please," she said.

Drinks in hand, he led her to a small, round table.

"I understand you work on cakes, Comical Cakes," he said, his voice smooth and his dark eyes penetrating.

"How do you know that?" she asked.

He laughed aloud. "Do you really think there's anything I don't know?"

"I'm fairly new in town." She placed her drink down and self-consciously tugged at her hem. The Baron's eyes narrowed ever so slightly, and she let it go. "I'm still learning who the Daddy Fish is in this pond."

"You're from Chicago," he said, continuing to make her feel as if she were under a microscope.

She grew more uneasy and cupped her drink. "I thought it was where all the real people hung out, but it's deader than sea scrolls compared to this place."

The Baron cocked his head and gave her a lazy smile, one that brightened his eyes. "You're an interesting woman, Zoe Vane. I will admit you puzzle me, but I like puzzles. I'm going to enjoy our time together."

Her mouth was dry. This Baron, the one who spoke to the heart, seemed far more dangerous, for more able to amass a devoted following, than a cold, passionless leader would be.

"There's nothing so special about me," she said, trying to come off as mysterious. If he liked mysterious, that's what he'd get. She needed to be close to him, to learn about him and others who were near.

"What do you say I order a Comical Cake?" He gave her a crooked grin. "Do you think you and your friend would make one for me?"

She couldn't help but laugh in return. "I'm sure we'd be honored."

Suddenly, his attention was caught by something

over Zoe's shoulder. His face tightened. "Excuse me. There's someone I must speak to."

Her gaze followed his. A young, pretty Oriental woman stood in the doorway, looking immensely self-assured and poised as she gazed out over the crowd, far different from most of the young people here.

The Baron hurried to her. Taking her hands, he pulled her close. The top of her head barely reached his shoulder. He wrapped his arm around her, and they disappeared into the shadows.

Concentrating on the Baron, Zoe realized with a start that his assistant, Fieldren, was standing beside her.

"She's a new member," he murmured. "Her name is Julie Sung."

Chapter 21

 Angie was beside herself. She'd been called to go to a house to discuss baking cakes for a party of twenty, and yet no one was there when she arrived. This was the second time that had happened to her. Was someone playing tricks, or were people really so careless as to make appointments and then not keep them?

She really didn't have time for this. But at least she was getting smart. She'd brought a cake with her that had to be delivered to a horse's birthday party not far from her appointment. She never thought she'd be baking cakes for a horse, but Heidi was being boarded some forty miles outside the city, and the owner visited her on weekends only. That was why the owner wanted a Comical Cake of the mare.

Angie couldn't imagine eating something that looked like a beloved pet or animal. She was meeting real ding-a-lings in this line of work.

Still muttering to herself about the thoughtlessness of the public, she got into her new car. A vaguely familiar yet disquieting smell hit her. A stain smeared the bottom of the cake box. She peered closer. The smell was stronger, and the bottom of the box was wet.

She opened the driver's side door, ready to jump out of the car as her hand slowly reached for the box top. Thoughts of flies and toads pounded her. What now?

She flipped back the lid and shrank away from it.

Nothing moved. Nothing jumped out.

Poor Heidi was now a bright-red color, but it wasn't frosting. The familiar smell was blood, and it had been poured on her cake. Shifting the box, she saw that it had seeped through onto the leather seat and was dripping to the floor mat.

OhGodohGodohGod! Disgusted and horrified by the sight, Angie didn't want to touch it, but the blood was ruining her car. The thought that the blood might be tainted scared her.

A trash bin stood on the corner. She drove to it and, holding an unbloody part, managed to whisk the cake to the trash can before it fell through the bottom of the box. Immediately, she drove to the auto detailer she'd used for her late, lamented Ferrari. Before even talking to him, she scrubbed her hands first with bleach and then Boraxo.

In the office, she phoned the horse's owner to tell her someone had vandalized her cake. Instead of offering sympathy, the woman threatened to sue. Angie wasn't worried; she was too frustrated to care. She'd have loved to hear what a judge would say about taking up a court's time because of a cake.

Next she called Rysk. He had kept her minivan after making the computer cake's delivery to Silicon Valley the day before, and she expected she'd have to leave her Mercedes at the auto shop overnight or longer.

He arrived fifteen minutes later to find her standing

at the door to the detailer's shop watching the owner trying every trick he could think of to get the blood off the car seat and floor mat. It didn't look promising.

"You were delivering a cake?" Rysk asked as he walked up to her. He wasn't looking too Goth today. She was glad. Her mood was black enough for both of them. "That's my job. You don't need to do that."

"It was on the way. I thought I'd save us both time."

"It . . . it's not a good idea for you."

She was surprised to hear him say that. "You're right. Somebody hates me, that's all I can figure."

"I don't think that's it, Angie." She was touched by his surprisingly caring tone. She hadn't expected kindness.

"I've had flies and toads in my house, now blood on a cake. Two people swore they hadn't made appointments when I showed up at their homes, and I delivered a devil cake to a customer, and he threw it at me!"

Rysk looked puzzled. "Why'd anyone get upset about devil's food?"

"Not devil's food. A devil. It was in the shape of a Halloween mask." She faced him, woeful. "Is it me? Is it the cake business? Nobody throws things at you, do they?"

"Let's walk," he suggested.

Just being on a sunny street filled with people looking carefree and not being plagued by creatures or blood made Angie feel a little better. "Thanks for coming to help me," she said.

"My pleasure. Anyway, you sounded pretty low, boss lady," he confessed.

"I was . . . I am." They were on Pine Street, and it

was a steep hike up to California. They began the climb.

"Is someone mad at you about something? A customer maybe?"

"The only one I can think of is Connie." She quickly told him about her former friend.

"Blond and pretty, hmm?" Rysk asked with a grin. "Think she'd be interested in going out with me?"

Angie knew he was kidding. At one time she would have automatically said no, but she had to admit that he cleaned up very nicely. She also decided he must be a good five years older than she thought when she first saw him in his Goth getup. Someday she might discuss with him the benefits of giving up that punk look altogether.

"I don't think so," she said finally.

"The story of my life," he lamented.

At the top of the hill a strong wind made the air crisp and clean, and the bright blue of San Francisco Bay painted a calming picture. "Connie used to be my best friend," Angie said softly. "It's hard to imagine her doing something like this to me."

"I've gotten a few women mad at me in my day," he said. "They turn from sweet little things to . . . to looking just like the cake that the guy threw at you."

She laughed. It felt good to stand in the sunshine and laugh. She hadn't realized how much she'd missed it.

"Tell me," Rysk said, his expression suddenly serious, "did Zoe know where you were going today?"

"Zoe?" She glanced at him with surprise. "I mentioned it to her, but so what?"

He nodded but didn't reply.

Angie didn't get it. He was interested in Zoe yet acted suspicious of her—just as Zoe appeared distrustful of him. It didn't make sense. "Zoe's done nothing but help and support me."

"You hardly know her," he pointed out.

"I hardly know you, either," she countered.

They walked through the Nob Hill park between the Fairmont Hotel and Grace Cathedral. A couple of elderly men walked tiny dogs, and a young woman in spandex jogged by.

"How did you two meet?" Rysk asked.

"It was . . . an accident, I suppose," Angie said. "We talked, and I found out she used to work in a pastry shop."

"She did?"

"Well, no, not really. But she needed a job. She must have seen me enter the restaurant, delivering a cake. I don't know, and I don't care. It's water under the bridge. She's a friend now."

"How much do you really know about her?" His gaze was serious, much too serious to suit her.

"Well," she lifted an eyebrow and grinned. "She's single . . ."

He grimaced.

Enough for now, she decided. "Let's go see what the bad news is on my car."

"We got him!" Calderon shouted as he strutted into the Homicide bureau. "Son of a bitch!"

"He squealed worse than a pig," Benson said, a big smile on his face. "Yelling he was innocent. Can you believe it? He tried to say he was the one who was going after the killer."

"Are you talking about Mason Markowitz?" Rebecca Mayfield asked from her desk.

"Paavo and Yosh found his apartment, or whatever you'd call it," Calderon said.

"If it was in a basement, it'd be called a dungeon," Bo added.

"Where did you find him?" Paavo asked, relieved that the suspect was in custody.

"It was easy." The two arresting officers poured themselves celebratory hours-old coffee and grabbed a couple of the morning's doughnuts. "We figured he'd be living on the streets after we found his room, so we put out word to patrol cops to be on the lookout for him. We got a call from one in Russian Hill who'd picked up a vagrant who was acting crazy. Bingo! It was Markowitz."

"Russian Hill?" Paavo asked, a sinking feeling in the pit of his stomach.

"Jones and Green. A nice neighborhood."

Yes, it is, Paavo thought. Angie lived on that corner. His gaze met Yosh's. Yosh knew where Angie's apartment was.

"He told you that *he* was looking for the killer?" Paavo asked after the two had settled at their desks.

"That's right. He's sticking with the story about being a demon hunter but swears he had nothing to do with any of those women's deaths. He admits to going to the area where Whitefeather and Sung were murdered, as well as to Sausalito, but he claims he was there only to 'feel' the demon who did it, whatever that means," Benson said before filling his mouth with jelly doughnut.

Paavo glanced up at this statement. "He admits to having been at the crime scenes?"

"You got it," Calderon said. "We didn't say a word, just let him talk. We've got his prints, plus he wears Kmart brand shoes. The Sausalito PD had a make on those at their scene. We've got the guy nailed."

"Along with his admissions," Bo added.

"His attorney must have had fits about that," Paavo said.

"He doesn't have one yet."

"And he's talking? That might mess up your case."

"I'm sure he'll find one soon enough," Benson said. "This is such a high profile case, I'll bet those guys will be crawling out of the woodwork to defend him."

"You've got that right," Yosh said. "He might be a vampire killer, but they're the bloodsuckers."

Chapter 22

 As Angie walked into the Jazz Workshop, Dominic Klee and his band cut the song they were practicing and launched into "Sophisticated Lady." She smiled and waved at him, then continued through the empty club to the back room.

Her sister Maria, Dominic's wife, was creating a mock-up of a newspaper advertisement. "Good to see you, Angie. Want to help?"

"Sure," Angie said, picking up a cutout of a trumpet, Dominic's instrument, and angling it. "I'm sorry to bother you, but I just don't know what to do."

"You're no bother, little sis." Maria was older than Francesca and Angie and younger than Caterina and Bianca. She was the sister Angie least understood.

She could understand Bianca's motherliness. Bianca was the oldest of five girls, and while they were growing up, their mother had worked long hours at the family's shoe store, selling, ordering stock, and keeping the books. Both parents worked hard until the business caught on and did a remarkable turnaround. Part of that turnaround, too, was because Salvatore Amalfi bought the little building in which his first store was located.

No one ever would have dreamed property in North Beach would take off the way it did. He didn't sell but used the appreciation to finance a second store in the financial district and more property. He now owned an apartment building and five commercial buildings in San Francisco, three of which continued to have shoe stores; he no longer operated them but leased to other people. He also owned a mansion in Hillsborough and a winter condo in Scottsdale.

By the time Angie was twelve, her mother had been able to stop working, and the Amalfi family began to enjoy the money they'd amassed.

Her second sister, Caterina, had, like Bianca, grown up with little material wealth. She didn't have the authority of the oldest sister, but was old enough to be conscious of all she'd missed out on compared to other kids she knew.

She became the most materialistic of all the girls, wanting the best of everything. She couldn't hold a conversation without talking about money or possessions. The world, to Cat, as she began calling herself about the same time as she decided to turn into a platinum blonde, was there for the buying.

Sister number four, Francesca, like Angie, had missed most of the hardship her older sisters had faced. Since she wasn't the baby of the family, she wasn't coddled and grew up resenting her baby sister while being fairly estranged from the older girls.

Her middle sister had always been a mystery. Maria was highly religious, and everyone thought she would become a nun. Instead, she ran off with a jazz musician. At times, Angie wondered if Maria didn't regard her marriage to Dominic Klee as some sort of penance, maybe for lust. She was happy, though, and Angie couldn't imagine a more disparate couple—except maybe herself and Paavo.

Maria was a blithe spirit. Or for want of a better description, she was New Age when it really was new. She didn't seem to see the world around her, but looked beyond it to a different plane. Nothing bothered her, and she was the complete opposite of Cat. She wore no makeup and rarely cut her long, black hair, wearing it loose or in a single braid down her back. Her home held the simplest of furniture and a few throw rugs on the floor, even though her own inheritance alone, without counting the proceeds from the nightclub, would have been sufficient for a much nicer place.

Even though Angie didn't understand her, she hoped Maria could give her the advice she was seeking. Since she and Zoe had finished up early and Rysk had completed his deliveries, she took the minivan to the nightclub before it opened to the public. The detailers were still working on her Mercedes's stained seat and floor mat. The blood had saturated both.

"So what's up, Angie?" Maria asked, pouring her a cup of peach-flavored tea, caffeine free, as she stepped back and studied the layout.

It was one of Angie's least favorite drinks, but she took it out of politeness.

"I want to know what it takes to be a good friend. How do you go about it?" Angie switched the lettering from the bottom to the top of the ad.

Maria cocked her head and straightened out the trumpet. "Me? I don't know if I am one, frankly. I have too many faults. I'm not a good enough person." That was typical Maria-speak. Angie knew her sister didn't believe a word of it. "Why are you asking about this?"

"I'm just feeling . . . a little down, I guess," Angie admitted. It wasn't as much fun not being able to call Connie all the time, and other people she got together with from time to time, like Nona, were acquaintances rather than all-around friends. "Maybe there's something wrong with me as a person," she said dejectedly.

"Who has you questioning yourself this way?" Maria asked, horrified by what she was hearing.

"Well, Paavo said—"

"Men! You can't listen to them. They just don't get it."

"Maybe it's my fault that I don't have lots of friends like you do."

"Me? Don't look to me as an example. I know what I'm supposed to do to be good and to live a good life." She sighed soulfully. "I'm afraid my friends aren't of this world, Angie."

That took her aback. "They're not?" She added a clipping of an old quote from Miles Davis.

"No. They're from . . ." and she cast her gaze heavenward.

"They are?" Angie said, forgetting her dislike of peach tea and swallowing a mouthful.

"The saints listen to me, listen to my troubles and woes and my happy times as well. They give me love and guidance. I couldn't do without them." Maria moved the lettering back to the bottom of the ad.

"I've heard of people saying they talk to saints, but you sound like they answer you back." Surely Maria was joking, Angie thought, as she stared dubiously at the tea. What did they put in these things anyway?

"Of course they do. Otherwise what would be the use of talking to them? I tell them all my secrets, and they never tell anyone else. They're very good that way."

"I would guess so," Angie murmured.

"Other people come and go in my life." She removed the quote. "Some are a pleasant surprise, others disappoint. But the saints are forever. They're my friends, Angie. My true friends. If you made them your friends, you wouldn't have to worry about them ever shitting on you."

"No," she gulped, shocked to hear her saintly sister use such a word. It sounded all but sacrilegious. "I guess not. I'd better get going."

"Wait." Maria reached onto a shelf on the back wall. "Take this. It'll help."

With a sinking heart, Angie read the title of the little paperback. *Living a Saintly Life.*

"Oh, and Angie, thanks for your help with the ad. It looks great now."

Without saying another word, she left.

She could have used a little one-to-one with Maria's martyrs when she came out of the nightclub and found all four tires of her van slashed. AAA had to load the van onto a flatbed and give her a lift to a tire shop, where she borrowed an avocado-green '69 Impala from one of the mechanics.

She had an errand to run.

"I've had all I can take!" Angie marched into Everyone's Fancy and straight up to Connie at the sales counter.

The heads of two customers browsing the gift items jerked up.

"Angie." Connie shushed her and glanced over at the women with a wan smile. "What's the matter with you?"

"It's become clear to me that you're jealous of my success and doing all you can to foil my attempts at creating a great and growing company," Angie declared as she leaned over the counter between them. She clenched her fists to keep from grabbing at her treacherous friend. Her reflection in the big mirror behind Connie only added to her fury. Her hair was a mess, her green Marc Jacobs dress smudged with grease from kneeling on the street to look at her tires, and sticking out of her Prada tote was the book Maria had given her. *A saintly life my . . . eye*, she thought. "I demand you stop it right now."

Connie stared at her a moment, then said in a high voice, "Are you nuts? Or have you been sipping the cooking sherry?"

"I know what I'm talking about, and I've had it." Angie's voice grew louder. "No more phony calls, no more bugs, no more slimy creatures—"

"Stop!" Connie fairly shrieked in outrage. "What are you talking about?"

The two women gaped from Angie to Connie and backed up toward the door.

"You know very well! You can't hide any longer!"

"I'm not!"

"You're jealous!" Angie shouted.

The bing-bong that sounded when the shop door opened rang now as the potential customers dashed out.

"Jealous?" Connie was beside herself and shouted back, "You think I'm jealous of your stupid comedy cakes? I just lost two customers!"

"They aren't comedy! They're comical."

"I said comedy and I meant comedy. Your business is a joke!"

"I didn't come here to be insulted!"

"Then go back to your cheesy business."

Steam was coming out of Angie's ears and nose. She teetered on her pumps to reach further over the counter. "Do you know what I'm grossing?"

"Do you think I care? What I do know is that you've been working too hard. It's affected your brain. What little there is of it!"

"Not that you've done anything to help!" Angie sputtered, furious.

"I did my part, and what did it get me? Not even a lousy thank-you. I talked to Stan, and he said you've dumped him as a partner, too, and that you found two new people to help and that you pay them. Maybe they're the ones causing you trouble. They probably don't like you as a boss any more than I did."

"What nerve!" Angie cried, unable to overlook the fact that Connie sounded just like Paavo in this distrust of her employees. "Why does everyone think I'm incapable of hiring good help?"

"You can leave now, Angie. I don't want to see you anymore."

"You're telling me to leave? I'm the injured party here! I came to tell you to stop meddling in my business."

"I never meddle in anything. That's your forte. If

meddling were an Olympic sport, you'd take the gold every time."

Angie was beyond furious. "I'm warning you, keep away from me and my tires!"

Connie folded her arms. "I wouldn't be caught dead anywhere near you or your precious car."

"Our friendship is over," Angie declared.

"Friendship? You don't know the meaning of the word."

Angie paled. "Is that so?"

"Yes, that's so."

"Well!"

"Well to you, too! Now get out of my store!"

"I just—"

"I never—"

"Fine, then!"

Angie marched out in a huff. It was all she could do to keep back the tears. What had gone wrong? The two of them had been so close, such good friends.

Not anymore.

Chapter 23

"Boy, is that guy looney tunes," Benson said as he stepped onto the elevator at the Hall of Justice with Paavo and punched the button for the fourth floor. Paavo had just returned from Angie's. He was sure he'd find her home, baking, but she wasn't there. On her cell phone, he learned she was at a tire shop and couldn't talk. Her movements were beyond understanding at this point.

"Who's that?" Paavo asked.

"Markowitz. The stories he tells about witches and demons are right out of *Beetlejuice*."

"Building his insanity plea, is he?" Paavo asked. Instead of heading toward room 450, he turned in the opposite direction.

"You got it." Benson stayed with him. "He keeps talking about spiders and blood and Goths and evil creatures walking the streets, posing as humans. I thought my view of humanity was bad, but he thinks there are even worse monsters in the world."

"What's that about spiders?" Paavo asked. "He doesn't also mention flies or toads, does he?"

"It wouldn't surprise me. He was raving about vampires and demons mostly. I think he even mentioned some count. Or was that Dracula? I'm not sure. All I know is we aren't going to get a confession out of him. I don't think he's capable of it, and even if we got one, it won't be easy to find a judge who'd let it stand. The guy's in the twilight zone."

Paavo turned into the men's room, holding the door open for Benson. "Would you have a problem if I talked to him?" he asked. "There are a couple of things I'd like to ask him about."

"There *is* no talking to the guy," Benson said. "He's beyond conversation."

"Do you mind if I try?"

"You shouldn't get involved anymore in this case. You've got other things on your mind."

"Not really. I'm wrapping up the Walters case. Everything points to suicide, probably brought on by drugs," Paavo said thoughtfully. "Actually, Markowitz just might know—"

"That's not what I meant," Bo interrupted. "I'm talking about Angie."

Paavo said nothing. As much as he wondered what Benson knew about him and Angie, he didn't want to discuss her. He walked up to a urinal.

Bo also positioned himself at one. Both zippers simultaneously descended. "You want to propose, and she's not giving you the time of day," Bo said.

"Where did you hear that?" Paavo's jaw was tight.

"Doesn't matter. Everybody knows it." Benson cast his gaze upward. "If I were you, I'd take all this as a sign from God."

"You would?"

"Right. A sign that there are a hell of a lot of women

out there, and you got no business limiting yourself to just one of them." Benson grinned as Paavo headed for a sink to wash his hands. "Especially one who would rather be baking cakes." His grin turned into laughter. "That ain't the type of woman I'd ever be interested in. No way!"

Paavo knew Benson was just giving him a bad time. Nevertheless, his comments grated.

He snapped a paper towel from the rack. "I'm going to see Markowitz."

"So much for my good advice," Benson said with a chuckle as a stiff-necked Paavo strode quickly out of the bathroom. "Man, it's your funeral."

Zoe paced the dingy room, impatiently glancing at the telephone. They'd always arranged to check in every four days unless something urgent came up. Where was he?

It all seemed so hopeless. Greta had last contacted her over a month ago. She sounded so happy. "The man of my dreams," she'd called the Baron. Mysterious and kind, guardian and lover, everything Greta could have wanted he was.

References to evil, witches, and vampires hadn't frightened Zoe at first. They were commonplace enough among Greta's age group in the subculture in which she traveled. After a while, though, her letters grew less coherent, her thoughts and actions much darker. Worried, Zoe managed to track her down by telephone, which wasn't easy the way Greta moved from one group of so-called friends to another. If she hadn't recognized Greta's voice, she would have thought she was talking to a stranger.

Soon after, nothing. No letters, and when she phoned, the people she talked to said they hadn't seen Greta either, but all assumed she was with the Baron. That was when Zoe came to the city to see for herself what was going on.

She could have just walked up to the Baron and asked him, but one look at his club and at the people going into it, and her gut reaction told her he'd clam up, have her escorted out, and her chance at finding out anything at all would be gone. It was best to get inside and look and listen for any clue as to her sister's whereabouts.

Hours were spent hiding outside the Baron's club, watching people, hoping against hope that one of them would be Greta. The third day, she discovered she wasn't alone, that someone else was curious about the Baron. They talked, and she learned that he had insights to the Baron, the happenings in the club, and the dangers surrounding it that she hadn't dreamed of.

The Baron scared her. He knew too much, and his followers were loyal and close-mouthed.

Seeing a woman who called herself Julie Sung at the Baron's club had rattled her badly. She'd read about Julie Sung's murder and Lucy Whitefeather's. Even the woefully dense young woman who called herself Mina Harker was eerily weird. People in these death cults sometimes took on the name of a murderer or someone who'd been horrifically murdered just to see what kind of reaction they'd get out of people. Charles Mansons, Jeffrey Dahmers, and even Donna Laurias abounded in these cults. The ironic part was that most people didn't recognize the names of the victims. The killers got the fame; the victims, a grave.

But Julie Sung's murder had been recent. To have

the name used by a woman in the Baron's club could mean the Baron liked to play some very sick games, turning living women into some necrophiliac's wet dream. Or it might mean something even worse; it might be something the police should know about. She hadn't met anyone calling herself Lucy Whitefeather, but she'd stopped asking. As despair over Greta filled her, she went less and less to the club. She was hiding—she knew it—but as much as she wanted to know, she was equally afraid of what she would learn.

Angie's boyfriend was a cop. Maybe she should tell Angie about her suspicions? Tell her what she'd been doing and all that was going on.

What if she told Angie and her boyfriend confronted the Baron? There was no proof of anything, just a drugged-out woman calling herself Julie playing a death game. The Baron already knew Zoe worked for Angie. If her cop boyfriend suddenly showed up asking questions, he might tie it all to Zoe. He might bar her from going to his club. As much as she hated everything about it, there was no denying it was her sole remaining link to Greta.

The thought that the real Julie's fate had also been Greta's plagued her. She sat, her hands shaking and her stomach churning.

She shouldn't think such a thing. Greta was alive and well. She'd show up again at the Baron's or at a friend's house, just like she used to. The Baron couldn't have had anything to do with the death of Julie Sung or anyone else. He had no need to. He had women galore around him, hanging on him, wanting him.

To say anything to Angie or Paavo could get in the

way of her goal: to find Greta and get even with the Baron for what he'd done to her. God, but she hated him!

Once Greta was safe, she would happily kill him with her bare hands.

She paced. What if the Baron had someone spying on her? It would have to be Rysk. His turning up at a place where she and Angie worked was far too coincidental. Delivering ice? How stupid did he think she was?

What was she going to do?

She sat by the phone, her head in her hands. Why didn't it ring? He was her best chance to find Greta, and now had he, too, abandoned her?

He must have thought she'd failed him. For some reason, he desperately needed to know about Angie and who her friends were. She was trying to find out, but everything took time.

He'd scared her at first with all his talks about demons, but the more she was learning, the more she was wondering if he was much closer to the truth than she'd ever dreamed.

Where was he? Where the hell was Mason Marko-witz?

Angie slammed down the phone. It was midnight. Who did that Baron Severus think he was? That was the third time he'd called and asked her to bake a cake for his club. Her body ached so much from baking and decorating five cakes today she'd had a hard time falling asleep, only to be awakened by that man!

Even if she had considered working for him, she wouldn't now.

She shut her eyes and rolled onto her side. Connie's voice screaming at her that she'd be a gold medal winner in meddling came back to her.

I should have said that she'd get the gold in back-stabbing! Angie thought. *That would have shut her up.*

If only she'd said that instead of standing there on the verge of tears. She rolled over to her other side.

Then, when Connie said she didn't know the meaning of friendship, she should have reminded her of all the times she'd lent a sympathetic shoulder when Connie came over crying about some new boyfriend who'd dumped her or who turned out to be a jerk or had a wife he'd forgotten to mention.

She should have said that!

Connie would have felt badly, and maybe she would have been the one ready to burst into tears.

Angie rolled onto her back and stared at the ceiling.

She wished she could talk to Paavo about this. Was she a bad friend? A bad person? How come she didn't have a zillion friends? Why only one special one whose hair color was out of a Clairol bottle and who wouldn't lift a finger to help her best friend in the whole world with her cake business and who was not only a dirty fighter but wouldn't even admit it when confronted?

She flipped onto her stomach, punched the pillow, and then dropped her head on it. She finally knew Connie as she truly was.

Why, then, did she feel so bad?

Angie glanced at the clock-radio on her bedside. One-thirty A.M. *Thank you, Baron.*

Chapter 24

Paavo walked into the small interrogation room outside the cellblock at City Jail. Markowitz would be a resident of the cellblock at least until his arraignment and possibly longer, since his attorney was arguing that he needed psychiatric evaluation and to be placed in a mental hospital rather than a high security prison.

Markowitz was perched on a metal chair at a plain metal table, his hands folded. He didn't look at all like the crazy killer Benson and Calderon said he was. His hair was stark white, and his blue eyes were more world-weary than Paavo had ever seen in a man before, making him look every bit of his sixty-eight years. A serial killer his age was almost unheard of.

"My name is Paavo Smith, Homicide."

His gaze met Paavo's and held a moment. Suddenly, the room felt smaller and oddly bright.

"Ah, you've come," Markowitz said.

Paavo took his time sitting down opposite him. "You were expecting me?"

"For centuries he's waited. You know he's out there," Markowitz replied.

207

"Who's out there?"

"*Ars Diabolus* warns against allowing a Dark Lord to take a Queen and gain power. In here"—he tapped his temple—"I know. We have little time."

"What do you mean by Dark Lord?"

Markowitz leaned forward and whispered, "Baalberith, high in the hierarchy of hell." He straightened, his voice louder as he said, "I must stop him!"

"Who is this Baalberith?"

"Behold Baalberith, beloved of the Ammonites. He has had many names. His bones are bronze, his limbs like iron. The wild beasts are his food, and he sleeps in the reeds and the marshes."

"Wait, I don't—"

"Behold!" Markowitz's voice grew louder, his gaze so intent over Paavo's shoulder that Paavo was forced to glance at the blank wall behind him just to make sure nothing was there. "He rides closer on his pale horse, eighty-five legions behind him, trumpets summoning all to his command. All his dominions are in darkness, and his purpose is wickedness and evil. He is destruction. He is nightmare."

"Mr. Markowitz," Paavo called, but still the man stared. "Mr. Markowitz."

Finally, Markowitz cast his eyes on him, the look so cold and dark, Paavo felt as if he'd fallen into an icy pond.

"I saw you with a dark-haired woman," Paavo said. "What is it you want with her?"

"Baalberith searches for his Dark Queen. The time is at hand."

Paavo's gut twisted at the words. "What Dark Queen? What do you mean?"

"Yes, yes!" His eyes sparkled. "There is such danger! I must find her, stop her. He brings their souls back, you know."

"Whose souls?"

"Only from the Dark Ladies. They and his Queen form a pentagram. Through it comes the power that is his." Markowitz suddenly clapped his hands.

"What about the dark-haired woman?" Paavo insisted, growing more irritated by these rantings. "What did you want with her? Why were you watching her apartment?"

"I know her soul. I must get out of here! We aren't safe. No one is safe! Just like that boy. He thought he could fly like a bat."

"What boy?" Paavo asked. The hair on the back of his neck stood up as a vision sprang to mind of Travis Walters with his black cape spread wide, standing on the top of that bridge and then letting himself go, hoping to soar, but instead falling.

"He was possessed. His demons were told by one more powerful to destroy him, and they did. You know! You were aware of the demon's presence. You knew he was watching you."

Markowitz began to rock, faster and faster.

Paavo didn't know what to think. "Flies and toads were in Angie's apartment. Did you put them there?"

Markowitz's eyes widened, and his body began to quake. "Alien eyes and evil presence. Rituals all around." He grasped the table, but his arms and shoulders shook from sheer intensity. "Hurry! You understand the danger."

Paavo decided to go along and hope that some of Markowitz's ravings made sense. "Tell me about it."

Markowitz began to wring his hands. "The evil one is creeping ever closer. He knows that we know. We must take care."

"Where can I find this evil one? Does he have a name?" Paavo decided to bring the conversation down to the mundane.

Markowitz gripped the table, leaned toward him, and shrieked, "Baalberith, I told you! Fool! You are as much a fool as the others! I must get out of here. The time is short. Don't you understand? I alone can stop him. *I must be free.*"

Paavo stared at the man's angry, tear-filled eyes and was jarred by what he saw. The man truly believed in this evil force. Whoever or whatever it was, it scared him badly.

"Do you understand that you're being held here for murder?" Paavo asked calmly.

"He's very clever! The cleverest of all, they say. He trapped me."

"You're accused of the murder of three women," Paavo continued.

"There will be more unless I can get out of here and stop him."

"More? How do you know?"

"Let me out!" His body rocked from side to side; he was almost keening. "I must act before he grows stronger. If he gains his ultimate power, all will be lost!"

"The only one who can set you free is a judge if you're found to be innocent."

"But that will be too late!"

"Your lawyer needs to explain the process to you."

Markowitz lunged at him. Paavo slid his chair back, and the manacles on the prisoner's legs stopped him from reaching the detective. "You don't know what you're doing!"

"If you know something about the murders, tell us," Paavo said. "Give us something to go on to prove you're innocent."

Markowitz lifted his gaze to Paavo's, his face contorted with rage. "You could see the evil around you if you would just open your eyes. If you don't, I can't help you. No one can. You will be lost. You! And all that you hold dear!"

Angie was walking out of the studios of KYME radio, a contract in hand for the station's ten-year-anniversary cake—one that would look like an oversized old-time radio—when a heavyset, wild-eyed woman ran up to her.

"I want to thank you!" she screeched.

The woman, with thick, curly red hair cascading over her shoulders, jiggled all over as she vigorously pumped Angie's hand.

"Thank me?" Angie asked as soon as she could extricate herself.

"We're all so glad you're in this business. We were afraid they'd order another of Lolly Firenghetti's cakes."

"You were?" Angie didn't follow.

"They're simply awful. Unless you add detergent to the batter, your cake will taste much better. We're all so glad—we love good cake!"

"Do you know Lolly?"

"Unfortunately, yes. She's made cakes for us for the

last few years. But they've just been flat sheet cakes
with drawings of radios in frosting. Yours will be ever
so much more clever. I just can't wait to take a great
big bite."

Well, she does have the mouth for it, Angie thought,
unsure of what to say. "Thank you."

"You're most welcome." With that, the woman
bounded away.

"It's not your case, Smith!" Lieutenant Hollins shouted.
He was the chief inspector over the Homicide bureau.
It was his job to keep the detectives in line and out of
one another's cases.

"I had questions," Paavo explained, "and Calderon
and Benson didn't seem to have any answers. Listen,
I'm sure this Markowitz knows about Travis Walters.
He said the boy thought he could fly."

"So what? It's still suicide." Hollins reached for the
roll of Tums he kept on his desk.

"There's a connection between the two. I want to
know what it is and what's going on here."

"Calderon told me Markowitz doesn't even know
Walters's name, let alone anything else about him."

"Markowitz claims that more women are in danger,"
Paavo said. The words *dark queen* kept echoing in his
head, along with Markowitz's interest in Angie—a
brunette.

"You believe this nutcase?"

"I don't know!" Paavo insisted. "I do know he said
the murders would continue. That plus his connection
with Walters"—he kept Angie's involvement to himself—"is good enough for me. I want to talk to him
again when he's calm."

"They upped his medication. He'll be beyond calm and into comatose for a while. Anyway, how do you know he doesn't have an accomplice? Why would you assume he's innocent?"

"I'm not assuming any such thing. I simply want to question him again about my case."

"Calderon and Benson are perfectly capable of asking whatever you need to know." Hollins glowered at his subordinate.

"They can ask, but will they get answers?"

"They're working on it. Better than you, I might add. It was all the shrink and his jailers could do to quiet him down again. His attorney had a shit fit that some cop not even involved in the case was up there questioning him. He's asking that Markowitz be put on a suicide watch because of this 'trauma.' Do you want the case thrown out before we even have a chance at it?"

"Of course not, but—"

"Look," Hollins visibly tried to calm his impatience. "I know you're upset because you're thinking about proposing to Angie—"

Paavo paled. "You know—"

"And I know she hasn't exactly been cooperating with your plans—"

"Who told—"

"I hear she's got a business—baking cakes. Tell her about the Chief's retirement party. It's next week. They'll need lots of cakes. Tell her the Chief likes mocha cakes. With buttercream frosting."

"I'll tell her," Paavo said, and did some mental eye-rolling. "But as for Marko—"

"Look, this is a tough time for you. Big decision

time. Hell, I remember when I was thinking about getting married the first time. I was a basket case. But you can't take it to your job. Boy, I couldn't sleep. Couldn't even drive. All I could think about was whether she'd like the ring, whether her parents were gonna have a fit."

"My wanting to propose or not has nothing to do with Markowitz. And I don't want to talk about Angie," Paavo said through gritted teeth. The fact that he also had been anxious about the ring and Angie's parents galled him.

"Good," Hollins said, with a paternal pat on the shoulder. "In that case, I'll repeat myself one more time. I don't want you to see Markowitz again. Knock it off, right now. As your soon-to-be in-laws would say, *capisce?*"

The combination of exhaustion, wine, and watching the city go around in circles beneath her was enough to make Angie's head swim. She sat across from Paavo in the Fairmont Hotel's Crown Room at the very top of the tower building. The tables of the circular restaurant were situated against the windows, and the seating area slowly pivoted, allowing diners to view the entire northeast section of the city.

Paavo wasn't helping her much. He had seemed glad to see her but distracted when he picked her up.

"How's your business coming along?" he asked after they had been served a salad of spinach, endive, and Gorgonzola.

"Busy," she said, and poked desultorily at her salad. "I don't know how Lolly Firenghetti handles so much business alone."

"Who?"

"My competition. Never mind. Tell me more about the Chief's retirement party," she said with a pretty smile.

The Chief's secretary, Carla, hadn't yet ordered a cake and planned on a traditional sheet cake. Angie had plenty of time to convince her to order something more personal and much more special. "Just keep in mind one thing," he cautioned. "The Chief has absolutely no sense of humor."

When the entrees arrived, veal scaloppini for Angie and oregano-crusted salmon for Paavo, he asked her about Connie.

"I haven't spoken to her since I said I didn't want to be her friend," Angie said. "The more I think of it, the more I really wonder if Connie is behind my cake problems. I mean, she's been a good friend for a long time. None of this makes sense to me. Why am I and my business targeted, and why is Connie so upset? I don't get it."

"Why not tell her the way you feel?"

"Why was she so snippy with me to begin with?" Angie asked, still feeling wronged.

"She'll tell you when she's ready. Or maybe she'll realize she was wrong and won't say any more about it. Talk to her. It can't hurt."

"I guess I can do that." She stifled a yawn. "You seem a bit distracted tonight, Paavo."

"Do I? I'm sorry."

"One of your cases?" she asked.

"One that's mine, one that's Calderon's." He gazed at her and thought of Markowitz's words. "Remember that panhandler who approached you outside Fugazzi Hall?"

She was surprised by the question. "Vaguely. Why?"

"His name is Mason Markowitz. Can you remember what he said?"

"Not really. He said there was danger, that he had to talk to me." She also remembered that he'd approached her a second time and that Zoe had chased him away. She could just see Paavo's reaction if she told him that. It was strange, but the more she got to know Zoe, the more convinced she was that the woman meant her no harm.

"Anything specific? Think hard, Angie. Did he mention anything else?"

"I don't think so."

"Did he use the words *dark queen?*"

"No. I'm sure of that." She tried to remember more but couldn't. "His appearance, more than anything, startled me. I hardly listened. What's going on? Should I worry about him?"

"He's behind bars. But"—how could he tell her Markowitz thought there were demons after her?—"be careful, anyway."

"I always am." Normally, she would have wanted to know more, much more. Who was Markowitz? Why had he been arrested? What was his connection to her? To Zoe? What in the world was a dark queen? But the man was behind bars, she had too much on her plate already, and she was *not* going to get involved.

"Good," he said as if in answer to her unspoken thoughts.

As he finished his dinner, his heart began to pound. It was almost time. He wasn't going to bother with the fancy crêpes suzette and all that he'd planned before. He was just going to wait until the table was clear, and before their coffee and dessert were brought out, he would ask her.

His breathing quickened. The waiter should be coming along soon to clear the table. He had to be ready. To be calm.

He needed a moment alone.

"Excuse me a minute," he said.

She yawned again and nodded. As he rushed off, he was reminded of the time he had to get up and make a speech in front of a school assembly after he'd won a civics award in middle school. In the men's room, he washed his hands, took several deep breaths, and in front of a mirror practiced his little speech about how much joy she'd brought into his life, how he wanted her with him forever, how much he loved her, and then asked her to marry him. A man entered the bathroom just as his proposal ended, gawked from Paavo to the stalls, and quickly backed out again. Ignoring him, Paavo pondered a moment whether to give her the ring before the speech or after asking his question. Sweat broke out on his forehead, and he washed his hands once more.

Taking another deep breath, he squared his shoulders and marched back to their table.

As he approached, his side of the table became visible. The first thing he saw was that the table had been cleared.

The next he noticed was Angie, her head against the windows, eyes shut, fast asleep.

After Paavo had driven a very sleepy Angie back to her apartment, he headed for Lobos Alley, where Lucy Whitefeather's body had been found.

No lights showed in the alley. The only doors led to the backs of buildings.

He got out of his car. The sound of the car door shutting echoed, as did his footsteps on a sidewalk glistening with mist. The alley was icy cold, so cold it was difficult to draw a deep breath.

The sense of evil, of something terrible here, was like a physical assault.

Next he went to the alley where Julie Sung's body had been found. There was the same sense of a presence. Not as if he was being watched, but that something had been in this area that was so evil the area still reeked of it.

He'd felt this before—at the site of Travis Walters's suicide. Markowitz's words played in his head. *You could see the evil around you if you would just open your eyes.*

He wasn't a man who believed in spirits; not even in good and evil. He practiced no religion, although he'd come to believe in a God of some kind. Although most of what he'd seen as a cop was pretty bad, there was good as well, and at times, the good fortune was so incredible, it went beyond luck. If he had been a religious man, he might say he'd witnessed a miracle; but he wasn't, and so the word didn't occur in his vocabulary.

If he could believe in a God, why was he so quick to dismiss evil? And why did he accept that Travis Walters's death was suicide?

Chapter 25

The creature walked the shadows of the Fillmore's decrepit flats in the heart of the city, staring at the gutters, the cracks in the sidewalk, the ants and spiders crawling everywhere, all around him, wherever he stepped.

At one time, most of the residents in this neighborhood were African-American. These days, newcomers from Asia and other parts of the world diluted his pool. Still, there were enough for him to choose from. A woman from the southern hemisphere, *Ars Diabolus* told him. He'd find her here tonight. He had no choice. Time was running out.

A car weaved toward him, then sailed past. A man and a woman were inside. The woman's arms were flailing. As the car crossed the intersection, it slowed, and the passenger door opened. The car jerked to a stop, and the woman got out, slamming the door shut behind her.

The driver, a young African-American man, also leaped from the car. He yelled something, but the woman didn't stop. She waved a backhanded middle-finger salute at the fellow and stomped toward the intersection.

Toward him.

The driver cursed and pounded the car roof with his fist, then climbed back inside and sped away.

The woman's step slowed a moment. She pulled her jacket tighter and tucked her head down, her heels clicking ever faster.

Two blocks away, a major street bustled with taxis and buses. That was her destination. He couldn't let her reach it.

She noticed him then in the darkness. Her eyes flitted from side to side. Big, lustrous eyes. Her cheekbones were high, her skin creamy-smooth with a honey-warm tone. Long legs tottered on high heels, and her body was enough to make him weep with joy.

He, with power over life and death, had chosen her to live forever at his side. To be his Queen's fourth consort. His mistress.

After this final deed, all that remained was for him to await the Ides of March. To await his Queen.

He had to stop her here, long before she reached Geary Boulevard. Too many people were on the lookout for him. He'd had to abort a couple of attempts because of busybodies. It was just as well. This woman was the best one yet.

Her shoes were the answer to his prayers. Once trapped, she wouldn't be able to outrun him.

"Lady, don't be scared," he said, stepping out of the dark shadows toward her. "Are you all right? This isn't the kind of neighborhood to be walking around in this time of night."

"I'm fine." She hurried past him.

"Do you want a ride somewhere?" He followed her. "Maybe just up to Geary, where you can catch a cab? My car is at the corner. I hate to get in and drive away, leaving you on this street. It isn't safe."

She shook her head and kept going.

He jumped in front of her, blocking her path. Her eyes widened, and her step slowed for just a moment, as if she couldn't quite believe he was still bothering her. She started around him. He knew she hoped to pass by without incident, that she was hoping he would give up.

He sidestepped in front of her again.

"Get the hell away from me," she said.

He smiled, reaching his hand toward her. She jumped back. "I feel bad about leaving you alone," he said softly. "I know you're scared, but believe me, I'm here to help you."

She took another step backward. He slipped his hand into his pocket, fingering the syringe. He just had to grab her and hold her long enough to jab it in her.

Her gaze dropped to his hand. "Go to hell." She glanced over her shoulder, then again at him. When he took a step toward her, she whirled around and ran.

He chased her.

She turned at the corner, and he followed.

He grabbed her arm, and she fought him, slapping him, socking, and kicking like a hellcat. He shoved her hard against the wall of a building, hitting her head.

It stunned her for a moment, just long enough to watch her boyfriend's car slowly go by to the street she'd just left, as if he'd felt bad about the argument and was looking for her.

She tried to run to him, to call for help.

He pressed his body against hers, his hand over her mouth. She wanted to bite him, but his hand pressed so hard, she couldn't move her jaw.

Tears filled her eyes, a look of horror coming over her at her first look at the syringe. Her fierce attempts to free herself began again, but he was too strong for her.

He jabbed the needle into her neck, and in a little while, her struggles ended.

Chapter 26

 "How have you kept your friends over so many years?" Angie asked her mother as the shoe salesman disappeared into the storeroom.

"I don't know," Serefina said dismissively. "Now, has Paavo hinted about proposing to you yet?"

"Not yet. But tell me about your friends."

"We keep each other. That's all I can say. They find me if they want to see me. Or I'll give one of them a call and see if we can get together. That's all there is to it. You can't make anybody like you, Angelina. Ah, my shoes."

The salesman sat on a stool and raised Serefina's foot to his shin. He took off her beige pump and put on a black one with a square heel.

"Hmph, it looks like a boat!" she cried, and reached for the box. "What size is this? Nine! Are you crazy? I'm a six and a half. I used to be a five and a half before I had my children."

The salesman was dumbfounded. "But I measured—"

"Take this *gondola* away and bring my correct

size. Oh, *aspetti*, I like my shoes loose now that I'm getting older. A seven and a half, double A, will be fine."

He shuffled off, scratching his head.

She faced Angie. "What's all this friend stuff about? Connie's your good friend. It's a husband you should be worrying over."

"I don't see Connie anymore," Angie confessed. "Once your friends move out of your life, do you just forget about them?"

"Of course not. I've got girlfriends, or lady friends, I guess I should say, that I don't see or talk to for years. When we do get together, it's as if all the time in between has gone in a poof. We feel like we saw each other only yesterday, and we talk and laugh like young girls again."

"Well, it's easy to keep friends like that."

Serefina's eyebrows popped up, then her eyes bored into Angie. "What's going on with you and Connie?"

"She's irritated at me. I don't even know why. I always have her best interests at heart."

"I'm sure you do . . ."

"Of course I do. So, what's wrong?"

The salesman came back and lifted Serefina's foot to the shoe. Her big toe went in, so did three others, but the little toe didn't. She turned the shoe, aimed all toes at the side, then tried to slide them into the vamp. It didn't work.

She put the shoe on the floor. Angie helped her to balance on one foot as she squeezed her foot into the new shoe. Once she got it in, nearly crippled with pain, the salesman had to practically stand on top of her to pull it off again.

"There's something wrong with that shoe," she complained, rubbing her toes and casting him a steely, black-eyed glare. "It must be mismarked. My husband used to own this shoe store, by the way. We never had mismarked shoes when he was here. Are you sure you know what you're doing?"

The salesman was pale now. "Let me see what I can do," he murmured, and rushed away.

"Maybe, at times, I took Connie for granted," Angie said as her mother cast daggers at the salesman's retreating back. "It's this cake thing."

"Are you sure it's what you want to be doing?"

"I'm good at it."

"That's not the same thing," Serefina said. "What's more important to you?"

The salesman came back with four other styles in size seven and a half. He showed them one by one to Serefina, who shook her head the more emphatically at each successive shoe. "I can't believe this," she bellowed. "I want to talk to your manager!"

Sweat poured from the salesman's brow. "I'm sorry, but—"

"Oh, wait," Angie said. "Look. Here's a size six in the shoe my mother wants." She picked up the very first shoebox the salesman had brought out and held it upside down. "You must have overlooked it," she said to him.

Mouth agape, his eyes jumped from her to her mother. "But that's—"

"Size six?" Serefina cooed. "Let me try it."

She put the shoe on. *"Bellissimo!* And it fits perfectly." She gave the salesman an arch stare. "It's good I have my daughter with me. At least she knows what she's doing."

As they walked up to the counter to pay for the shoes, Serefina said, "Now, I want to know why Paavo hasn't proposed yet. You talk about your business and your girlfriend. Angelina, *cara mia*, a girl must have priorities."

Paavo wasn't about to let Markowitz's comments go by without trying to determine what he meant by them, no matter how upset Calderon and Benson might be once they found out what he'd done. The talk about demons sounded nonsensical, but he had to learn what was behind it. Clearly, Markowitz believed what he was saying, which meant he might well have acted on his beliefs. To understand the actions, Paavo had to understand their cause.

He went down to the Property Control section in the basement of the Hall of Justice, where Markowitz's papers had been stored as evidence.

Notebooks, scraps of paper, and newspaper clippings had been gathered into oversized manila envelopes. Paavo checked them out and sat in one of the cubbyholes. His interest lay in the notebooks. Simply getting past the handwriting was a challenge.

Once he could read most of the words, he realized it wasn't the handwriting per se that was so confusing, it was their meaning. They didn't fit together in a normal way; but after a while, he began to understand, and soon found himself caught up in Markowitz's world.

It was a world of evil, a world where children could be born with no souls and people could bargain with the Devil for worldly success and otherworldly damnation. It was a world of complete darkness and amorality, in which humans were chattel and food.

Markowitz wrote of the alienation of youth and the lure of those who tempted the deepest, darkest parts of human nature with promises of power, wealth, and immortality. For those who were lost, Markowitz saw little hope of redemption, and his cold calculations and logic left even a cynical cop shaking his head.

Mason didn't want to save souls, he just wanted to stop the demons. His notes told of those he'd hunted. He was clearly insane.

Paavo read on. Much of the material was ravings and rantings, drawings and doodles. Then something caught his eye. Scribbled along a margin were strange words: Crypt Macabre.

"Well, now that we're all here, I can announce my big news," Angie said to Stan, Zoe, and Rysk standing in the kitchen. She and Zoe had just finished a camisole—the lingerie company had liked the garter—and two teddy bears and one pair of breasts for a plastic surgeon's conference on silicon implants. The thought of eating a cake that looked like an ad for Hooters made Angie squeamish. Stan was munching his way through a plate of cake that had been cut from the decorated portions, Rysk was ready to go on his deliveries, and Zoe was loading the dishwasher.

They all stopped and turned her way.

"We've been given our biggest job yet," she said proudly. "Paavo told me the Chief of Police is going to retire. I contacted the woman in charge of the retirement reception, and guess what? She wants us to bake a cake for his party!" The other three applauded, and Angie took bows.

"We'll need to do one big sheet cake that's in the shape of a police badge," she said.

"That's supposed to be funny?" Stan asked, and reached for another slab of cake.

"It isn't, but neither is the Chief of Police. Apparently, the man has no sense of humor. The secretary, whose name is Carla, and I tried to think of something humorous that wouldn't offend him, but she was too nervous about that. The more we talked, the more she decided Comical Cakes wasn't such a good idea. So, I suggested the badge. She loved it and even gave me his old patrolman badge number. She said he'd love it as well, and there's no place else she could get a cake that way at such a reasonable price. I'm giving them a good deal because of Paavo and because the police deserve it. I don't want to make a profit off them."

"You aren't getting paid?" Zoe asked. Stan gawked, so appalled he even stopped stuffing his face.

"They'll pay for our costs, but that's it. Don't worry—it'll be great publicity. Other than the badge, we need to make six plain sheet cakes, all with dark-blue icing. It'll be quite wonderful."

"Shit," Rysk said under his breath.

"You have a problem helping the police?" Angie asked.

"Oh, no. Not at all. It's just what I always dreamed of doing," he mumbled.

"Look, if this makes you uncomfortable, I'm sure Stan could help me and Zoe deliver the cakes. You'll help me serve, won't you, Zoe?"

"The police?" she asked, looking thoughtful. "Where is this party going to be given?"

"It'll be held in the Hall of Justice," Angie replied. "They have a cafeteria, and they'll be putting up banners and balloons and flowers, trying to make it festive."

"Got it," Zoe mumbled.

"Come on, you won't back out on me, will you?" What was it with these two? This job should be the proverbial piece of cake, given the other cakes they'd had to do.

"Most of the cops will be at this party?" Zoe unexpectedly asked.

"A lot of them. It's a reception. They'll come in a few at a time. We can't deplete the entire force, after all. And this is just for the police and Bureau of Inspectors housed in the Hall of Justice. Each of the police stations out in the community will have their own parties for the Chief. We don't have to try to take care of them. Oh . . . also, the secretaries, clerks, and the guards at the City Jail will be invited, since it's connected to the Hall of Justice. Some of them might show up, too. Of course, they can't leave the jails unattended."

"Of course not," Zoe said, brightening up. "I'll help. It sounds like a big project."

"It will be. And a fun one, I'm sure."

"Yeah, I'm sure, too," Zoe murmured.

"I'll help," Rysk said, as if coming to a decision. "You'll need me and Zoe both."

"Great," Angie said. "Stan, that leaves you off the hook."

He paused, fork in midair, long enough to say, "Can't say I'm sorry."

"When is it?" Zoe asked.

"It'll be Friday, starting around five. Most of the people will be coming by right after work."

"Beware the Ides of March," Stan said, putting down his fork and contentedly rubbing his stomach.

Zoe dropped a metal bowl. It clanged against the wooden floor. "What did you say?" she asked, suddenly even more pale than usual.

"Friday. It's March fifteenth." He turned to Angie with a grin. "Do you really think you should be doing something like this on the Ides of March?"

Angie laughed, but no one joined her. "What's this about some old Roman date? Who cares?"

"Maybe someone should care," Rysk said, giving Zoe a strange look. "Didn't Stan just say to beware?"

"That was a joke," Stan said, looking at all of them as if they were crazy. "I was quoting Shakespeare. Shoot, that's the last time I'll try to be literary."

"First to last in one fell swoop," Angie said.

Stan just shrugged.

"It's a copycat." Calderon slammed his fist against his desk and glared at Bill Never-Take-a-Chance Sutter, who'd earned his nickname because of the way he approached his work now that he was close to retirement. Sutter got up from his desk and walked to the water cooler without a word.

"You don't know that at this point!" Rebecca Mayfield shouted. She and Bill had found the most recent ritual murder victim. "You haven't looked at any of the evidence."

"You don't know enough about my case to know that this murder is nothing like the other two. Nothing at all!"

"Whoa, you two," Yosh said, entering Homicide with Paavo right behind him. They had just returned from testifying in court, a homicide inspector's most frustrating activity. "What's going on here?"

"We've had another ritual murder," Rebecca said.

"You don't know that," Calderon countered immediately.

"You don't, but I do." She walked over to them. "Another young woman. African-American this time. Her name is Tashanda Reed, twenty years old. She was killed last night. Apparently, she and her boyfriend got into a fight, and she got out of his car heading north on Steiner. He figured she'd go to Geary Boulevard for a taxi, but he couldn't find her. That was the last time she was seen alive."

"She was found like the others?" Paavo asked.

"In an alley, surrounded by candles, nude. No heart."

"The boyfriend did it, I tell you," Calderon nagged. "They fought, he killed her, then set it up to look like the stories in the paper."

Paavo glanced at Rebecca, who scowled and shook her head.

"We've got Markowitz cold," Calderon continued. "You couldn't ask for better evidence, including the statement of an eyewitness—now deceased—who placed him at the scene. We've got enough evidence, in fact, to go for the death penalty. It looks like the DA is going that route."

"But those weird, smelly candles were used," Bo said. "We didn't let anyone know about them."

"Smelly?" Yosh asked.

"Like the kind of stuff your grandmother might have rubbed on you when you had a sprain. It also keeps away bugs. What did they call it? Liniment? No, wait. Camphor. That's what it was. Anyway, we kept that fact from the press."

Paavo mulled it over. The camphor-scented candles did make it even less likely to be a copycat.

"Too many people could have talked about them," Calderon interjected. "The case is too sensational to keep everyone's lips sealed. One person blabs to two, they each tell two more, pretty soon, it's all over town." He faced Rebecca. "Lean on the boyfriend, I tell you. He'll confess. I know it."

Paavo couldn't help but wonder what Mason Markowitz would say about this. Markowitz had predicted the murders would continue. Looked like he was right.

Paavo waited until late that night, long after the other homicide inspectors had left for home or hit the streets to talk to snitches and others who only came out after the sun went down.

He went to City Jail and asked to speak to Markowitz, showing his credentials. The guard remembered him from the last visit and gave him a dirty look, but he led Markowitz into an interview room.

Markowitz's hair was tangled, and he appeared even more haggard than previously. The orange jail suit hung from his bony frame. His eyes bulged, and he was too excited to sit. "I can't wait here any longer! It's soon!"

Here we go again, Paavo thought. "What is?"

"All the signs were there, and now with the alignment of Pluto and Aquarius, we must act."

An astrology lesson wasn't the reason Paavo had come there tonight. "Mr. Markowitz, I don't understand."

"It's the Ides of March."

All right, Paavo thought, *we've gone from bad satanic movies to bad Shakespeare.* He remembered reading *Julius Caesar* in high school English.

"Why did you say the murders would continue?" Paavo asked.

"Why? Why not?" Markowitz raised his hands out at his sides, palms up. "Of course they would. What would stop them?"

"You're here."

"So?"

"Your fingerprints were found at one murder scene, your shoeprint at another."

"We must stop Baalberith before he kills again."

"He has," Paavo said, and then wondered where *that* had come from. He had no idea about any Baalberith.

Markowitz's eyes were bright and watery. "Who did he kill?"

Paavo shook his head.

"A woman? Was it a woman?"

"Yes."

"The fourth! The Dark Ladies are his. I must get out. I must stop him. Stop him before he takes his Queen." Manacled, he stood and shouted, "Let me out! Only I can handle him! Only I have the power!"

As much as Paavo tried to calm him, he couldn't. Finally, he gave up and called the guard. Maybe Markowitz really should have been in that psychiatric hospital instead of a jail cell.

Chapter 27

Angie had a bunch of magazines spread in front of her. She had received a cake order from the father of a man who had just won a mechanical engineering award for coming up with an improvement to some kind of sophisticated diode. She couldn't begin to understand what a naïve diode was, let alone a sophisticated one.

Or what could possibly be comical about it.

Head in hand, she flipped through the pages of *Popular Mechanics,* hoping something might jump out at her.

The ringing phone was a welcome diversion from tools and building plans. Between cakes, her mother, and agonizing over Connie, her head was splitting.

It was Paavo. He told her he was hung up on a case and hoped they could go to dinner tomorrow night or the night after that.

"That's fine," she said. Her voice was flatter than the bottom of a springform cake pan.

"Is anything wrong?" he asked.

Everything, she wanted to say. Aloud, she replied, "No," and heaved a weighty sigh.

"You haven't seen any strange characters hanging around your apartment, have you?"

"No one stranger than Zoe and Rysk," she answered.

"Any more flies or toads?"

"No."

"Have you talked to Connie?" he asked.

"Me?" Her bottom lip trembled as their argument came back to her.

"Angie, you've got to call her. The two of you need to have a calm, adult talk. Find out if she is the one behind the troubles you've been having."

"I'll think about it," she said.

"Listen, we arrested the guy we thought killed those women, what the press called the ritual murders, but there was another murder last night. We're all trying to piece this mess together."

"My God, Paavo, be careful."

"Me? You're the one I'm worried about. Since Markowitz was interested in you, be doubly careful. Go nowhere alone and keep your doors locked all the time."

This so-called interest of Markowitz's just didn't make sense to her. "It's got to be a mistake. There's nothing special about me. All I do anymore is bake cakes." *And fight with friends and blow off my boyfriend . . .*

"He was caught lurking around your building. He might have been looking for you or maybe Zoe. There's some tie-in between him and the Goths. It's not clear yet."

The thought of a potential killer having been nearby was unnerving. "You said he'd been arrested," she said, searching for assurances.

"He might not be the killer or not the only killer." Paavo didn't even try to hide his worry. "Why don't you go stay with your parents for a while until we can tell what's going on here?"

She rubbed her forehead. "I don't get it. I'm not *doing* anything."

"I know. That's the part I'm having the most problem with in this whole mess."

"I can't just walk out on my business. I've made promises to people. They're depending on me for important special occasions in their lives."

"Angie—"

"I can't leave. I'm sorry. I'll be careful, Paavo. I promise. Now, don't worry so much and go find the killer."

She hung up, depressed and frustrated, and knew Paavo was feeling the same way. It didn't help.

Sorry, Mamma, she thought. *No proposal anytime soon for me.*

She went back to searching for engineering humor in the magazine and was trying to concentrate when the phone rang again. Hope that Paavo was calling back welled up in her. She didn't know what had gotten into her, why she was so touchy and in such a foul mood all the time. This perpetual PMS was getting old.

Or just maybe it was Connie.

"Hello," she said brightly.

"It's Zoe." Angie pressed the phone tighter against her ear. Loud heavy metal music played in the background, and she could hardly hear Zoe's voice.

"I can't come in tomorrow," Zoe said. She sounded upset. "I've got to try to visit someone, and I think it'll take me most of the day."

"What's wrong?" Angie asked.

"Nothing," she said. "Nothing at all. Has Rysk contacted you?"

"Rysk? No, why?"

"Just wondering."

"Zoe, did you know you left your backpack here today? Will you need it tomorrow?"

"I did? That's right! I forgot. I thought I just took my wallet with me today. I don't think I'll need the backpack. Thanks for letting me know. I've had a lot on my mind."

"It's okay." Angie knew the feeling, and Zoe was even more distracted than usual today. "Take it easy, and I'll see you day after tomorrow."

"Thanks, Angie."

She hung up. Another vaguely unsatisfying phone call.

Who could Zoe have to "try" to see that might take all day? Paavo's warnings and Rysk's uncertainties about Zoe came back to her.

She wandered into the kitchen and saw the backpack under the chair where Zoe always tucked it.

Hmm. She really shouldn't . . .

On the other hand, what if Paavo and Rysk were right? What if she was being shortsighted, naïve, dumb—all their unspoken insults.

She sat on the floor and slid the backpack toward her. Unzipping it, she folded back the front flap to peer inside.

An unopened bottle of water. A sealed package of Ritz crackers. Something told her she was looking at what would have been Zoe's dinner tonight.

An old sweater. A large manila envelope. Nothing else.

Being careful not to tear it, she opened the envelope and slid out the contents. Newspaper clippings about the ritual murders were the first things that caught her eye. What would be Zoe's interest in that?

A small white envelope was included. Inside were photographs. One was a young woman, blond with pink and purple streaks. Except for the hair, she looked like a young version of Zoe. This must be the sister she'd lost contact with. The combination of the sister's photo and the newspaper clippings made Angie's spine tingle.

The sister's eyes were painted black, and she wore lots of cheap silver, or possibly tin, jewelry. A knit top of white and black zebra stripes was worn under a black jacket. Beside her stood a couple of geeky-looking young men, scrawny and pimply, and behind them others danced near small tables—a club scene of some kind.

The other photos were of Goths. A street scene of people entering a basement room stopped her—she recognized the street and house. It was the Baron's. This must have been the club he'd talked about wanting a cake for.

More pictures of people entering the club spread around her. She didn't recognize any of them, and many were a bit blurred. There was a streetlight in front of the Baron's house, but still, the camera had to have been on a very slow shutter speed to get the night scene. She doubted Zoe would have used a flash, and these didn't look like the type of people who'd want their pictures taken.

All of this had to be part of the reason why Zoe was so private and often wore such a sad expression.

Loud music had played in the background when Zoe called. She wondered if Zoe was at the club now. Poor woman, she probably needed someone to talk to.

Angie was tired of not being a friend, of being too busy with her cakes to care about those around her. She would go to Zoe and ask if she could help.

Chapter 28

 Paavo knocked on Zoe's apartment door. He was sure she knew a lot more than she was letting on. No answer. He knocked again and was waiting when his cell phone began to ring.

He answered, hoping it was Angie. It wasn't. He listened to the woman's upset tones and agreed to meet her immediately.

Zoe was walking out the door of The Crypt Macabre when Rysk caught up to her.

"Leaving already?" he asked, joining her on the sidewalk.

"Yes." Zoe shook her head. "Sometimes this girl finds that whole scene hard to take."

"Me, too," Rysk said, falling into step beside her. "Why do you go there?"

She stopped walking. She shouldn't want his company, should say something to cause him to turn away in a huff the way she usually did, but when she met his gaze, harsh words melted on her tongue. "I wonder that myself," she admitted. "Have you been going long?"

"A little over a month."

They began to slowly stroll toward the three-hundred-dollar Dodge Omni she'd picked up when she first arrived in the city. Amazingly, it still ran. "I guess you've met a lot of women at the club," she said, trying to sound casual.

"I'd like to hope the thought makes you jealous," Rysk said cockily, "but I don't think that's why you're asking. Looking for someone?"

Dismay struck her. He was too clever by half, but she already knew that. "I was told a friend used to hang out here. Did you ever meet a young woman named Greta? Seventeen. Pink and blond hair, blue eyes, slim, pretty."

"Greta? No. The name's not familiar. I've seen girls who look like that—several, in fact."

"I know. It's a type, isn't it? I was told she and the Baron were an item, but I haven't seen her with him."

"The Baron goes through his women pretty fast. He's got a new one every week, minimum. I saw him make a move on you. What happened? Did the lady-killer strike out for once?"

They reached her car. "He's not the type that makes this girl's heart beat faster," she said with a grimace.

"Oh? What is?"

She couldn't keep her gaze from drifting over him and liking what she saw, despite herself. It was the last thing she'd ever admit. "Three-piece suit. MBA. Tom Cruise hair and looks."

"Ouch."

She unlocked the car door, trying to stifle her smile. "I won't be at Angie's tomorrow. See you the day after."

He regarded her quizzically. "Okay, see you."

*   *   *

With a quick tug at her black miniskirt as she got out of the taxi, Angie faced the Baron's house. She wondered if she shouldn't have dressed up more Goth.

No, she wasn't going there to snoop around. She was going as a friend, with no need for disguises or trying to fool anyone. With the mini, she wore a black turtleneck, black nylons, and high, strappy heels. Okay, so she didn't normally dress this way, but as far as she was concerned, it was more New York than Goth.

Two women, one in a floor-length hooded black velvet cape, the other in a man's black suit, shirt, tie, and Florsheim wingtips, both looking more dead than alive, walked past the front door of the decrepit Victorian, its walls and eaves dark with soot. Two gray gargoyles leered down from above the doorway. At the side of the house, they walked down some stairs. A door opened, then quickly shut.

Angie was suddenly far less sure of herself than a moment ago. How much nicer it would've been if Connie had been with her. They could have dressed up in wild Goth clothes and makeup, laughing at themselves and each other. A heaviness descended on her heart as memories of the crazy times they'd spent together came back to her.

She knocked softly on the door. A puffy, bald-headed man with a pasty, bluish-gray skin tone, wearing a black Nehru jacket buttoned snugly against his oversized neck, opened it. "Yes?"

"I'm a friend of Baron Severus," Angie said.

His eyes lighted as he took in everything about her. "You are?"

"Yes. I bake cakes. He wants me to make him one."

He looked ready to laugh at her. She squared her shoulders, ready to argue.

"I see," he said quietly. "Do you have any, uh, identification?" He held out his hand.

She ignored it. "I didn't drive, so I left my license at home." She'd learned that going to strange places like this, she was better off not bringing much with her. The thin handbag held only lipstick, compact, comb, money, cell phone, and apartment key. "You don't think I'm under age twenty-one do you?"

He frowned.

"Look, all I want to do is check out the scene," she said, trying to sound like Zoe. "I was told this is a neat place, and the Baron is a friend. You can ask him."

The blue-toned doorman raised an eyebrow. Something was vaguely familiar about him, but she couldn't imagine where she might have seen anyone who looked like him—except maybe on TV.

"Do I need someone to vouch for me?" she asked. "The Baron's assistant knows me, too. I just wanted to go inside for a simple little visit. I won't bother anyone, I promise. If I do, you can throw me right out of here, okay?"

Glaring fiercely, he continued to hold out his hand.

"I won't hurt anybody." Angie widened her eyes innocently. "I promise."

He dropped his hand to his side with a loud smack. "Are you a cop or undercover agent?"

"A cop? Me?" What would Paavo think of that? She couldn't wait to tell him! "Of course not."

"Remember, it's illegal for you to lie when you're asked that question. It could jeopardize your case."

"I don't know what you're talking about," Angie

said blankly, shaking her head in bewilderment.

He suddenly broke into a chuckle. "Go on inside. This should be interesting."

She walked around, canvassing the room and smiling while searching for Zoe. The more she saw of it, the more horrified she was that Zoe hung around a club like this. Angie could understand why she'd never talked about it. The place was creepy.

"Hi," she said to a grungy young fellow who'd propped himself against a wall.

"What's happening?" he mumbled. He looked stoned.

"I'm looking for Zoe. You know her?"

"If she's a friend of yours, she's one of mine, too. I'll help you find her. I'm Fred Limore, and you're . . . ?"

"Thanks, Fred, but I'll just have to find her on my own." Angie backed away from him.

"Wait."

She waved a hand in a way he couldn't mistake for anything but a brush-off and went to a woman this time. "Hi," she said. "I'm Angie. Are you a friend of Zoe's?"

"Zoe? No, my name's Mina Harker."

In a pig's eye, Angie thought. The woman was ten miles high, but then, so was just about everyone else here. Where was the Vice Squad?

"Do you know Zoe Vane?"

"You're not very friendly." The woman wandered away, leaving Angie gaping after her.

So I've been told.

"Miss Amalfi?"

Angie turned to see a tall man with a kind of soft, squishy look about him. After a moment, despite the red lipstick and black eye shadow, she recognized Wilbur Fieldren. She'd know those particular black fingernails anywhere.

"What a pleasant surprise," he said. "I had the distinct impression you weren't into this kind of thing."

"Live and learn," she replied.

"My sentiments exactly."

"I'd like to meet the Baron," Angie said.

"Wonderful!" Fieldren said. "He's been most anxious to meet you for some time. Come with me."

Connie smiled at Paavo as he walked into the coffee shop. "Thank you for coming," she said when he joined her.

"I'm glad you called," he said. "How are you doing?"

"I'm okay." They made small talk until the waitress took his order, then Connie said, "I called because, I guess, I was wondering about Ang— I mean, I noticed some guy lurking on the street across from my house. He's out there every evening after dark until eleven or so. Should I call the police? Can they do anything?"

"There are laws against loitering and vagrancy. You can call the local station. Is the guy watching you?"

She picked up an empty sugar packet and smoothed the paper. "It's hard to tell. Maybe it's nothing. He makes me nervous, though." Suddenly, she crumpled the packet and pushed it aside. "Hell, that isn't why I called. How's Angie?"

"She misses you and your friendship," he said bluntly.

Connie's face fell. "I was so furious at her, it amazed

even me. I wanted to stay mad at her, I really did. Life is much easier this way. I don't get involved in any of her wild plans and outrageous schemes." She stirred her coffee. "I just go along my quiet way, running my shop, seeing nearby shop owners and neighbors, watching TV, cleaning up the apartment, trying to find a good man. . . ." She glanced up at him bleakly. "I miss her, too."

"What happened? Was it her cake business?" he asked.

"In part. You know how one-track her mind is when she starts something. A team of rampaging bull elephants couldn't divert her attention. That made me mad, but if I hadn't been so upset about her—and you—I'd have kept helping her out. I wouldn't have been so touchy."

"Me?" he asked.

She nodded. "I knew that after all you went through with your family you'd come to realize how important Angie was to you. I knew you were going to ask her to marry you and she would and then"—Connie yanked a napkin from the holder and dabbed the corner of her eye—"and then she wouldn't have time to be my friend anymore."

He was stunned. "You thought that?"

Her tears flowed harder. "I was feeling sorry for myself, thinking about my divorce and the guys I tried to get together with and how nothing ever seems to work out and how you and Angie are so perfect together and how she wouldn't need me anymore. And then Stan said—"

"Stan?" he blurted.

She nodded. "He said she was taking advantage of my good nature. That she only pretended to be my friend because I worked for her."

Paavo shook his head, disgusted. "I should have known he was behind this. Angie's got to keep that weasel out of her life."

Connie's sniffles grew louder.

"Listen to me, Connie." He put his hand on her arm. "Angie would never give up your friendship. She's talked my ear off because she thinks you don't like her anymore. She's been asking all her sisters how to be a good friend—not that she's gotten very good advice, mind you. You're very important to her. Nothing can get in the way of that."

"Really? You wouldn't know it from the way she talked to me at my shop. She has quite the mouth when angry."

He grinned. "Don't I know it. Although, to hear Angie tell it, you more than held your own. She was licking her wounds for days afterward."

She chuckled. "It got pretty ugly, you're right."

Paavo was glad she could laugh about it. "Do you think you'll be able to forgive her?"

Her eyes widened. "I'm afraid I already have."

"I'm glad to hear it," he said warmly. "One more question. Do you think Angie also suspects I'm thinking about proposing?"

"Well . . . Normally, she'd be picking up the cues just like I have. But she's so consumed with this cake business, I don't think she knows which end is up. Is that why you haven't asked her yet?"

He nodded. "I've been waiting for the right time. You know Angie. I might not be the one-knee-on-the-floor type, but I'd like the setting to be memorable for her."

"But you will ask her?" Connie said.

"If she ever stops working with those damned cakes long enough for me to get a word in."

Connie ran around the table to hug him. "That's good. I'm glad for you both."

"You're pretty sure she'll say yes, then?"

Connie laughed. "Try to stop her!"

Angie was surprised that the Baron wasn't a bigger man than he was. He was fairly tall, although everyone seemed tall to her. His hair, like almost everyone else's here, was black. If she hung out with this crowd, it would save her a fortune in highlighting costs. And if she wanted color, she could buy a can of spray and do it herself.

He stood as she approached. His hair was pulled back into a rubber band, emphasizing a deep widow's peak, and his eyes were a strange purplish color. She suspected tinted contact lenses. He blinked slowly, as if he didn't always view the world through rose- (or purple) colored glasses.

"My favorite city's favorite cook," he said, holding out both his hands.

"You're very kind, especially since you haven't tried my cakes yet," she said, placing her hands in his. He pulled her closer and kissed her cheek, then smiled down at her. She could feel him taking in her sapphire and gold earrings, the matching ring on soft, mani-cured hands, the cut of her clothes, her Fratelli Rosetti shoes, her tiny Gucci handbag.

"I'll try anything you'd like to offer." His voice was

a deep rumble. "You are very special. Very special indeed. I am honored that you finally chose to come to me. I've been trying to lure you here for days, as you know."

"You've been most persistent."

"I'd still like you to create a cake for me." His eyes were surprisingly soft, and something about the way he looked at her, even with the tinted lenses, made her feel warm and wanting to please him. It was weird. "Perhaps not a comical one but a serious, Goth cake."

"Black on black, in other words?" she asked.

"Ah . . . a joke. Yes, I can understand why you do comical cakes."

He had a nice laugh. She was getting some insight to his club's popularity. "Actually," she said, "I came here looking for a friend of mine, Zoe Vane. Do you know her?"

"Of course I know Zoe: A very nice young woman. I also know she works for you. Why are you looking for her? Is she missing?"

She was sorry to learn she'd been correct in her assumption that Zoe frequented this club. It gave her a picture of Zoe she didn't want to have. "I just wanted to say hi. She suggested I come. You've got a great spot here."

"I'm most grateful to her, but I'm afraid I haven't seen her tonight."

"So, she must come a lot?"

"Fairly. I'm surprised she said anything to you about us."

"Only that it's pretty neat and I should give you a try."

He smiled suggestively. "Feel free to try me in any way you like."

He had charm, but not *that* much. "What do people do at your club besides dance?"

"We enjoy each other's company."

"In other words, nothing special."

An eyebrow cocked. "If you're looking for a more unique experience, at times we take part in ritual. Do you like ritual?"

"Of course. I love it. What kind of ritual?"

"We don't do it here but in an old, abandoned church. It's got a great atmosphere. We pretend we're something we're not. You can pretend to be anything you want. Most of the people here dress up as vampires. Vampires are in these days, as you might have heard."

"Yes. I did hear that, not that I understand it, though."

"No? Actually, that's perceptive of you. Vampires simply regard humans as food. Others have much more interesting ideas about humans."

"What kind of others?"

His face, his whole demeanor, grew more intense. "Demons, for instance. They see humans as a challenge."

"Oh?"

"A challenge to win over to the side of evil. A challenge to tempt and see how much, or more often how *little*, you need to offer a human to get them to submit."

Her breathing quickened. "You sound as if you aren't human yourself."

The Baron laughed, a strong, loud laugh that caused heads to turn. "I suppose I do. I've role-played a demon so many times in our rituals that it comes naturally to me."

"I hope you haven't sold your soul, Baron," Angie said with a smile.

He glanced at her. "Now, why would you say that?"

"Isn't it obvious? If you had, you would be doomed to hell for all eternity."

The Baron's eyes sharpened. "Some of us who live in the night would say that the real hell would be to spend all eternity with the good people in heaven."

"Oh, dear," Angie said. "I think on that note, it's time for me to leave."

He took her hand, stopping her. "I do hope I haven't frightened you with this talk."

"You haven't frightened me." She pulled her hand away.

"It's just an act, you know." He waved his arm over the group. "All this is. By day, these people are as normal as you . . . and me."

She doubted that.

"Give us . . . me . . . a chance." He lightly placed his hand on her arm. "You'll enjoy it here. We have many ways to help with your enjoyment. Something that will bring great *ecstasy*, shall we say?"

This made her curious. "You do?"

His hand tightened, and he drew her toward him. "Why don't you come with me? We should talk more privately."

Angie blanched.

"Well, look who's here!"

She turned at the familiar-sounding voice and saw Rysk. Relief and astonishment swept through her. What was he doing here?

"I didn't know you were into this scene," he said.

Tonight he wore tight leather slacks and a flowing white shirt.

"Zoe told me about it," she replied. "I thought I'd check it out. I didn't know you came here, too."

"You know both Angie and Zoe?" the Baron asked Rysk, his eyes hard.

"Sure." Rysk folded his arms and smiled at Angie. "I know all the beautiful women in the city. Angie's an old friend."

Angie saw that for some reason, Rysk didn't want the Baron to know he also worked for her. Maybe it was a macho thing. Driving around Comical Cakes wasn't, she guessed, a job to proudly tout to anyone.

"I was just trying to convince your friend to come back to us," the Baron said, giving Rysk a penetrating look before he turned once again to Angie. "She has much to offer, and I know we have much to offer her in return."

Rysk glanced from one to the other. "You're quite right, Baron." Angie didn't think she heard much conviction in his voice.

"I'll keep it in mind," she said to the Baron, then turned to Rysk. "I was just about to leave. I'm going to call a taxi. Want to wait with me?"

"Oh . . ." Rysk glanced at the Baron, who nodded once curtly. "Sure," Rysk said.

"Nice to have met you, Baron." She held out her hand.

He took it and kissed the back of it, then continued to hold it as he said, "I will not feel alive until you return. Come back soon."

"I will." She turned away and Rysk followed. Both

missed the nod the Baron gave to Fieldren.

"I didn't know you came here," Angie said as they headed for the door. She wanted his explanation.

"This is a way for me to spend my nights. I like the music, the conversation, the women. What can I say? What brought you? I don't see this as your scene."

"I was hoping to find Zoe. I talked to her on the phone this evening, and she sounded so down, I was worried about her."

"She told you she comes here?" he asked.

"Not exactly." A reason for being here popped into her head. "The Baron wants me to do a cake for him. He mentioned it to Zoe."

"Really?" Rysk obviously saw right through her story and didn't seem to approve.

"You see Zoe here, don't you?"

"This is where we met," Rysk said, avoiding her eyes.

"Do you like it here? The Baron?" she asked.

"He's not anybody I'd mess around with."

She peered at him curiously. If he didn't care for the Baron, and there were plenty of other places to go for music and dancing, why come here—if not because of Zoe?

Yes! That must be it!

She took out her cell phone to call a cab.

Rysk obviously was more interested in Zoe than he pretended to be. She knew it! God, but she was good.

Chapter 29

Paavo felt a distinct affinity for the terror in facing demons that Markowitz had spoken of as he approached the front door of Angie's parents' home. He knew he'd been taking the coward's way out, wanting to talk to Angie first rather than her Old World parents. Maybe that was why his plans just weren't working. He decided to make amends.

The housekeeper let him in, and in a moment, he was wrapped in a warm greeting from Serefina. *"Buon giorno, Paaverino. Come stai?"*

How Angie's mother, who was all of about five feet two, could call him "little Paavo" was beyond him. Angie swore it was an endearment.

"I'm not so good, Serefina," he said, sitting down on the sofa.

She sat beside him and took his hand. He could feel the calluses and lines that had permanently formed in her bent fingers from years of hard work before the family wealth grew. "It's about you and Angelina, I take it. What's wrong?"

"I want to propose to her," he said after a while.

"*Bravo!* I knew it! I'm so happy, Paavo," she gushed with sheer happiness, giving him another rib-breaking hug and kissing him soundly on both cheeks twice. Tears glistened in her eyes. "You're a good man. *Buonissimo*. When will you ask her?"

"That's the problem. She's so busy with her business, I can't seem to find the right time."

"When you ask her, it'll be the right time, no matter what. I know my Angelina."

"I'd like to do it the right way, in a nice setting," he said. "Also, I'd like to talk to Sal. I know he objects to me marrying Angie."

She laughed heartily, took his face between her hands, and shook him tenderly. "Salvatore is no problem. Don't worry. He pretends he doesn't like all his daughters' husbands except for Bianca's husband, Johnnie, and that was only because Bianca was so bossy with him, he was glad to get her out of the house."

Paavo knew Serefina was trying to help, but it didn't do anything for the knots in his stomach. Angie was Salvatore Amalfi's baby girl, his princess. "Thanks," he said. "Is Sal here? May I see him?"

When Angie's father entered the room, his hangdog expression told Paavo he had a good idea why Serefina had called him. Despite that, he had, as always, a distinguished air about him. He was almost as tall as Paavo, although frail from a heart condition. His nose was Roman in an olive-complected face, his hair almost completely gray, and his eyes as piercing as a hawk's.

"Paavo has come to us, like a good man should do," Serefina said as she rejoined Paavo on the sofa, patting his hand. "He came to tell us he wants to marry our Angelina."

"Hmph," was Salvatore's only response.

"Sit down! *Madonna santissima!* Didn't you hear what I said? Be civil."

He sat on an armchair on the far side of the room. "I knew this was coming," he grumbled to Serefina, as if Paavo wasn't in the room. "What do you think I am, stupid? I knew him and Angelina were thinking of something like this. I can't say I like it, but nobody cares anymore what I think. In the old country, girls listened to their fathers. We'd say who they should marry. Not anymore. Not here."

"I know you have particularly high hopes for Angie in many areas," Paavo said, heart thumping.

Salvatore nodded. "*É vero.* We sent her to good schools, even the Sorbonne for a year. That cost so much I couldn't believe it. I thought she'd accomplish many things. I keep waiting."

"She tries, Sal," Paavo said. "She tries very hard to please you."

"I know, but nothing works. Maybe I put too much pressure, I don't know. Or she puts too much on herself."

Paavo drew in his breath. He could do this, he told himself, despite feeling like he was tussling with a porcupine. "You've made it clear you think she can do a lot better for herself than to marry a cop. I don't want my job to be a problem for Angie, not another area for her to feel pressured or feel she's failed in her father's eyes. That's why I'm here to talk to you."

Sal went to an antique sideboard and poured himself

a straight shot of Jack Daniels. He gestured toward the Baccarat decanter and Paavo shook his head.

Sal sipped the whiskey and then sat again. "Why don't you get out of her life? It'd be so much easier."

Serefina clucked her tongue in annoyance but kept quiet.

"I've tried," Paavo admitted. "It hasn't worked. I love her. She . . . she makes my life worth living." He stared at the floor a moment, then raised his eyes to Sal. "She loves me, too. If I had any doubt of her feelings, I wouldn't be here. I might not have the world's greatest job, but I'm the best man for Angie. I'll spend my life doing all I can to make her happy."

"Ah, *amore!*" Serefina's eyes were shining. She clasped her hands together and smiled mistily. "You must give your consent, Salvatore."

Sal tossed his drink back and returned to the bar.

"Enough! Your heart!" Serefina ordered.

"My heart. Who cares? I'm old. All my girls are going to be married. They don't need me. Who the hell cares anymore about an old man." He nevertheless left the decanter alone.

"I have to listen to you feeling sorry for yourself when Paavo is telling us he loves our *bambina?* Our youngest little girl? Oh, such a pretty baby she was. It seems like only yesterday." Serefina heaved a deep sigh and dabbed her eyes with a small handkerchief she pulled from her pocket.

"Hmph. Love is easy to talk about when you're young. There's more than that to make a marriage work," Sal said, sitting down again without the drink he wanted.

"Nothing is more important than love." Serefina's

hands fluttered to her heart. She sighed, and with her eyes gleaming and her face rosy, Paavo could see the young woman who had caught the eye and heart of a proud man. "You were crazy about me when we got married."

"Yeah, I was, but I was crazy about a lot of women. That doesn't mean I wanted to marry all of them."

"Che dici?"

"It's not what you're thinking, Serefina. You were always special to me." Salvatore threw his hands up in exasperation.

"Hmph!" She glanced at Paavo. "We didn't have a big wedding. No, we had no money. No nothing. Not even my father and mother standing there watching me. We took a train to Reggio—that's in Calabria. It was such a mess of a city. But we were young. In love, despite what Salvatore says now."

"I didn't say we weren't!"

"No, just that you could have had your pick of women, and somehow I was the lucky one," she snapped. *"Madonna!* Where is *l'amore?* At least, it is with you, Paaverino." She stood up and gave him another hug. With a new tear in her eye, she said, "I'll leave the two of you to work things out."

Paavo and Salvatore faced each other in the ensuing silence, both feeling they'd just been caught up in a tornado.

"Angelina is a lot like her mother," Sal said. "It's quite a bit to put up with, you know."

"I know. I love them both."

"When Angie told Serefina the story of your mother and father, it brought tears to her eyes. Serefina will mother you. You know that, too?"

"I'll enjoy it," he admitted.

"I suppose there's nothing I can say to change your mind."

"I'm afraid not," Paavo said.

"Have you asked Angelina yet?"

Paavo drew in his breath, then shook his head dejectedly. "I'll admit that I tried to, even before talking to you. I thought we'd face you together. That wasn't right, and my plans didn't work out."

"I appreciate your honesty." Sal looked Paavo over even more carefully. "So, what's keeping you from asking Angelina?"

"She's been too busy with her new business."

"She's that involved in her work?" Salvatore's eyebrows lifted. "Does that mean I might get a son-in-law and a business woman for a daughter at the same time?"

"Could be," Paavo said, with not a little wonder.

"No." Sal sighed. "That's not my Angelina."

"I'm glad you called," Angie said, clasping Paavo's arm as they walked along Fisherman's Wharf. He'd asked her if she had time to join him for a late lunch. After talking to Serefina and Salvatore, not to mention Connie, he knew he had to act. He couldn't wait for the perfect romantic set-up. He and Angie had had some of their nicest times together strolling along the water's edge. He should have thought of coming here sooner.

"I hoped you could get away from a hot oven for a while. I needed something bright and pretty in my day."

"The Wharf?" she asked with a smile.

"Exactly," he said teasingly.

They stopped and bought shrimp cocktails from a sidewalk vendor, then walked along a pier. As they ate, she told him she had been given the job of creating cakes for the Chief's retirement party. "The thought of serving cake to a bunch of cops must have really gotten to Zoe. She couldn't make it to work today," Angie said with a laugh.

"I still don't care for her or Rysk," Paavo admitted. "They're both mysteries."

"You were a mystery for a long time." Angie smiled. "But I stuck with you, didn't I?"

"That's different. Anyway, I wasn't the mystery, it was my family."

"I'm afraid that in many ways you're still a mystery to me, Inspector Smith. That's one of your many attractions."

Cocktails finished, they stood against an old wooden railing and peered down at the water and a couple of fishermen making their boat ready to head out to the Pacific. Paavo reached over and took her hand, running his thumb over her knuckles. "If I'm such a puzzle, why do you stick with me?"

"Because of your nature." She squeezed his hand and turned toward him. "You aren't a man to lie or cheat."

"Never with you, Angie. That's how we should always be with each other."

"Absolutely." A thought struck her. How much did she dare tell him? Well, if they were being honest . . . "Actually, Paavo, even though I joked about Zoe earlier, I found out a bit about her," she said. "Maybe it'll help you understand her better."

"What's that?" he asked, interested.

"She's looking for her sister. Apparently the girl is one of the many runaways who seem to find their way to this city. She sounded so upset, so troubled, that last night I went looking for her."

Something in her tone must have conveyed to him that he wasn't going to like what she had to say because his hand tightened on hers. "You went looking?"

A seagull cawed and swooped right by their heads. They ducked, then began walking once again. "I found out that she goes to a Goth hangout. It's called The Crypt Macabre. It's at the house of this weird guy who calls himself Baron Severus. The Hugh Hefner of the Goth set."

He froze. "The Crypt Macabre?"

"You've heard of it?"

"Just the name. Where is it?"

She gave him the location. "It's weird, kind of spooky, and some of the people there seem to be living a Dracula fantasy." She chuckled.

"It's nothing to laugh about. I've seen it in connection with—"*Demons and insane serial killers.* "Things that are dangerous. If they knew you were there snooping around—"

"I was not snooping!" She hooked his arm and tugged at him. He fell into step at her side. "I've given all that up. I was minding my own business, just looking for my friend. And anyway, Rysk was there. He even walked outside with me and waited until my taxi showed up. I knew what I was doing and I was perfectly safe."

"Rysk! That's even worse! I already told you, Angie,

Edward Bowie doesn't exist. He's a fake. And if he and Zoe both go to that club . . ."

Angie stopped walking. His reaction to her little adventure had been making their stroll less than enjoyable, and the turn it had just taken killed her enthusiasm for it completely.

"Look, I don't know why Rysk and Zoe go to a place like the Baron's. They aren't even Goth, or not really."

He leaned toward her. "What are they, then, *really?*"

Her hands clenched. "I don't know!"

"That's what I mean. I don't like them around you. I insist that you fire them right now."

She gaped at him, scarcely believing what he'd just said. "Are you telling me how to run my business?"

"I'm telling you how to be safe," he all but shouted.

"And I'm telling you where you can go!" She turned and stomped away, not looking back when he called.

When Angie got out of the taxi, she was shocked to see Rysk across the street from her apartment building, studying the building next door. After fighting with Paavo, she didn't feel like talking to anyone, but it wouldn't have been nice to ignore him.

He seemed equally surprised to see her. "What are you doing here?" she asked as she approached him.

"Just looking around. You weren't home, so . . ." He slid his hands into his pockets. "You haven't mentioned any more pranks. Is everything okay?"

"Nothing new, thank goodness." Her head swiveled from side to side. She didn't like the thought of some malevolent prankster in her neighborhood. "Have you seen anything or anyone suspicious?"

He laughed. "Don't worry. No bogeymen are out here."

"That's good. See you tomorrow," she said.

"Right." His voice held more resignation than enthusiasm.

Paavo was in one of the foulest moods he'd ever been in when his feet hit the concrete stairs leading into the Hall of Justice. His head was muddled with the heartburn-inducing walk with Angie, and he wondered whether he was in his right mind to consider a lifetime with a spoiled, stubborn, sassy, smart aleck.

So lost in thought was he, he almost missed spotting Zoe as she walked out the main door. Seeing him, she stopped in her tracks and turned to reenter the building. He sprinted up the steps and grabbed her arm.

"Hey!" she yelled. "Watch it!"

"What are you doing here?" he demanded.

"I came to pay a parking ticket. What's it to you?"

"Do you know Angie went looking for you last night at The Crypt Macabre?"

She paled. "I don't know what you're talking about."

He kept his hand on her arm and pulled her out of the doorway to the side of the building. "Start talking. Who's Baron Severus? What's The Crypt Macabre? And why do you go there?"

She jerked her arm free. "My sister is a runaway. I knew Greta went there when she was in the city, so I've gone to try to find her or someone who knows her. I've had no luck so far."

"That's it?"

"That's it."

"What about this man?" He pulled a couple of photos from his inside breast pocket and showed her one of Markowitz.

She shook her head. "Never saw him."

"He's right here in city jail. Are you sure you aren't here to see him, to talk with him?"

"Of course not!"

"What about this one?" He held up Travis Walters's photo.

There was a long pause. "I've seen him at the club," she said softly. "He was complaining . . . um . . . I don't know. I don't remember."

"Was it about an old man following him?"

"No. Maybe. I'm not sure."

"Did anyone there tell him the old man's name?"

Her eyes were wide, looking everywhere except at him. "I don't know. He talked to the Baron. I don't know anything more. I'm sorry."

She practically ran down the steps in her hurry to get away.

Chapter 30

 "What do you want?" A bleary-eyed, heavyset man with short brown hair, smudged eye makeup, and a sickly, gray-tinged face opened the door of the big Victorian on Vallejo Street. He was wearing a bathrobe and slippers.

"Inspector Smith, police," Paavo said as he flashed his badge. "Are you the owner of this house?"

"No. He's still sleeping."

Obviously the owner wasn't the only one who'd been asleep. It was four in the afternoon. "When will he be up?" Paavo asked.

"Around six."

"I'd like to speak to him now." Although Paavo had left messages for both Calderon and Benson to check out Markowitz's connection to The Crypt Macabre, he had a few questions of his own for Severus.

"What's this about?" the man asked arrogantly.

"Who are you?" Paavo retorted.

The fellow straightened his spine. Had he been wearing shoes instead of slippers, Paavo wouldn't have been surprised to see him click his heels. "I'm Wilbur Fieldren, the Baron's assistant."

"I'm here on a homicide investigation. I want to see Severus now."

"One moment." He shut the door. Nearly ten minutes went by before the door opened again and Fieldren waved Paavo inside.

Stepping into the house was like entering a meat locker. The sense of evil he'd had at the crime scenes struck him tenfold. He followed the assistant through a gaudy hallway to a small, dark parlor. The room had a strong, almost medicinal smell. He couldn't quite place it, but it was disagreeable.

The Baron was seated by the fire. He wore a heavy brocade robe, and his head was flopped forward, chin to chest. He slowly lifted it as Paavo entered the room. At first, Paavo thought he was an old man, but then he realized the Baron was simply dissipated and in need of sleep.

Paavo explained who he was and then said bluntly, "I'd like to ask you about Mason Markowitz."

"Never heard of him," the Baron grumbled. Obviously, being pulled from his bed didn't agree with him. Frankly, Paavo wasn't in the world's best mood either, and if this guy wanted trouble, he was ready.

"He's heard of you," Paavo said coldly. "And your club."

"That's no concern of mine. What's this about?"

"It's about murder, Baron Severus. What's your real name?"

"I don't see that as any concern of anyone but me. Why am I being questioned?"

"I'd like to know why Mason Markowitz is interested in you and your club and why you deny knowledge of him."

"I'm not denying anything. The man is a stranger to me."

"Have you ever seen this man?" He handed a glossy lineup photo of Markowitz to the Baron.

"Never." The Baron handed it back. "Is he Markowitz?"

"What about Travis Walters?" Paavo asked as he placed the photo back in the envelope.

"Travis . . . Oh, yes, the boy who killed himself. I was sorry to hear it but not surprised. He was very troubled."

Paavo was finding the Baron an interesting liar. He seemed to deal in half-truths and had a shell that was difficult to penetrate. The Baron, he was sure, had a lot of practice in deception. "In what way?" he asked.

"I didn't know him well enough to say. He was unhappy, with few friends. That's all I can tell you."

"Did he tell you about an old man leaving holy water at his house?"

"I heard about it. He was extremely upset by it—unnaturally upset, if you ask me."

"Someone told him the name of the old man who was after him. Who could that have been?"

The Baron yawned. "Your guess is as good as mine. Probably better, Inspector, because I don't give a damn. Ask Fred Limore. The two were thick as thieves."

"What do you know of Zoe Vane?"

"She's also troubled—and trouble. I have no idea why she hangs around. She's too uptight for our group. I'd be just as glad if she stopped coming. In fact, she won't be admitted anymore. This *is* a private club, after all. Happy now?"

"What about her sister?"

The Baron looked at him curiously. "Who *is* her sister?"

"Greta. Greta Vane."

His frown didn't come quick enough, and Paavo saw a twinge of something flicker across his eyes before his nonchalant mask descended once more. "Months ago, a Greta came here. I scarcely remember her, and I have no idea where she is now."

"And Rysk?"

"I'm tired of these questions. He's a jerk. I pay no attention to him."

"Where were you on the night of March third?"

"I'm here every night. I rarely go out. I have no need to. Everything I want is right here."

"You have parties here nightly?"

"What's your problem, Inspector? It seems to me you're just fishing, and I don't have time to waste."

"Thank you, Baron." Paavo stood. "Our talk has been most enlightening."

"No, it has been most disagreeable." The Baron stood. "I don't want to hear any more from you now or ever, Inspector, unless you are here with a warrant."

"A warrant for what reason?"

"That's just it—there is no reason."

When Paavo went out into the sunshine, he breathed deeply, trying to fill his lungs with clean, pure air.

An awful night's sleep, reliving his argument with Angie in his dreams, didn't help Paavo's mood one bit the next day.

Another bout of rants and raves was the last thing he

wanted to deal with as he strode into the interview room and scowled at Markowitz and Markowitz's attorney, Cecil Zeller.

In fact, he'd never felt less like doing his job than he did now.

"Well, well, well! The good inspector," Markowitz said with a friendly smile.

Paavo scowled at Zeller. What had he done to his client? Drugged him? Zeller, however, was gaping at Markowitz in surprise.

"I want to ask you about Baron Severus," Paavo said.

"Ah, yes. A terrible man. He deals with drugs, you know," Markowitz said brightly.

"He does?"

"Demonic masters use surrogates to do their bidding." His voice dropped to a whisper. "You have to beware of people. All of them. They're all evil."

Paavo glanced again at Zeller, who shrugged.

"What about the Dark Queen?" Paavo asked, hoping to find some common ground with Markowitz in order to get some answers.

"I know she is being watched," Markowitz said calmly after a long while. "I felt the evil around her. Poof!" He laughed. "Poof! It's all around us. All around."

Paavo wasn't sure that he didn't prefer the ranting Markowitz to Little Miss Sunshine. "You mentioned surrogates," he prodded, his thoughts on Zoe and Rysk. Were they surrogates? Or were they something more? "Tell me about them."

"You shouldn't worry, my boy," he said with an eerily peaceful smile. "Help is on the way."

"It is?"

Markowitz's gaze was fixed somewhere on the far wall, and he seemed not even to hear Paavo's question.

"Mr. Markowitz." Paavo decided to try again. "Can you tell me about The Crypt Macabre or Baron Severus?"

"Don't go there, young man. Evil lurks. Our time of trial is at hand."

Markowitz bowed his head, eyes shut, and began to speak in what sounded like Latin.

Why wasn't the man screaming about leaving, as he had done before? What was going on?

After a couple more unsuccessful attempts to get Markowitz to respond, a completely baffled Paavo left.

The librarian gave Paavo a strange look as she handed him several references on the demon Baalberith.

He sat at a table and read them. All told a similar tale of a demon who weaves a net of fornication and wealth to trap his victims. Scorned by a beautiful young woman, who throws herself into a fiery pit rather than endure his love, Baalberith goes on a rampage of killing and possession of souls while searching through the centuries for the one woman who will love him, the one who will become his Queen and raise him from the second order of demon to the first—to become a Dark Lord.

Paavo was unsure of what to think of all this. Supposedly, demons were capable of taking over a human body, overwhelming its original soul, and making it act in uncharacteristic ways.

Demonic possession was, all in all, an easy excuse for a lot of evil. He was just about to leave the library when the fiction section caught his eye. Curious about

Angie's comments about The Crypt Macabre, he found Stoker's *Dracula*.

Mina Harker's journal entries were prominent in the book, as were writings of her friend, Lucy Westenra. Flipping through the pages, he came across the name Renfield, the crazy minion of the Count. Renfield—Fieldren.

Markowitz had talked about demons having surrogates.

Paavo placed the book back on the shelf with a shake of his head. He was becoming a little too comfortable with all this. He felt like he was caught in a cross between *The X-Files* and *The Exorcist*.

Angie was surprised but relieved to see Paavo at her door at nine o'clock that night. She had just indulged in another long soak in the tub, aching and weary from baking cakes all day for the Chief's reception. At this rate, she was going to become waterlogged.

"I thought you were busy working on a case," she said, leading him to the living room. She was upset by the way they'd parted at the Wharf, and when he hadn't called all day, her unhappiness grew. His showing up was a good sign, but when she sat and he didn't, the good sign took a turn south.

"I came here for two reasons. The first is to apologize. I was wrong about Zoe and Rysk being behind your troubles. I still don't trust them, but nonetheless, I'm sorry."

"That's wonderful news," Angie said, thrilled, yet unable to hide her confusion. "But how do you know?"

"That's the second reason. We caught the woman who has been trying to harm your business."

She stared at him. The woman? Was it Connie after all? "What woman?" she asked.

"Lolly Firenghetti. She'd taken to following you, doing damage to your cakes, pretending to be customers with phony orders."

Angie's head reeled. "She did that?"

"Someone called in an anonymous tip. We caught her on the roof next door with a cage filled with live mice. She knew someone in the building, and once when she was visiting, managed to swipe the key to the main door. With it, she could get into the apartment building and go up the fire escape to the roof. That roof isn't much below yours. She'd climb up onto it and then lower herself to your back door. You don't have a double lock on it, so she was able to let herself in, do whatever mischief she planned, and then leave."

"Mice! Oh, my God!" She shivered. "I've never even seen Lolly! How could she hate me that much?"

"You were cutting into her business, and she hated that fact."

"I've heard she's an overweight, middle-aged woman. How did she manage to climb around on rooftops?"

"She was plenty angry, and the cop who went up there to arrest her has the bruises and bite marks to prove it."

Angie shook her head in amazement. "I can hardly believe it's over. And to think she's Italian!"

He grinned. "So much for Cosa Nostra." He was actually quite relieved to learn the mishaps were caused by human mischief. For a while, he'd even considered an unnatural source. He definitely was spending too much time around kooks like Markowitz and the Baron.

She held her arms out to him. He walked up to her, drew her to her feet, and pulled her close. They had a lot of celebrating to do.

Chapter 31

Angie awoke in the middle of the night. Paavo was no longer at her side but had quietly left while she slept. She wrapped her arms tight around the pillow he'd used, holding it close.

In the kitchen, blue-frosted cakes covered every counter, even the top of her range. An attack of paranoia caused her to run in and look for flies or toads, despite Lolly Firenghetti's arrest. Imagining what mice would have done to those cakes was heart-attack time.

No strange creatures were there, just a sea of blue.

Tomorrow was the reception, and she prayed everything would go well for Paavo's sake as well as her own. She wanted him to be proud of her.

It would be nice if someone was proud of her.

Maybe after tomorrow, things would be better.

Rysk left The Crypt Macabre and stared up at the stars a moment. Not many were visible above the lights of the city, but he knew they were there, just as he knew of the many levels of activity going on around him.

Zoe hadn't been allowed inside the club tonight, but

to his amazement, she'd asked for him to come out to talk to her. She had a request. An outrageous idea he should have run from as soon as she started talking. But he couldn't.

He'd given her a promise, and tomorrow, no matter what, he was going to keep it.

Mason Markowitz paced his cell, unable to sleep. Tomorrow was the day. He had to get out of there—the safety of humanity depended on him.

Would his plan work? Dare he depend on others? He had no choice. He could only wait for tomorrow and pray.

Paavo drove home through the quiet streets. Tomorrow, when the big reception was over, somehow he'd get Angie to have a dinner with him that was free of arguments or interruptions—even if he had to take her to his house and cook it for her himself.

He was tired of waiting, tired of not being sure if she'd say yes, despite what everyone else had to say. He wanted to hear the words from her lips.

Tomorrow, whatever it took to get her attention, he'd ask her to become his wife.

"Where are you, Greta?" Zoe whispered, even though, in her heart, she had no more hope. Her mind swirled in too many directions to sleep, and she paced around her small rented room.

Tomorrow she would put the plan Mason gave her when she visited him at city jail into action. She'd used a pseudonym and fake ID's to get in to see him. It would be dangerous, but she didn't care anymore—or did she?

She'd met someone who made her *want* to care, who made her feel there might possibly be something enjoyable about this crazy life. At a time like this, though, how could she even acknowledge such stirrings, let alone consider acting on them?

She had no business acting on anything until she found Greta. To the outer limits of her ability and beyond if needed, that's how far she told Mason she would go. Tomorrow would be the test.

She must not fail.

One more infernal day until night fell and everything the *Ars Diabolus* predicted would come true. The Dark Queen would be his, and with her ascension, he would gain the ultimate power. He would become Dark Lord.

Behold Baalberith! All the angels and saints would bow down before his power.

Tomorrow all would become his.

He looked at the not-quite-completely-full moon and raised his arms high to it. In twenty-four hours, all the world would know the truth of his prophecy:

I am Destroyer. I am Beast. I am Nightmare.

Chapter 32

 "The cake and the set-up look great," Angie said, smiling at Zoe and Rysk. "You two have been simply terrific."

The secretaries and clerks from the police chief's staff had joined Angie, Rysk, and Zoe to transform the cafeteria into a party room. Helium-filled balloons along with streamers festooned the ceiling. More were used as centerpieces on each table, and a colorful banner across the entire back wall read, "Happy Retirement Chief O'Malley. You're the Greatest."

The pièce de résistance, however, was Angie's cake. It was four feet across by five feet long and was a perfect replica of the San Francisco Police Department badge, complete with the Chief's number.

It might not have been comical, but the oohs and aahs it received did her heart good. She was glad she'd gone with serious rather than funny.

Not only did she know the Chief of Police had no sense of humor, but hers vanished as well when she eyed Rysk. He was dressed more garishly than usual. His glow-in-the-dark green spikes were gelled to hard peaks; eye shadow was smudged all the way around his eyes. His nails were painted the same dark crimson as his lips, and tonight he wore earrings in every one of his three ear holes, not to mention a nose ring. Dressed head to toe in black, he was an incongruous sight amidst all the blue uniforms and suits.

She could have spit when he showed up at her apartment that way. The urge to act like a school principal and send him home to scrub his face and wash his hair tempted her, but there wasn't time. If she hadn't known better, she'd have thought he was in disguise.

Zoe, thank God, was at least normally dressed in navy slacks and a white blouse. So far, no one had paid any particular attention to Rysk, all being in a party mood. Besides, this *was* San Francisco.

"I never thought I'd be waiting on a bunch of cops," Rysk admitted as he studied the room, which was just beginning to fill up.

"Everyone I've met here has been a great guy or woman," Angie said. "Give them half a chance, and you'll like them."

Rysk tightened his lips. "I'd like to think they'd do the same for me."

"What? That spiked green hair doesn't make them warm to you?" Zoe asked with laughter in her voice. It was the first time that evening she'd shown any sparkle. She seemed preoccupied, as she'd been yesterday while they baked. Angie had hoped to talk to her about what was bothering her, but time and Zoe's mood hadn't allowed for it.

"What's more important is how you feel about it," Rysk said to her.

"You can shave it all off for all I care." Zoe went about her business putting out plates and paper cups.

Rysk looked so crestfallen, Angie couldn't help but
laugh.

Paavo wanted to check the incoming faxes before going down to the police chief's party. The others, except
for Rebecca Mayfield, had already left. She gazed
glumly in his direction as he went to the fax machine.

A transmission from the FBI had his name on it.

Before visiting Baron Severus, he had wiped the
glossy photo of Markowitz free of prints. When he
gave it to the Baron to look at, he only touched its
edges. He didn't think the Baron would be so careful,
and he wasn't. A perfect thumbprint resulted.

The FBI produced a match. George Arthur Hyde,
age forty-three, born in Ithaca, New York, arrested
three times for possession of narcotics and twice for
dealing. Each time, he'd gotten off for tainted or lack
of evidence. Markowitz had been right when he'd
called the Baron a dealer. What else had he been right
about?

As he carried the report to his desk, he noticed Rebecca Mayfield dabbing her eyes with a Kleenex.

"Rebecca," he said. "What's wrong?"

"Is it true?" she asked in a wobbly voice.

"Is what true?"

"That . . . that you're going to ask Angie to marry
you?" The tears welled up again.

He sat down on the chair beside her desk. "Rebecca,
don't do this."

"I can't help it! She's so wrong for you. I'm not saying I'm right, but I care about you. I don't want to see
you hurt."

"Angie won't hurt me."

"Won't she? It's easy to put up with a cop when you're just dating. During that time, we're exciting—our jobs are dangerous, we're clever, in the know about lots of the wild stuff going on in the city. If we stand up our date, well, it's obviously because a life-or-death matter came up. They understand. Then you get married, or even engaged, and your partner suddenly isn't half so understanding."

"Don't you think I know all that?" Paavo asked. "Don't you realize it's the reason I've put off this decision for so long?"

"You know it, but only intellectually." She dropped her gaze to the crumpled tissue. "I speak from experience. Been there, done that."

"You're divorced?"

"No. Never got that far." She lifted watery eyes and sniffed. "I was engaged, though. I didn't listen to all the cops who said I'd be best off if I stuck to others like me when I dated. I found a civilian, and damn it all, I fell in love with him. In the end, he couldn't deal with my job—not the hours, not the danger, and not the fact that if we went out together, he knew I was much more capable of protecting him than he was of me. His ego couldn't handle it, and it destroyed us."

"I'm sorry," he said.

"Me, too," she whispered. "But that was then. I've gone out with cops ever since. Of course, now that I'm in Homicide, where most of them want to be, they kind of see me as way up the ladder from them, almost a boss, and that brings its own set of problems. Good God, why am I telling you this?"

"Because we're friends," he said.

She met his eyes. "Yes, and that's all we've ever been."

He nodded.

Elbows on the desk, she folded her hands and smiled wanly. "God, but I hate that!"

He grinned. "You'll find the right guy, Rebecca. Want to walk down to the Chief's reception with me?"

She shook her head and gazed around the bureau— the ratty steel desks, the ancient computers, the stacks of papers and books and file folders. "I think I'll sit here awhile. I worked hard to get here. May as well enjoy it."

Zoe snuck out of the reception. The room was slowly filling with people, but the Chief hadn't yet arrived.

She hurried through the hallways to the opposite side of the floor and went in search of a pay phone.

Making sure no one saw her, she stepped inside the booth, pulled the door shut, and dialed.

"Richards, Adams and Blaustein," the receptionist answered.

"I'd like to speak with Mr. Zeller," she said, asking for the firm's junior attorney.

"May I tell him who's calling?"

"My name is Dolores Rice. Mrs. Dolores Rice. I'm calling about his client, Mason Markowitz. I believe I have some information that will be very useful to him."

Zeller came on the line quickly.

"I can't keep my mouth shut any longer," she said, trying to make her voice high and nasal. "Mason Markowitz is innocent. He was with me the night Lucy

Whitefeather was killed. We were together all night, and I can prove it."

There was a long pause. "How can you prove it?"

"I've got a receipt from the motel we stayed at. Mr. and Mrs. it says." She spoke hurriedly. "He signed it, and I took his copy. I was supposed to throw it away. My husband was out of town that night, you see."

"Why didn't you give me this information sooner?"

"I didn't think it would go this far. Mason and me, we agreed this was our secret. It's because of my husband. We're retired, and I get a wife's pension. I can't afford a divorce, but I can't let Mason stay in jail for something he didn't do. It's hard to do this, Mr. Zeller. Very hard."

"You're now willing, however, to come into the open with this information?" he confirmed, excited.

"I wouldn't be calling if I wasn't. Mason is a good man. He believes that there's evil in the world, but he's no killer. He wants to rid the world of evil, to rid it of demons. Okay, I'll admit that's a bit strange, but don't we all have little quirks now and then?"

"It's more than a little quirk to some people."

"I don't care. He's innocent, and I can prove it. Now, do you want my information or not?"

"Of course I do, but let me talk to my client."

"I'm leaving town, Mr. Zeller. I can't take this. It's got my nerves all jangling. I'll call you in a couple of hours. You tell me what I can do now, right now, 'cause I won't be here later."

"Wait. Try to relax. We'll keep this as quiet as possible, I promise."

"I know what lawyer's promises are worth."

"How can I reach you?"

"You aren't listening to what I'm saying. This will end my marriage, the life I know. I'll call you at eight o'clock." With that, she hung up.

Zeller was a young lawyer and a hungry one. He'd be working to become a partner, trying to make a name for himself, so that he wouldn't be stuck with the kind of pro bono work that the firm meted out to its junior associates. Having been given a possible way to win a case that everyone suspected was a slam dunk for the prosecution, he'd find a way to meet with Markowitz immediately. Of that she had no doubt.

Smiling, she went back to the reception. Time to find Rysk.

Angie was ecstatic. The reception was a resounding success. She stood beside Paavo as the various dignitaries made speeches about the years of able service Chief O'Malley had given the city and the department.

Last of all, they waited through an interminable speech as O'Malley recounted said years of service—one by one.

Finally the time came when Chief O'Malley had to cut the cake. Paavo smiled proudly at Angie as the Chief praised her cleverness and had a number of photos taken standing beside it. Angie hoped that one of the photographers was from the *Chronicle* and that a photo with her cake would be chosen for the city's major daily. That should bring lots more business her way.

She had to admit she almost cried when the Chief made the first cut after all the hours she'd put into making the badge perfect. And now it was going to be eaten. *Sic transit gloria.*

She and Zoe soon took over cutting and serving. She'd learned quite a bit about who was who in the police force from Paavo, and she gave out pieces to the bigwigs first. That seemed to please them.

After the dignitaries wandered away with their cake and coffee or punch, Angie and Zoe put a number of pieces of cake on plates and cut up the remainder to make it easy for latecomers to serve themselves.

"You know, Angie," Zoe said, pouring more punch, "I've heard that there are a number of police next door at the City Jail who aren't able to leave their posts to come over here for a piece of cake. I was wondering if it would be all right with you if Rysk and I brought them some."

"How very thoughtful," Angie said, surprised that they'd come up with such a suggestion—and that she hadn't—considering how alienated from the police they'd both initially acted. "There's a corridor between this building and the jail, so you won't have to go outside."

"Yes. I know," Zoe said.

Carla, the Chief's secretary and the one in charge of the party, agreed to the proposal. Zoe and Rysk sliced up a sheet cake, put paper plates, forks, and napkins onto a cart, and left.

Angie slowly surveyed the crowd. People seemed to be enjoying themselves, and her cake was a big hit. Zoe and Rysk should return soon, the party would end before much longer, and the clean-up would be relatively fast. Almost all the cake had already been eaten.

Paavo, too, was pleased by what he saw. "This party is a winner," he said proudly, as he stepped to Angie's side. "You've done a great job. Everyone is impressed." The smile she gave him was beautiful. No vestige of the unpleasantness between them remained, nor did any doubt of his love for her—although she probably always would drive him to distraction. And tonight she was distracting enough in a long-sleeved black dress with discreet beading at the square neckline and cuffs.

"Thank you," she murmured.

"When it's over, shall we go celebrate?"

Her smile deepened. "Wonderful idea. I'll be ready to relax. I'll admit to having been quite nervous about this. I particularly wanted everything to be perfect for your sake."

"You're always perfect to me."

"You know what I mean. I wanted you to be proud of me. Also, there's something else I've been thinking about."

"What's that?"

"This cake business. With a lot of hard work, I know it can be profitable, but I don't think it's what I'm looking for." She took his hand. "Zoe has a natural gift for it. Lots of the designs were hers. I think I'll ask her if she'd like to take it over. Maybe with Rysk's help . . ." She winked at him.

Relief poured through him, and he pulled her closer. "That sounds wonderful."

As they spoke, the buzz of voices in the room grew progressively louder. Lieutenant Hollins caught Paavo's eye, and gestured for him to approach.

"What's going on?" he asked, after excusing himself to Angie.

"Mason Markowitz escaped." Hollins took his arm and led him away from the others. "Markowitz had been taken out of his jail cell and placed in a much lower security interview room, where he was talking to his attorney. Apparently, a woman gave the cop guarding the room a piece of cake at the same time as a man pretending to be a plumber showed up to take care of some problems in the cells. Between the two of them, the guard was so distracted that while the plumber was looking for his identification, he took a bite of cake and went out like a light. It was laced with knockout drops.

"Next thing, the couple opened the door to the interview room, bound and gagged the lawyer. Zeller said it was clear the woman and Markowitz knew each other. The guy had black jeans and a T-shirt under his plumber's uniform. He gave the uniform to Markowitz, and the three walked out of there pushing the cake cart, easy as you please."

"What the hell?" Calderon was standing behind Paavo and had heard the whole thing. "A spiked cake?" He turned and glared at Angie.

Her eyes widened as she looked questioningly from Calderon to Paavo to Lieutenant Hollins. All three were staring at her. What had she done?

She started to walk over to them when Paavo bolted from the other two. He whisked her to a corner and quickly told her what had happened.

The room began to spin. "This is a joke, right?" she whispered, no coherent thought in her head. "Some kind of sick cop humor?"

"No joke, Angie. Sounds like Zoe and Rysk helped a serial killer escape."

Paavo's boss and Calderon approached. Noticing the activity, Yosh also joined them. Angie felt faint and weak. "I can't believe it," she whispered.

Calderon stuck his angry red face in hers. "Who the hell are those people you hired?" he barked. "Are you part of this, too? I know Paavo didn't agree with my arresting Markowitz. Is this your way of helping him get even with me?"

"Leave her alone," Paavo said, putting his arm protectively across Angie's shoulders and drawing her closer to his side.

"Why should I? Look at what she's done!"

"I didn't do a thing, and neither did my people." Her cheeks burned, and she was sick to her stomach. "I can't believe they were willingly involved. Someone made them do it!"

"Who? You?" Calderon sneered.

"She's got a business to run," Yosh said. "She's not interfering in anything anymore."

Nothing like damning with faint praise, Angie thought.

"Let's see what we can find out." Paavo went with Angie in search of the two helpers but the jail had been locked down, and they weren't admitted.

"There's no reason for them to have helped Markowitz escape," Angie insisted.

"Did Zoe ever mention knowing him?"

"Never."

Paavo stopped and thought a moment. All Markowitz's strange warnings came back to him. The full moon, today's date, that more women would be killed, and that Angie could be a victim. "I want you to go to Connie's place and stay there."

"What? I can't go home? What's going on?"

He couldn't tell her what Markowitz had said. It didn't make sense to him, and he sure hoped it wouldn't make sense to her. He had another, much more plausible reason to give her. "If Zoe and Rysk are behind this, they might go to your place to hide out and might even bring Markowitz with them. I don't want you facing the three of them. It's best if you aren't alone. Stay with Connie. You'll be safe there."

"But Zoe and Rysk are my—" She swallowed the word. She'd been saying all along that they were friends, and now look at what they'd done. She could have cried.

"People you consider friends wouldn't help a serial killer escape, would they?"

She chewed her bottom lip. "Maybe he isn't the killer everyone thinks he is," she said weakly.

Her thought mirrored his own, but now wasn't the time to admit it. "That isn't for them to decide. It's for the law. They're obstructing it and will be arrested when caught. I want you far away from them."

She nodded.

"I'll get one of the uniforms to escort you."

"Escort me?" She paled. "What aren't you telling me?"

"Nothing. I just want to be sure you're safe so I can concentrate on finding Markowitz."

She eyed him dubiously but held her tongue. It was better not to make a scene. Besides, she was beginning to feel more and more responsible for the escape.

Officer Crossen, who knew Angie from past cases, had just stopped in to give his best wishes to the Chief and to eat some cake when Paavo approached him.

Before long, Paavo was gone, and Angie and Crossen went to the parking lot, where the second nasty surprise of the night awaited her. "It's not here," she said, frozen in place, staring at the empty parking spot where her van had been.

"What kind of car is it?" Crossen asked.

"It's a minivan, a white Ford something-or-other." Panic set in. Any minute now she was going to start hyperventilating. What unlucky star was she born under? "There are no white vans out here of any make."

"Are you sure this is where you parked it?"

"Of course! I parked near the door so we wouldn't have to carry the cakes too far."

He just nodded and scanned the parking lot as she spoke. "Did the two people who worked for you have keys to the van?" he asked.

"No. I let Rysk drive it to make deliveries, but he didn't have his own set of keys."

She held up a bundle of keys for him to see.

"What would have stopped him from having a duplicate made while he was on a delivery?" Crossen asked.

Her face fell. "Nothing."

He put his hands on his hips. "I think we know what they used as the getaway car."

Chapter 33

Angie rode in silence beside Officer Crossen, too upset to say a word.

Not only had the Chief's retirement party been ruined, but her employees had released a serial killer back into the community. Once word of this got out, her business would be a shambles. Forget Zoe—she wouldn't even be able to give it away to anyone. And the damage to her good name would be even worse! She'd have to move somewhere far away where no one knew her name. Somewhere like . . . Idaho, maybe.

Going to see Connie was the only good thing about this. How could she have doubted her friend? She never should have fought with Connie but should have been sensitive to her, talked about whatever was troubling her. More than anything, she wanted to see Connie and beg forgiveness, even if she had to get on her knees to do it.

Crossen walked with her up to Connie's apartment. She knocked on the door. No answer.

"If she isn't home," Crossen said, "where do you want to go next?"

"Don't worry. I've seen Connie do this many a time." She walked to the decorative round knob at the top of the banister right across from Connie's door. Wiggling the ball slightly, she worked it off. Underneath was a key. "Voilà!" she said.

Taking the key, she unlocked the door, and she and Crossen walked inside. She was trying to find the light switch when she saw a movement in the dark, felt a rapid whoosh of air toward her head, and all went dark.

Lieutenant Hollins called Paavo into the meeting with Calderon, Benson, and Zeller. Zeller told them that as they'd talked, all Markowitz's attention had been focused on stopping the ascension of the Dark Lord's Queen.

"Ah, yes, his mysterious Dark Lord," Calderon sneered. "And did he happen to say who's been chosen as the Queen of this master demon?"

"Tell him," Hollins demanded of Zeller.

Zeller loosened his tie as he took in Paavo's scowl. "Markowitz said something I didn't understand. Well, one thing among many that I didn't understand. He said the one who believed him must watch his woman to keep her safe. We . . . uh . . . Lieutenant Hollins thought you might have some idea what he's talking about."

Hollins's eyes narrowed at Paavo. "Aren't you the one he thinks believes him?"

Paavo's breath came quickly. "It sounds like Angie could be in danger."

"No, no, no!" Calderon yelled. The others faced him. "None of you get it. Angie was a part of it. She helped him escape. It's all part of the game that's going on with Markowitz. He says these outrageous things and gets gullible people to believe him."

"Wait a minute—" Paavo began.

"No, you wait. He's only saying this because Angie's friends helped him. That's how he knows her. The rest is all nonsense—scare talk to get everyone worked up."

"If you really think the man is a serial killer," Paavo said to Calderon, "I should think you'd be very worried about Angie and Zoe both. Or do you suddenly believe Markowitz is a lot less dangerous than you were saying?"

"Of course he's dangerous, but not to the ones who help him. Serial killers don't work that way."

"You're wrong. They do," Zeller said. "I've been doing a lot of reading since I took this case. They've been known to turn on their own mothers."

"Angie had nothing to do with this!" Paavo insisted. "She was as shocked as anyone else by what happened. She's perfectly innocent."

"Let's see how helpful she is to us," Calderon said. "I want you, Paavo, to find out from Angie all you can about her two workers, where they live, everything else that might be useful. Don't bother about anything else. I'll handle it."

Paavo glanced at Hollins, who nodded in agreement with Calderon. Paavo left quickly before he said anything he'd regret.

Inspector Pamela James, who he'd worked with a number of times, was at her desk in the Missing Person's bureau. As Paavo had listened to Cecil Zeller, he had been trying to sort out the connection between Zoe and Markowitz. He was afraid he might have the answer.

"Pam, I need help," he said, then went on to explain what he was looking for.

She did the search as he'd asked. Location: Chicago or San Francisco. Sex: female. Age: 16–18. Name: Greta Vane.

A school picture came onto the screen of a smiling teenager.

As he studied the picture, his stomach churned and his shoulders sagged as if with the weight of it all.

Now that he was looking for it, he could see the resemblance. If Zoe's hair wasn't dyed black and if she didn't wear all that dark Goth makeup, she would look a great deal like this girl, and he would have seen the resemblance between her and the first victim, the one who called herself Mina Harker.

He went up to Homicide to show Calderon and Benson this latest piece of the puzzle. Zoe clearly didn't know her sister was dead and may have thought Markowitz would lead her to Greta. Or to an answer to her disappearance. Perhaps Zoe, too, believed in demons.

Homicide was in a stir as each inspector pushed his own theory of how the breakout had happened, why, and most importantly, what to do about it.

Connie stood up from his desk as he entered. He was stunned to see her and quickly looked around for Angie. A sense of dread filled him.

"What are you doing here?" he asked. "Didn't you see Angie?"

"Not yet," she said. "I heard she would be here serving cake, and I thought I'd come to see her, to talk and hopefully make up, but when I got to the reception, it had already ended. I thought she'd be here with you."

"I'll try to reach her on her cell phone," Paavo said, punching in her number. If she couldn't get into Connie's, where would she have gone?

"Have you proposed yet?" Connie whispered to him so the others wouldn't hear. He shook his head. "She'll be so happy when you do. Me, too. For both of you."

Angie's line was busy. "She's talking to someone." He scowled at the phone.

"I didn't call anyone about my so-called stalker." Connie babbled nonstop. "I think I scared him away. The night after I talked to you, I got home a little later than usual, and he was already across the street, looking up at my apartment. When he noticed me, I stared right at him. It scared me half to death, but he hurried away. I've been looking and looking, but so far, he hasn't returned that I've noticed."

"That's good news. Just another nut case."

He tried Angie's line again. Still busy. Who could she be talking to? And where was she?

"I hope so," Connie continued. "Although I still have this eerie feeling of being watched. Maybe I just need a vacation."

The Greta-Mina photo lay in the center of Paavo's desk. He had to tell Calderon about it as well as give him the background information—or lack of it—that he'd already gathered on Zoe and Rysk. He excused himself.

"Hi, there," Benson said to Connie. "You a friend of Paavo's?"

"Yes. Angie's my best friend, or was. We had a stupid fight. I won't say it was all her fault, but it wasn't all mine either. I hope we can make up with each other."

He put the Markowitz folder on Paavo's desk. "I'm sorry to hear that. I'm sure she'll come around. Have you two known each other long?"

"It's not like we're old school friends or anything. I'm . . . a little older." She smiled at him.

He pushed the folder to the side and sat on the corner of the desk. "If you and she run around together, does that mean you're also single?" he asked, smiling back.

Paavo picked up his phone to try once more to get through to Angie.

"Well, does divorced count?" Connie asked coyly. She reached for the cup of coffee she'd helped herself to while waiting for Paavo and Angie to show up, and as she did, she bumped Bo's folder. It toppled to the floor, and several papers and photos slid out.

She bent over to help him pick them up. Suddenly, she let loose with an eardrum-splitting scream.

Everyone started. Calderon pulled out his gun, and Bill Sutter dived under his desk.

Paavo ran to her side and took hold of one arm, while Bo grabbed the other. "What's wrong?" Paavo asked.

"There." A wildly shaking finger pointed at a picture taken inside the Baron's club. "It's him! It's my stalker!"

"Tonight." Markowitz rocked back and forth in the backseat of the minivan. "We've got to stop him tonight."

"I know already!" Zoe shouted nervously. She sat behind the wheel, ready to drive off at a moment's notice. "We will as soon as Rysk comes back and tells us what he sees."

"I can't wait. If he gets the Dark Queen, he will be too powerful to fight. I must go now." He tugged on the door handle. Luckily, Angie's minivan had a child safety lock, and Zoe had used it. Markowitz wasn't going anywhere.

She needed him to find Greta. He'd promised that at the same time as he took care of this Dark Queen business, in his confrontation with the Baron—or Baalberith, as he always called him—he would somehow force the man to tell him where Greta had gone.

Now that she'd been barred from The Crypt Macabre for some unknown reason, she had no one but Markowitz to help her. He'd needed her help with Angie, and she'd needed his with Greta. If only Markowitz didn't talk in riddles, it would be a lot easier to follow his instructions.

All she knew was that Greta seemed farther and farther away from her with each passing day.

"Holy Michael the Archangel, defend us on this day of battle," Markowitz muttered. "Be our safeguard against the wickedness and snares of the Devil—"

"Damn it, stop already!" He was spooking her, just like the Baron's quiet house. With its Gothic tower piercing the night sky and a half-moon with wispy black clouds looming overhead, it could have been part of a Wes Craven movie.

Rysk had snuck into the back of it over ten minutes

ago and hadn't returned. Where was he? "Rysk should be back by now," she said. "I don't like this."

Markowitz seemed so much crazier to her now than he had before being imprisoned, it scared her and made her wonder why she'd ever listened to his cockeyed scheme for breaking out of jail and confronting the Baron. So far, to her amazement, it had worked, but Rysk's prolonged absence was making her very nervous.

"May God rebuke him, we humbly pray—"

"Hey, cool it!" She twisted in the seat and faced him. "What do you think is happening inside? Do you think the Baron's hurt Rysk?"

Markowitz stopped his mutterings and looked at her strangely. "The Baron? Why should we care about the Baron?"

Zoe froze. "What do you mean? The one you call Baalberith. Isn't—"

Before she could finish, shots rang out.

"Go back into Homicide. You'll be safe there," Paavo said to Connie as she dogged his footsteps to the parking lot. He was sick with worry. Not only had he been unable to get through to Angie, but Crossen wasn't answering his page either.

"No. I'm going with you," Connie said, jumping into the passenger seat when he unlocked the city-issue car. "We're going to find her. She's in trouble, and it's all my fault."

"I wouldn't say that," Paavo said.

"I would! Where can she be?" Connie twisted her fingers. "It's my fault she's out there with those crazies running around. But she should be safe at my place.

She knows where I keep an extra key. I don't understand why she didn't simply go inside."

"She might have," he murmured. What he didn't voice—and didn't want to tell Connie—was his fear that going into the apartment was exactly what she did do, and that's why she was now missing.

Now that he had put the pieces together, he wondered how he could have been so wrong.

Chapter 34

 When Angie opened her eyes, it was so dark she had to blink several times to be sure they were open. She was sitting on some kind of chair, her wrists bound to the arms of it.

Nearby, someone was crying.

She remained still, not making a sound.

Suddenly, two bright-red eyes came out of the darkness at her. She tried hard to hold herself steady, to not move. But as they came closer, she couldn't stop her scream.

Paavo parked a half-block from the Baron's house. The street was empty and quiet. A light shone in the front window of the house. It was nine o'clock, and the club-goers hadn't started to arrive yet. They never showed up until close to midnight.

Connie's eyes were wide with fright as Paavo began to make calls on his cell phone. Angie's was still busy. Yosh had just entered her apartment with Paavo's key. No one was there. The place appeared undisturbed.

Calderon and Benson were inside Connie's. They'd found the apartment door unlocked and inside, Officer

Crossen knocked unconscious. All he could say was that there was more than one person involved. As he followed Angie into the apartment, someone had struck him from behind, and as he tumbled forward, he felt another blow from the front. After that, nothing until Calderon's ugly face yelling at him to wake up.

Paavo rang the bell, then pounded on the door to Severus's house. No one answered. Along the edges of the drapery-covered windows, he was able to see that some lights were on inside.

"The hell with it," he said, and took out a lock pick. In a moment, the door sprang open. He turned to Connie. "Go sit in the car. Be ready to call for help if needed."

Connie backed onto the street, her eyes wide as she took in the aged, gaudy furnishings in the house.

He unsnapped the strap over his gun holster and went in, leaving the door open. Immediately, the sense built of something cold squeezing his lungs, trying to steal his very breath. He gasped, fighting it, and continued toward the parlor.

Candles lighted the room. Hundreds of votive candles, all reeking with a familiar smell. Camphor, that was it—the same kind of candles found at the ritual murders. In the shadows, near the window, sat Severus. His back was toward Paavo, and he seemed transfixed by his unlit fireplace.

One hand over his gun handle, Paavo entered the room. "Baron?" Was the man asleep?

He walked up behind him and lightly touched his shoulder. "Baron Severus?" A cold prickle went through him as he whirled in front of the man and looked at his face. The Baron was dead.

* * *

A young man in a black robe silently walked around
the windowless chamber, lighting candles. When he
finished, he walked up stone steps built against a wall.
No railing protected the open side, and he stayed close
to the wall.

In the chamber, on one side stood a long table, a
wooden chest beside it. Against the opposite wall, on
the floor, their arms and legs tied, were Zoe and an old
man. *Mason Markowitz,* Angie thought. Where was
Rysk?

Whatever was happening here didn't make sense to
her. She remembered the Baron's talk of rituals and
Paavo telling her about Markowitz and a Dark
Queen—and her. The Baron had to be the one behind
this. But wasn't Zoe his friend? Why had he tied up
Zoe? Had Rysk, for some reason, double-crossed her?

Her eyes caught Zoe's, and the fear in the other
woman's made her blood run cold. Angie could tell by
the bruises on her face she'd been beaten. Dried blood
was caked at her mouth. She'd put up a fight and lost.
The old man looked dazed.

Maybe somehow Rysk had escaped. She knew he
cared for Zoe. He wouldn't have allowed the Baron to
do this to her, unless . . . No! He was out there. He'd
call Paavo. She was sure he had enough sense to do
that. But how would Paavo know where to find her?

Somehow she had to take care of this herself if she
and Zoe were to get out of it alive.

Mason Markowitz was muttering. She understood.
She, too, had learned to say the rosary in Latin. Hearing him shook her. His were not the words or demeanor of a serial killer.

"What's this about?" she asked.

"He's going to kill us," Zoe said. Her voice was hoarse. Angie wondered if she'd been yelling for help. The walls were so thick no one outside could have heard.

"He is the demon Baalberith. With his Dark Queen, he will rule the world," Markowitz said. "She will make him stronger than he's ever been. Through the centuries he's searched for her, and now, finally, the hour is near. He's killed four women, and now he plans to kill his fifth. His Dark Queen."

"The ritual killer?" Angie asked, her voice tiny.

Zoe nodded.

"Where's Rysk?" Angie asked, hoping against hope they'd tell her he was rounding up the police as they spoke.

Zoe's tears began to fall again. "I don't know. I heard shots. He's got to be all right, Angie, he's just got to be."

"The fifth victim will become the Dark Queen," Markowitz's pronouncement cut through Zoe's sobs.

"After she's dead?" Angie asked.

Markowitz nodded.

Just then the door at the top of the staircase began to open.

Paavo heard a stifled scream and turned around to see Connie standing in the doorway, gawking at the body. She pressed her back to the wall, hand to her chest. "I saw you just walking around," she whispered, "and thought it would be okay to come in. I had no idea. Who is he?"

"Severus. Stay back." He continued down the hall. She followed.

He glanced back and frowned at her.

"I'm afraid to stay alone," she whispered. "What if the murderer is still here?"

His experience with Angie told him it was easier not to argue. The two continued through the house, Connie watching the hallway as he searched one room after the other for more people or victims.

At the back of the house, beyond the kitchen, he opened the door to a room whose only furniture was a table set up as a sort of altar with candles, incense, rocks, and goat horns atop a black cloth.

In the back corner of the room was a door, and in front of the door, another body.

A man wearing a heavy black robe and a black full-face mask came down the stairs. He didn't look at any of them but went straight to the large table.

He lifted the wooden chest onto it and drew a key from the pocket of the black trousers he wore under his cape. Opening the chest, he took out a syringe and a bottle of serum.

"By the power of God," Markowitz shouted, "thrust down to hell Satan and all wicked spirits that wander through the world for the ruin of souls."

Behind the mask Angie could hear the man's laughter. She could scarcely breathe as she watched him. What was the serum? And who was he going after?

"Why am I here?" she demanded.

He didn't answer but muttered and set up an old book and candles in what resembled a makeshift altar.

"I don't know either," Zoe said. "Unless . . ."

Angie realized what Zoe was thinking. "Not me," she cried. "I haven't done anything. I've minded my own business! It's not even Paavo's case. All I've done is bake and bake and bake, until I'm sick of it." As the so-called demon prepared the syringe, her hysteria grew. "Isn't it bad enough that my business is ruined, that I have no friends, that my boyfriend doesn't even think about getting married? I tried to be a good person, I really did. Is it my fault that I screwed up? I don't want to end this way!"

He whirled on her. "Shut up!" he demanded.

"Please, Baron," she said on the verge of tears. "I don't want to be your Dark Queen."

"You're mistaken, young lady," Markowitz called. "That's not the Baron."

"He's not?" Angie asked, stunned.

"And you're not the Dark Queen."

Paavo hurried to the body and turned it over. It was Rysk. Bullet holes pierced his shirt, and blood puddled on the floor.

Paavo felt a light pulse and handed Connie his cell phone to call for an ambulance. He tore open the shirt to see the damage and found a bulletproof vest. The kind cops wear. The vest had protected him from the heart shots he'd taken and had saved his life. So far, at least. The shock of being struck in the chest was sometimes enough to kill.

The leg wound looked bad. He'd lost a lot of blood. "I'll get a rag or sheet for a tourniquet," Connie said and ran to a bedroom.

As Paavo checked him over, Rysk opened his eyes. He looked startled, dazed, then shifted as if he wanted to sit up. Paavo put a hand on his shoulder, stopping him.

"Who did this?" Paavo asked as he ripped the sheet Connie gave him.

"There were several, all wearing robes, masks. I think they were from the club. I'm pretty sure I recognized the way a couple of them moved. The shooter was older, bigger."

"He also wore a mask?"

"Black. Shiny. Full face."

Paavo bound the leg and tied the tourniquet tight. "You saw Severus dead?"

"That was when I heard the others. I pulled out my gun, headed for the back door. Two moved closer, acting like they didn't even care if I shot them. I hesitated, and that's when the shooter got me. I went soft. Stupid of me!"

"Did you see Angie?"

"Angie? No." His eyes cleared a bit. "Where's Zoe? Is she here?"

"No. Neither is Markowitz."

"Damn! I've got to find them. The Baron talked about an abandoned Catholic church for ceremonies." He tried to sit up. "Maybe there . . ."

Paavo held him down and asked Connie for blankets and a pillow. "You aren't going anywhere. What's this about? Why did you spring Markowitz?"

Rysk refused to lie flat. Paavo helped slide him back so he could lean against the wall. It was clear he was in terrible pain, and his eyes would cloud from time to time. He put his head back and shut his eyes a moment.

"I'm DEA. We got a tip about a dealer—Severus. I

was elected for undercover, to build a case against him and his suppliers. Met Zoe at The Crypt and tagged her as a fraud. She interested me—I couldn't figure her out, especially when she got a job with Angie. I followed her, knew her story was phony, so I kept after her. Big mistake."

"Tell me."

Connie brought the bedding, and they covered Rysk as he spoke, trying to keep him from going into shock.

"I fell for her hook, line, and sinker. She's strange but good-hearted. She thought Severus was behind her sister's becoming a junkie and disappearing. She wanted to find the girl and wanted revenge. Markowitz was supposed to help her, but he got arrested."

Paavo waited while Rysk gathered his strength.

"He kept talking about the full moon. He had to get out of there—stop some demon. Zoe believed him. I went along to make sure she didn't get herself killed. But also, I came to believe that Markowitz was innocent. And you know what?"

"What?"

"I think there are demons here."

Paavo flinched.

"The man in black with the mask, I think— No." He shut his eyes again. "Forget I said that. I'd like to keep my job."

The medics showed up, and Paavo backed away from Rysk. "You were the one who called in the tip about Lolly Firenghetti weren't you?" he asked.

He gave a slight nod. "Find Zoe for me," Rysk whispered as the paramedics began to work on him. "Please find her."

"Get better," Paavo said, then to Connie, "I'll call

the diocese, find out if there's an abandoned church in the city."

Connie's eyes were wide. "I know exactly where one is."

The Dark Lord turned from the altar with a sneer. "You? You thought you were my Queen?"

"I'm not the Queen?" Angie said, astonished.

"You're a pushy little thing. Not even a virgin." His voice was tinged with disgust. He shook his hand lovingly over the book. "My Queen is beautiful and pure. Twenty minutes before midnight tonight she will become mine, and the commandment of the *Ars Diabolus* shall be met."

"Midnight where?" Angie asked, not understanding who or what he was talking about. "Your book sounds like Latin. If it's talking about Italy, that time is long past. You lose." She hoped she'd bought them all some time and hadn't just signed their death warrants.

He laughed. "You are clever. Perhaps you will tell me where my Queen has gone tonight."

"Me?"

"Once we find her, you and your friends will be let go. If we don't, you will all die."

"Don't listen to him," Markowitz said. "If he finds her and gains her power, everything will be lost. Sacrifice us, but don't give her to him." He stared at the masked man. "I exorcise you, Most Unclean Spirit! Be uprooted and expelled from this Creature of God."

"You filth!" the masked man roared at him. "Vomit-eating pestilence! Abandoned by your own wife, flesh of your flesh, you have no one! How does that make you feel? You are nothing! And I . . . I am Dark Lord!"

Angie stared at them both, wondering which was craziest. "What am I looking for?" she asked, afraid the old man, who continued his prayers, might be torn limb from limb.

The Dark Lord spun toward her. "Your friend, damn it!"

"What friend?" Her voice was hardly a whisper.

His chest heaved. "The beautiful one. The most perfect being on the planet. My other half, my love, my completion."

"You've got the wrong person," Angie insisted. "I don't know anybody like that."

"Connie," he said.

"Connie?" She was flabbergasted. "You want Connie to be your Queen? *My* Connie?"

"She isn't home tonight!" He pounded his fist against his hand. "She's always home every evening. I've watched her night after night. I don't know what happened, but you're her friend. Or were. You *will* find her for me."

Angie thought quickly. If she convinced him not to go look for Connie, then he might choose . . . Oh, dear! "Okay," she said. "She's a fine choice. Excellent. In fact, I always could see an aura of royalty about her."

"Connie—so that's her name," Markowitz murmured to Zoe. "I'm sorry. I never could see her clearly." Then he faced Angie and said, "She really does value your friendship very much."

Angie's spine tingled with his words at the same time as realization struck. She faced Zoe. "Your questions about my friends, looking in the Rolodex—you were trying to find Connie, weren't you? All this time, it was all about Connie."

"I never wanted you involved," Zoe said.

"Quiet!" the Dark Lord demanded. "We don't have much time."

"Let me use my cell phone to call hers," Angie suggested. "She's probably got it with her." She'd try to put in the call to Paavo, and if that didn't work, somehow she'd get a message to him or Connie that she was in terrible danger.

"Your cell phone is in your handbag?" he asked.

"Yes." She glanced at the wrist bindings. "I can't use the phone with these."

He slashed through them. "Don't try anything. I have a knife—and a gun."

Angie shrank back. She was free of the bindings—now she had to come up with something smart to do to save them all . . . somehow. She stood up to go to her handbag and get her cell phone, but he pushed her back into the chair. "I'm sure we'll find her. Let me try."

"Wait. Let me think. I already have my four consorts, but perhaps I will allow you to be one of her handmaidens."

Connie's handmaiden! It was on the tip of her tongue to protest, but she thought better of it.

Chapter 35

 Siren on, Paavo raced through the city streets toward St. Michael's. He called Yosh and Calderon to let them know what was happening and to ask for backup.

"She'll be all right, won't she?" Connie asked, her voice cracking.

Paavo forced himself to a place where no emotion could reach him. He couldn't think about that now, couldn't think that whoever had taken her didn't need her. Connie had been the one he wanted. Angie was just in the wrong place at the wrong time. Her captor had no reason to let her live.

"She'll be fine," Paavo said firmly.

Within a couple of blocks of the church, he shut off the siren. When the statue of St. Michael the Archangel on the church top came visible against the night sky, he turned off the headlights as well.

He was suddenly freezing, so cold that his hands could hardly grip the steering wheel. He could see his breath with each exhale.

* * *

Holding the knife in one hand, from the wooden chest the masked man lifted a flask, scissors, and pliers, and placed all on the table. From his pocket he took the syringe he'd prepared earlier and put it on the table. Angie nearly choked on an involuntary hard swallow, but she remained still, hoping he'd forget he'd untied her.

He lifted the glass top from the flask. "This is the oil of purification," he said. "We will bathe my Queen and her handmaiden in this oil to make her ready to receive me."

"I don't think so," she murmured. Her heart pounded with fear. "People are looking for me right now. They'll find me."

"The cop won't be helping anyone ever again," he said.

No! Her mind screamed as the world tipped. "Paavo?" she whispered, unable to breathe because of what he was suggesting.

"Not him. The other one. The one who hung around and pretended to be one of us. Did he think I was so stupid I couldn't tell? I could smell it on him."

"Rysk?" Zoe cried, her eyes betraying her pain. "Oh, my God, no!"

Angie stared at him, holding back tears close to the surface, her mind whirring between relief over Paavo and horror over Rysk. Rysk a cop? Strangely, it made sense to her. But she wouldn't believe he was dead. She couldn't. He was too young, too full of life and laughter. *Please, God,* she prayed, *let him live*.

In the background, Markowitz continued to speak the rite of exorcism.

A plastic sheet lay folded in a corner. Finally, he put the knife down, spread the sheet on the floor, and placed a stack of towels beside it. The once white towels had a rust-colored stain, the color that appears when blood is imperfectly washed from cotton.

He drew aside a cloth that covered a portion of a wall. Painted in silver on the wall was a five-pointed star with the fifth point facing straight up. Nailed to each of the other four points was a heart.

Angie stared in frozen horror at the sight. "Here are my Queen's consorts. The empty space is hers. Here are Julie and Lucy and Tashanda and Mina, my first." He ran a finger over the desiccated heart, then faced Zoe. "She preferred that name to Greta." He'd known who she was. All this time he'd known.

Zoe screamed hysterically and somehow pulled her hands free from their bindings, stripping away her skin as she did so. She rose onto her knees and lunged at him.

He knocked her to the floor, but she was beyond caring.

Still shrieking, she clawed at his legs, his stomach, crawling up him. He put his hands to her throat. She tried to pull his hands off her, but he squeezed harder.

Angie hurled herself at him, breaking his hold. She tried to punch him, but he let Zoe fall and turned toward her. She jumped back, away from him.

Even through the round holes in the mask, she could see that his eyes burned red. As he moved toward her, she attacked again, hoping to catch him off guard, and reached for his mask.

The mask came off in her hand. She looked up, and the pallid, fleshy face of Wilbur Fieldren, the Baron's assistant, stared back at her.

This was no demon, no Dark Lord, just a weak,

homely man trying to make himself into something important at the expense of women like Zoe and her sister, Rysk, and her own dear friend.

Fieldren grabbed Angie's arms. "Look at my eyes, and be lost to God."

Paavo shouted a warning as a Goth-looking woman leaped from the shadows of the unlocked back entry to St. Michael's Church and grabbed a handful of Connie's hair. Connie reared back her fist and smashed the woman in the jaw, knocking her out cold.

At the same time Frederick Limore, dressed in a long, black robe, flew at him, hands fisted and skinny arms outstretched. Paavo made quick work of Limore, but two other Goth teens, the ones Limore had named as Travis Walters's friends, attacked, each swinging heavy four-by-fours of wood and aiming at his head.

Suddenly, Connie leaped on the back of one of them and stuck her thumb in his eye.

Fieldren! That this monster, this very human monster, had inflicted so much destruction and pain was more than Angie could stand. She'd pay him back with her tongue if nothing else. "You think you can control people with those little piggy eyes? Look at you? Only if I want to throw up!"

"Quiet!" he ordered.

"You're so pathetic! A disgusting blowhard who needs a Thighmaster and a serious diet—"

"I said—"

"You're a ball-less, fat lump of gristle, not worth the water to flush away."

"Damn you!" Momentarily stricken by her assault,

Fieldren shoved her away from him. His face turned crimson. He tore off his black robe and picked up a wooden chair. "I'll crush you! You are not worthy to be anything for my Queen! I'll beat you until there's nothing left."

"Oh, I'm so scared. Lord of the stupid and craven, that's what you are. Put down that chair and leave us alone before you find yourself being strapped to a different chair—an electric chair."

"You will rue today for eternity!" He lunged at her, trying to jab her with the legs of the chair. She stepped between them, two on one side of her body and two on the other. She grabbed hold of the stretcher between the legs and tried to yank the chair out of his hands.

He pulled it back, but she wouldn't let go. He jerked it at her again, then swung the chair from side to side, but no matter what he did, she held on, preventing him from getting enough leverage to hit her with it.

Finally, he pressed forward with determination, pushing the chair with Angie trapped inside toward the wall.

"Begone, Most Evil Serpent!" Markowitz thrust his foot in Fieldren's path. Fieldren tripped on it, falling hard onto the cement floor.

Angie let the chair drop.

Furious, Fieldren grabbed it again and whirled on Markowitz, beating him until the chair cracked into several pieces and Markowitz lay in a bloody heap. Fieldren tossed aside the part of the chair he still held and turned to Angie.

She wasn't there.

He slowly turned in a circle. One of her shoes lay on the stone steps leading out of the basement, and the door at the top was ajar. Had he left it that way? Or had she gone up there?

After a quick sweep of the cellar, he picked up the shoe and ran up the stairs to the top landing. There he stopped and made another search of the cellar.

Suddenly, he gave a sharp laugh and pointed.

By the sound and the direction he was pointing, Angie, who had been peeking out from the discarded robe she'd burrowed under, realized he'd spotted her. She looked down at herself and saw that her shoeless toes were jutting out from beneath the material.

His laughter turned hollow and then into a roar. Unconcerned with hiding any longer, her eyes were fixed on him. He stood on the landing, bending down toward her, his face contorted, his eyes slanted into those of a serpent, his nostrils flattened, and his mouth and jaw rimmed with sharp, uneven teeth. He reminded her of a drawing of a demon she'd seen as a child in a Classics Comic book of Milton's *Paradise Lost*. She stared, unable to move, expecting fire to spew from his mouth at any moment.

"You are mine." A deep voice reverberated through the cellar, the most chilling, unearthly, and unholy sound she had ever heard.

Petrified, she screamed, kicking the remains of the broken chair in front of her as a meager protection.

Behind Fieldren, a familiar figure charged through the door at the top of the stairs. Connie!

The door hit Fieldren square in the back and knocked him off the landing. Arms and legs spread wide, he fell straight down and landed atop a broken chair leg. The leg impaled his heart.

He jerked once, twice, and then collapsed. Angie

stared at Fielden's face. In death, it was again the flabby, nerdish face she'd known. She must have just imagined the strange transformation at the top of the stairs—a hysteric reaction on her part, nothing more. Of course, nothing more.

"Angie!" Connie shrieked and bounced down the steps. The door had blocked her view of Fielden's fall, so the one selected to be Dark Queen had no idea what she had wrought. Behind her, standing on the landing, was Paavo.

Next Yosh pushed in behind him, followed by what seemed to be a whole squadron of blue uniforms. Although they hurried down, Paavo stayed still. She saw his astonished gaze go to Zoe and Markowitz, both bloody and unconscious, to Fielden, who now looked very dead, and to her, standing amidst it all.

She held his gaze, smiling tearfully, until she was swept into a bear hug by Connie.

"Angie, I'm so sorry! I was so scared." Connie burst into tears. "My wonderful friend! Are you all right?"

Angie started to cry as well. "Connie, how I've missed you. I don't know what got into me! I'm so ashamed of myself."

"And I've missed you," Connie sniffled. "I'm the one who should be ashamed."

"No, me! Shall we fight again?"

They both began to laugh through their tears, all the while hugging and patting each other.

Yosh was checking out the very dead Fielden, while police officers were administering first aid to Zoe and Markowitz, who were both stirring.

"Are you all right, Angie?" Paavo asked, hovering nearby. He'd retrieved her shoe and handed it to her.

"Yes," she said, her arm still around Connie. "Thank God you got here when you did. Both of you."

"I'm so sorry I ever doubted our friendship," Connie said, tears in her eyes. "Thinking you were in danger told me how important you are to me. I love you, girl-friend. I'm sorry I've been such a pill."

"You were out looking for me?" Angie asked.

"Absolutely," Connie said.

"Thank God!" Angie realized that was why Fieldren couldn't find her. In that same instant she decided never to tell Connie how close she had come to becom-ing royalty—dead royalty.

"I didn't know you could take out three people all by yourself," Connie said with awe.

"Oh, I didn't—"

"Good work, Angelina," Calderon said, as he and Benson marched into the chamber, trying to see what was going on with *their* case. "You caught the escapee and the one who helped him, plus some nutcase they were working with."

"No, that's not—"

"Wow, you are some babe," Bo Benson said. "You got some cool woman here, Paavo. You ever get tired of her, give me time to line up." Despite his words to Angie, he smiled at Connie and winked.

"I don't know if I'd want a woman who could do all this," Calderon said with a chuckle. "What if she got mad at me?"

He and Benson laughed and then moved in to begin the preliminary steps for a homicide investigation. At the same time, the medics arrived to take care of Zoe and Markowitz.

Angie watched over both while the cops around her told the paramedics of her bravery.

She finally got a chance to explain to Calderon and Benson that Markowitz wasn't the serial killer after all, that Fieldren was. She pointed to the hearts of the four women.

This caused even more of a stir as the cops realized that she had stood up to a serial killer and a deranged one at that. She was remarkable.

That didn't stop her knees from shaking as she realized just how close to dying she had come. She wasn't really courageous, she simply had had no choice. Yet as the compliments continued, she couldn't help but stand a little straighter and even tried to smooth her hair and dress.

Paavo felt about as useful as a potted plant. A warm potted plant. From the time they walked into the chamber, at the time that Fieldren died, the aching chill he'd struggled against vanished. It had to have been a bizarre coincidence, nothing more.

None of that mattered as he grew increasingly agitated watching one after the other of the homicide inspectors, uniformed cops, paramedics, coroner's teams, and even the crime scene inspectors stop and tell Angie how incredible it was that she had not only found the serial killer, but had managed to keep her cool long enough to give them time to get there and prevent any more murders. There were all sorts of brotherly and sisterly pats on her shoulder as cops and paramedics circled around her, and Krazy Glue couldn't have stuck Connie more firmly to her side.

The way they were talking, she sounded like some

Superwoman or something. *Xena, move over,* he thought, *not to mention Buffy.* But she wasn't any of those things. She was just Angie—the woman he loved and wanted to marry.

The woman he never seemed to be able to find the right time or place to tell those words to. And now, with this madman, he'd nearly lost her. What the hell was he waiting for?

"Angie, let's get out of here," he said, taking her arm.

She pulled back. "Get out? But my friends. I can't leave Zoe. I'll have to go to the hospital."

He didn't want to wait. No more delays. No more nonsense. Just him and her, so that he could tell her all he'd wanted to say and hadn't for far too long. "We'll go later. She'll be under doctors' care for a while. As will Rysk. She'll have his company there, whether she wants it or not."

"Rysk is alive? Thank God!" Angie smiled down at Zoe. "She'll want his company, that's for sure."

"Let's go, then," Paavo said once more as he reached for her.

She turned away, scanning the room, gazing with affection again at Connie. "Calderon wants my statement. He said for me to wait right here."

"He can get it later."

"Later we're going to the hospital, remember?"

"Angie—"

Just then, Officer Crossen ran down the steps and stopped in front of her, a huge bandage on his forehead. "I was sent home from the hospital, but when word came over the police band about the action here, I had to make sure you were all right."

"I'm fine. Thank you for coming." Ignoring Paavo

once more, she kissed Crossen's cheek, then hugged him. He hugged back.

Paavo couldn't stand another minute of this. "Angie," he called.

"This woman should win the bravery award for the year. Maybe for the decade," Crossen said to another blue uniform as Angie beamed.

"Angie, let's go."

She glanced at him. "I've got things to do here. Whatever could be so important?"

He blurted out the words. "Asking you to marry me!"

Her face drained of color. He had her full attention now. "What did you say?" she whispered.

Suddenly, every cop, inspector, and medic froze in place. All eyes turned toward him in stunned silence. He'd blown it, he realized. All his plans for moonlight and roses and a romantic setting had fizzled, and he'd ended up practically shouting at her. A first-class idiot would have shown more sense. But as she looked at him with those big, brown eyes, wonder and hope and surprise and love on her face, he knew he couldn't back down.

He drew in his breath, his voice much softer now. "I said, Angie, will you marry me?"

Her eyes widened, her jaw dropped, and suddenly, Angie the Demon Slayer keeled over in a dead faint.

From the kitchen of Angelina Amalfi

 ANGIE'S MOCHA PECAN TORTE

Angie knows her cakes, and this one is her absolute favorite. It's wonderfully rich, made with only a little flour and lots of ground pecans, coming as close to perfection as ever a cake can be.

3 tablespoons sifted all-purpose flour
1 teaspoon baking powder
12 oz. pecans, finely ground
6 eggs, separated
2 tablespoons instant coffee powder
1 1/2 cups sugar
1/8 teaspoon salt
Dry bread crumbs

Preheat oven to 350 degrees. Butter two 9-inch cake pans and dust with dry bread crumbs (or, if none available, flour).

Place ground pecans in a large bowl. Sift flour and baking powder over pecans, stir to mix. Set aside.

In a medium-size bowl, beat egg yolks at high speed for three minutes. Reduce speed while gradually adding instant coffee powder and sugar. Increase speed to high and beat 5 minutes until very thick. Set aside.

Using clean beaters and bowl, beat egg whites with salt until stiff but not dry. Using about a quarter of the whites at a time, gently fold them into the yolk mixture. Pour eggs over nut-flour mixture and gently fold together until blended.

Divide the mixture equally between the two cake pans. Bake 35–40 minutes. Cakes are done when the top springs back when lightly touched and the sides begin to pull away from the pan. Let cool 10 minutes, then remove from pans.

 ## MOCHA PECAN TORTE ICING AND FILLING

3 oz. (6 tablespoons) butter
4 oz. (4 squares) unsweetened chocolate
1 tablespoon plus 1 teaspoon instant coffee powder
2 cups confectioners' sugar
$^1/_3$ cup milk
2 eggs
1 teaspoon vanilla extract

Use a double boiler. Place butter and chocolate in top, water in bottom. Stir over medium heat until melted. Add instant coffee and stir to dissolve. Set aside to cool.

Mix sugar, milk, eggs, and vanilla in a bowl. Add *cooled* chocolate mixture and beat at high speed 3–4 minutes until fluffy and light in color.

Place four thin strips of wax paper to cover edge of cake plate. Place one cake layer upside down on plate. Spread filling half an inch thick on it. Cover with the second cake layer, right side up. Spread icing on top and sides of torte. Carefully remove wax paper. Refrigerate 2–3 hours before serving.

 CRANBERRY CREAM SCONES

This simple recipe is one of Angie's favorites.

2 cups flour
$1/4$ cup sugar
1 tablespoon baking powder
Dash salt
1 cup dried cranberries
$1^1/4$ cups whipping cream
2 tablespoons melted butter
Raw sugar

Preheat oven to 400 degrees. Stir flour, sugar, baking powder, salt and cranberries together. Add cream. Stir to mix thoroughly, then knead on floured board 7 or 8 times.

Pat and shape into a circle about 8 inches across. Divide into 8 sections as you would cut a pie.

Rub salad or vegetable oil on cookie sheet. Place the scones on the sheet, giving them space to spread. Brush the tops with melted butter and then sprinkle with raw sugar. Bake at 400 degrees about 18–20 minutes or until lightly browned.

Award-Winning Author

CAROLYN HART

THE HENRIE O MYSTERIES

DEATH IN LOVERS' LANE
0-380-79002-5/$6.50 US/$8.50 Can

DEATH IN PARADISE
0-380-79003-3/$6.50 US/$8.99 Can

DEATH ON THE RIVERWALK
0-380-79005-X/$6.50 US/$8.99 Can

THE DEATH ON DEMAND MYSTERIES

SUGARPLUM DEAD
0-380-80719-X/$6.99 US/$9.99 Can

YANKEE DOODLE DEAD
0-380-79326-I/$6.50 US/$8.50 Can

WHITE ELEPHANT DEAD
0-380-79325-3/$6.50 US/$8.99 Can